Southern Fried Women

Southern Fried Women

Stories

PAMELA KING CABLE

SPOTLIGHT PUBLISHING, INC.
Madison, NC 27025
www.spotlightpublishing.com

Spotlight Publishing, Inc.
P.O. Box 621
Madison, NC 27025

ISBN: 0-9768469-3-4
Library of Congress Control Number: 2005939185

First Edition

10 9 8 7 6 5 4 3 2 1

Some version of the story *Old Time Religion* has appeared in the publication *Original Sin: The Seven Deadlies Come Home to Roost*, published November 2004. *No Time For Laura* was an award-winning story, April 2004, Burlington Writers Group.

Book design and composition by Julie Murkette
Photography and photography restoration by Michael Cable

For Michael

Acknowledgments

To me, the word *acknowledgment* is trite and simplistic. My deep desire is to give more than a proper *acknowledgment*. The emotions I feel for the following individuals expand inside my heart and mind and ooze out my pores. I find what I'm thanking them for has everything to do with my own well-being in addition to their belief in the book itself. As a writer, my most valuable assistance has come from people who cared a great deal about me.

I feel an overwhelming need to thank two authors for their support. Cassandra King, you are my inspiration. Gail Cauble Gurley, dear friend, thanks for every syllable and your support.

I'm forever grateful to Dena and Blair Harris for being there when I needed you.

Thank you Deborah Bryant, publicist extraordinaire, for reading and believing.

Julie Murkette, I'm thankful for your expertise and willingness to go the extra mile to make this a beautiful book. You are a true professional and fantastic artist. And thanks to Joe for lending me his eagle-eyes.

What would a Southern Story Goddess be without her Sister Story Goddesses . . . Betsy, Lisa, Beth, Jody, and Jolee for their loving support and unfailing encouragement . . . I'm truly blessed.

To the Writers' Group of the Triad novel critique group, a thanks for not insisting I forsake my Southern accent, and special thanks to Ed Schubert, Dena Harris, Judy Glazier, and Rudy Daugherty Clark for your support. Thanks to Sisters In Crime and my local High Point Chapter, Murder We Write, you made my research easier.

To Hannelore Hahn and the International Women's Writing Guild, for your words of wisdom and the opportunities only the Guild can give, I thank you.

My heartfelt gratitude goes out to the North Carolina Writers' Network for the many conferences, and networking and promotion opportunities that have made a difference in my career.

And a gracious thank you goes to the High Point Literary League for your inspirational Author Luncheons that have made me feel like a Southern belle at a cotillion.

For all the lunchtime words of love, I thank my dear friends Lil, Angie, Susan and the rest of the WSP staff. Your Southern mannerisms, speech, and way of life have inspired me on this journey. I'm still laughing.

"She don't pick her peaches before they's all fuzzed up." I adore you, Bette Lou Nicholson, for every Southern phrase that unknowingly came out of your mouth. I wrote many down when you weren't looking.

Beth Hanggeli, your editing has been a special gift, a typical offering of your love. I cherish you.

To Tina and Tim Rich — thank you for being there all my life and believing in me when nobody else did. Without you, I would've died on the vine a long time ago. I love you both.

Grateful thanks to my mother-in-law, Bobbie Sue Rossi, for giving me the gift of time, a stress-free environment in which to write, and posing for the cover in 1947.

Thanks to my parents, Darrel and Joyce King, for birthing me in West Virginia and for their love. I thank them for their deep storytelling well from which to draw.

Loving hugs to Aaron, Jillian, Christopher and Nicole for only rolling their eyes when I'm not looking.

And to Michael, a gentle thanks doesn't cover it. If not for your unconditional love, self-sacrifice, and confidence in me, this first book would never have been written. This is as much your work as it is mine. You are the true meaning of the word, *husband*. I love you twelve times.

Contents

No Time For Laura
11

Vernell Paskins, Mobile Home Queen
17

Punkin Head
47

Cry
55

The Homestead
99

Old Time Religion
107

Pigment Of My Imagination
117

Beach Babies
141

Coal Dust On My Feet
175

What Is A Southern Fried Woman?
250

I originally wrote this story in 1985. No Time For Laura is based, in part, on a true story. Laura was my best childhood friend, a once sweet memory now immortalized in words and a few old snapshots.

After a couple of rewrites, the story won an award at the Burlington Writers Club Awards in April 2004. The judge's comment on the manuscript stated, ". . . you have a way of touching the hearts of your readers." As a writer, I want to inform and enlighten a reader's mind — what I wish for even more is to jolt the reader's heart.

In this story, my desire to find the true meaning of friendship begged the question—how far will a person go for the love of a best friend? For the past twenty-five years, Tina has been my best friend. We've been through tough times — together and apart — but one thing remained constant — her love for me never lessened, no matter what I did. She loved me unconditionally. That's how it is with best friends. They never leave you.

As I edited this piece for *Southern Fried Women*, the character of Laura remained steadfast in her appearance and personality. She refused to let me change her. I gave in. Laura will always have a special place in my heart. This story is dedicated to her.

No Time For Laura

Lightning flashed near Macon, Georgia the afternoon I drove my truck down a red dirt road to Mamaw's funeral. A week later, I boxed up her belongings. Rummaging through her old-lady junk drawer I uncovered a Polaroid picture, discolored and cracked with age. Mamaw had titled it at the bottom, "Laura and Patsy with Popsicles – July 1968." Laura — a forgotten piece of my past. I had no siblings; we were sisters by default, hooked-at-the-hip best friends.

I imagined God laughed when He loaded a kinky mass of sweet-potato-orange hair on Laura's head. At twelve, freckles blanketed her baby fat while nasty black glasses slid down her adult-sized nose. By the time we experimented with make-up, Laura announced she was the long-lost sister of Bozo the clown. Peering into my mouthful of perfect teeth she hissed through her braces, "At least I can tune into WDEN." We busted up. Life was a joke: we laughed at everything, right along with God.

"I wanna be the skinny blonde in the Mamas and the Papas," she said. I stared at her wondering if she was serious, until she snorted and giggled. Deep down, Laura knew what she was. Cass Elliot and Pipi Longstocking rolled into one. A face only her grandma loved, but I loved her too.

Picking at the label on the old mayonnaise jar, Laura's dirty fingernails scratched and scraped the glass.

"The perfect size," she said. Satisfied, she plopped it in my lap.

"We used this jar for lightnin' bugs." I shrugged. "I suppose it'll work." We launched our latest summertime project in Mamaw's backyard in a tent made with old quilts over a rusty clothesline. Weekly sleepovers turned brilliant ideas, like time capsules, into adventures. A memento to the Star Trek alien in the future who would dig it up and learn about the two most groovy girls that walked the planet.

The next afternoon, by the climbing tree, I dug a hole up to my knees. "That'll do," I said, shaking the dirt out of my Keds.

I laid the jar stuffed with paper and shiny trinkets into the earth. Filling the hole with dirt, I put its grassy hat back on then gazed up to find Laura dangling upside down by her legs from a tree limb. She giggled as gravity gathered her shirt around her armpits, revealing her flat chest. The sun blinked around her and through the leaves of the tree.

That was over thirty years ago.

Staring at the old photo, I tried to feel guilty for not missing her. Except for the raging storm outside, Mamaw's house was quiet and I was alone with my memories. I had forgot Laura on purpose. I closed my eyes, recalling our perfect childhood and the anticipation of a most excellent future.

But there would be no future for Laura.

"I'm off to the new Dairy Queen in Macon with Aunt Rose, wanna come?"

"I'm grounded. Take notes," I said. "I'll talk to you tomorrow."

"Okay your highness, see ya, wouldn't wanna be ya!" I heard her giggle as she hung up the phone. It was the last time I would talk to my best friend.

In a Volkswagen speeding down a wet highway, her aunt lost control and the car rolled like a bowling ball. We didn't wear seatbelts in 1968. Laura was dead.

At thirteen, I hadn't learned the art of taking life seriously. I wasn't prepared for this. When I staggered into the funeral home, her grandma grabbed me and wailed. Her face strained, I wanted to retch. Mama nudged me to hug her. I could not. Numb, my arms remained at my sides.

I glared at the casket. My legs moved but the rest of me did not. I swallowed hard. No tears came. I had shut Laura out. How dare she leave me to face my future alone? Enraged, I could hear her laughing again.

Trudging through the stormy afternoon, I finished packing Mamaw's kitchen. I picked up the picture again; lightning flashed and cracked outside the window. The electric popped and went off. But in that blinking instant, grief showed up. I knew what I had to do. Find her. Tell her I was sorry.

Bolting to the garage, I grabbed a pick and a flashlight. In the near darkness, I ran to the old tree, ignoring the sheets of cold rain stinging my skin.

After three unsuccessful attempts, I yelled into a rain-filled sky, "Where'd we dig, Laura?" *The lilac bushes . . . further to the left.* I moved and dug faster. *Clink.* I hit something. The pick was heavy and muddy like my body. *Clink.* The black night surrounding me, I tunneled through cold March mud. Excavating with my hands and feeling the jar, I dug around it. After some tender tugging, I heard the sucking sound of the mud as I pulled it up.

I hurried into the house, lit a candle, and bathed the jar in Mamaw's kitchen sink. After a couple hard turns, it moaned and opened. Rust fell on the carpet.

Our "valuables" slid out first. The adjustable decoder ring I found in our church parking lot, and Laura's contribution — a string of plastic pop-together pearls. I smiled, dropped them into my pocket, then pulled out the papers that had yellowed over time. Secret lists of everything reading like the pages of nostalgia they were. Our favorite TV shows, food, teachers, boys we had crushes on, and the current events of 1968.

Then I saw them. Essays we'd kept a secret, even from each other. Mine was just more sweet rhetoric of the time in which we lived and played. I pulled Laura's essay out of the jar, opened it, and gasped. It was a letter.

Dear Patsy,

I think someday you might dig this up. So, I'm writing to you, not to some dumb alien klingon.

Do you still watch Peyton Place? How old are you now? Do you have kids? Are you married? To Paul McCartney, I hope. Are you rich and famous?

I have so many questions. Are we living side by side like we promised? Am I old and wrinkled with gray hair and do I look more stupid than I do now? Maybe I'm prettier than you and have bigger boobs. Ha Ha. I can't picture myself grown up. I think adults are goofy.

You are my one true friend. I hope we will always be best friends, but I don't think I'll ever get old like you will. So if you read this and I'm not around, remember you are my best friend forever, wherever I am. I'll never forget you.

A bushel and a peck and a hug around the neck.

Laura, 1968.

I crumbled to the floor with Laura's letter in my lap, holding it. Holding her. I pressed it to my heart. I said I was sorry she had died and that I didn't cry at her funeral. My lost tears found their way to my heart and I sobbed to the depth of me.

The lightning flashed in the darkness. In some strange Star Trek cosmic fashion, I felt her there. She accepted my apology.

VERNELL PASKINS, MOBILE HOME QUEEN, spoke to me in ways I never dreamed a character could.

While studying a map of North Carolina one day, I saw a tiny town (a crossroads, really) named Needmore. Not living far from there, my husband and I decided to drive to the area. A beautiful little rural spot in the country, but there wasn't much to see. The place did 'need more' to be called a town. Still, the name of the locale intrigued me.

What type of person lives in Needmore and do they really . . . need more?

Over the next several days, a character popped into my head and I placed her in Needmore, with a dose of humor, hopes and dreams, and huge disappointments in her life. A woman with little education most people would look at and call "low life" or "white trash." Although Vernell struggles to make a way where there seems to be no way . . . living from paycheck to paycheck (like so many women I know), the deck is stacked against her.

I asked myself, what if . . . she lived in a doublewide and worked at the interstate flea market . . . what if . . .

Vernell Paskins, Mobile Home Queen

I gaze up at the sky and wonder if it's rain or pee from Victoria's diaper that's dripped on my leg. I hold my ten-month-old grandchild on my hip and pull out a nice rose-colored quilted bag to show my next customer.

The clouds that've rolled in this afternoon look like handfuls of dryer lint from a load of blue jeans. I hate bad weather. I won't make much money if it rains. I'll have to dip into my savings next week for the rent. It's money I got from Floyd's employer when I sued him for exposing my husband to asbestos, and it's dwindling.

Victoria rubs her eyes and kicks her feet into my side. Her legs have rolls — they're bitable. So damn cute. I call her Mamaw's little tubby tuba. Still cutting them back teeth. Got a touch of diarrhea and a raw bottom. I need to rub Jack Daniels on her gums when I get her home. Maybe stop at the drug store for some Paregoric. Help her sleep. Hell, help us both sleep. She smiles up at me; I imagine she's done forgot her Momma by now. She looks like Vernise and I choke back a few tears. What'd I do wrong? How'd I end up 40 and raising a baby again? Mmm-mmm.

Two women stop at my table. Typical city gals. They talk in circles and say things like, "Carolyn, I can make these purses and sell 'em at our Christmas church bazaar!" Opening the bags, they check out my double knot stitching. Damn snooty women come to waste my time asking stupid questions. Ain't going to buy a blasted thing. Not a stitch of their padded blazers, linen trousers, or leather loafers comes from the Wal-Mart. Real gold rings squeeze every one of their fat fingers. But they sure smell better than me and their hair is freshly permed and styled like Sue Ellen Ewing on Dallas. If I'm lucky they'll go bother Flossie.

I worry about my daughter, Vernise. She up and run off with that low life redneck Lenny I-can't-remember-his-last-name. I wish I could've hog-tied her to the trailer's hitch. After Vernise had herself a baby, she couldn't keep her job at Eckerds Drug Store. They fired her after three weeks. Flossie said she'd heard Lenny about drove Vernise nuts. He showed up at the store every day, acted like a crazy man — stalked up and down every aisle until he found her. Ain't no wonder Eckerds kicked her butt out of the store after the fight she and Lenny had in the middle of the health and beauty aid aisle. Flinging boxes of Band-aids and Kotex at each other, screaming loud enough to wake the dead — Flossie said.

One night she came home all lovey-dovey, kissed Victoria, and then packed her bags. I'll be damned if she didn't leave me a note in the middle of the night.

Dear Momma,

I got to go with Lenny. I can't live in this place no more. Please take care of the baby. I'll come back to get her when I've found me a job and a place to live.

Love,
Vernise

That was five months ago. Ain't heard hide nor hair from her since. And I ain't got the money or the energy to go looking for her neither. Hmmph. Vernise is a grown woman. She's making her own bed right now, I guess.

"For ten dollars this here purse will make a nice present for your Momma," I say and watch the Saturday crowd meander past my tables; their eyes peer down at what I'm selling and seldom see me. They hear my voice, but never bother to acknowledge my existence. I'm used to it. Sometimes a nice old lady stops and chats. But mostly it's tourists or folks out for a drive, or yard sale hopping. They see the sign for the flea market and end up here, buying things they don't need, junk they end up selling in their own yard sales next year. A few hope to find a rare antique. But ain't too many antique dealers here. Just junk dealers and crafters like me. Years ago, my daddy collected ashtrays and yardsticks and sold them here. God only knows why. I still collect and sell them — in his memory.

I've rented a booth at the I-85 flea market for the past ten years. Some folks call it Spencer's Garbage Dump. I don't care what they call it, as long as they see the sign at mile marker 82 and stop.

My name is Vernell Paskins and I make purses and bags from old ragged quilts I buy cheap from estate sales and thrift shops. My friend, Thelma, works over at the Jesus is Lord Thrift Store in Salisbury. She keeps an eye out for quilts and calls me when one is donated to the store. Thelma lets me buy them cheap. My bags usually sell out over a weekend.

I live in Needmore, North Carolina. In the land of the doublewides. It's about twenty miles from the interstate and the flea market. The town's name fits perfect because everybody here is needing more. I raise my youngest daughter and my granddaughter in a place called Tub's Trailer Park not far down Pot Neck Road. My friend Flossie calls me the mobile home queen of Needmore. I suppose that's because I've lived in one all my life. First with Momma and Daddy in a singlewide that's done rusted and has long since been hauled to the landfill. Then later, my husband Floyd and I rented the doublewide I'm still living in.

I tended bar in Statesville when Floyd worked construction until he died back in '69. He'd been wounded in Vietnam. Had constant headaches and night sweats. But asbestos is what killed him. I'm still trying to get over it, all these sixteen years later. My oldest daughter, Vernise, was four when he died. Vivi, my youngest, was a baby.

I make do. The money I earn from the flea market keeps a roof over our heads and food on the table. I ain't complaining.

Flossie says I should pray about my Vernise. I don't pray. I don't believe in using God as a wish book or some cosmic errand boy. When I lived with Momma, I'd flip through the JCPenney catalog and make a wish list as long as my leg for things I couldn't afford. That's the way it is with most folks and God, I think. Always wishing, never getting. He supplies our needs, I've been told. I guess He figures me and the girls don't need much.

Flossie Muldaney rents the booth next to mine. She pedals her handmade jewelry, washcloth slippers, and crocheted doll toilet paper covers. The dolls' eyes open and close and they come in all colors of yarn and hair. In the summer, Flossie sells peaches when her trees are in season.

Lin Wang, Chinese woman, has a booth on the other side of mine. She can't speak a lick of English. Sometimes I worry a customer is taking advantage of her. But old Lin, she knows American money. She sells paperweights and silk shirts with dragons and little oriental kids on them. Once I tried to tell her she priced her stuff too high. Then Flossie butted in, as usual.

"Leave her alone, Vernell. Them people think they know everything." Flossie's dangly earrings shook with her head and her fists were burrowed so deep into her hips they disappeared.

So I gave up, until one day Lin's granddaughter stopped by and I heard her speak perfect English. Her name was Ming, I think. Friendly gal and more amiable than her grandma. I told Ming to tell her granny if she lowered the price of her shirts a dollar, she'd sell more. I'll be damned if the old lady didn't do it. The next weekend, she sold a right smart many. She smiled and gave me a nod at the end of the day. We been friends since.

I think it makes Flossie mad. She'll get over it.

Victoria is heavy on my hip again; her diaper's soaked.

I see the kind of woman I despise out of the corner of my eye. She tries to be friendly, like the hypocrites that come from the Baptist church on Sunday to the flea market and pass out them Bible tracts. I know she's going to try and make me feel bad because I work on Sunday. She wears a cotton print shirtwaist dress with a crooked zipper that hangs below her knees: clothes only the Pentecostal women wear. Her curly chestnut hair is unruly; her enormous brown eyes are liquid and pour themselves through her thick eyeglasses into mine. Her big teeth are a little crooked and her smile — weak.

"That your baby?" she asks.

"No, my granddaughter, Victoria Jean. Excuse me, I gotta change her." The dense, molasses-like strands of my drawl become obvious compared to the soft Scarlett O'Hara tone of her own. I'm hoping she'll move on to Lin's tables.

"Pretty child, pretty name, Victoria." The woman reaches over the table to stroke my grandbaby's chubby legs. "You don't look old enough to have a grandchild," she says.

"I ain't. You interested in buyin' a bag? I make each one myself. Made this here bag with a quilt what come from Tennessee. An elderly widow lady had it stored in her attic. The material's in great shape." I move the baby from my left hip to my right. She's starting to fuss.

"Where's her mother?"

"What?" I ask. I'm distracted as Victoria pulls my hair, wanting down. Then my baby granddaughter makes a swiping pass for my sunglasses. I lightly smack her chubby hand, kiss her, and then put her dolly in her fat little fist instead. She throws it to the gravel lot and cries.

"Your grandchild's mother?" she asks a second time.

Now is that any of her business? I stare at the woman. I've been asked these questions before. Maybe Child Services sent her. Then again, most women can spot a needy woman a mile away. Especially if you've been one yourself.

So I lie — again. Try to hide my need and not spout off. "My daughter's out of town, she's job hunting over in Raleigh. I take care of my granddaughter."

She smiles at me — again. "My name is Rosalyn Boudreaux. Pleased to meet you." She offers her hand.

I shake it but hesitate before I turn on my own smile. Now I remember. The tent revival is back in town. "I know who ya're."

"Yes, well, my husband's the Evangelist Jimmy Boudreaux. We're in town from New Orleans. We're having a tent revival in Lexington all next week."

"I seen your tent." I shift from one foot to the other like I'm four instead of forty.

"I'd like to invite you to the Say Yes for Jesus Crusade. We've been having big crowds. The Burger King is letting us use their parking lot."

"Well, ain't that just super," I say. "I suppose I can say yes to Jesus and grab me a Whopper on the way out."

Rosalyn won't wipe her sinner-radar grin off her Pentecostal face. She ignores my ignorant statement.

"We set up a nursery in a nearby trailer. You're welcome to bring the baby."

"Yeah?" I feel my holier-than-thou-self shift into high gear. "You sellin' any tambourines, T-shirts, bumper-stickers or them King Jane Bibles?"

She doesn't flinch. "No, Sugah. We don't even sell Jesus. We give Him away. If you get the chance, come on over next Sunday."

"Sure." I laugh. *Like I'd give up a day to sell my bags for some pencil stick evangelist to shove religion in my face.*

All smart-alecky, I point to Lin Wang. "Why don't you go ask Ms. Wang over there to come to your tent meetings. Now there's a soul that needs savin'. She's one of them Buddha worshippers." Inside, I laugh harder at the thought of this evangelist's wife trying to speak Lin's language.

She stretches her neck towards Lin's tables like she's looking for Buddha himself. Then she says, "I'd love to speak to her. I'll take the rose-colored bag, by the way."

I mentally stuff my fist in my mouth and bag up my sale. Then I watch Sister Rosalyn stroll over to redneck Chinatown. I decide Flossie

would enjoy watching this religious woman make a spectacle of herself
and I nearly knock my table over rushing to find her.

Flossie is a big, fleshy woman who laughs from deep in her belly.
She can be downright imposing when she chooses. She's also a woman
with no filter between her brain and her tongue. She says exactly what
she thinks.

"Hey . . . Flossie!" I am plum out of breath with excitement.
"Flossie!"

"What now, 'Nel. I'm busy. Maynard just brought in a truck full
of peaches."

I point to Lin's booth. "That's the tent preacher's wife, solicitin'
for revival."

Flossie smirks. "I already heard what revival foolishness is fixin' to
take place over there in Lexington."

"You gonna go shout with all them Holy Roller do-gooders next
week?" I ask.

"Lord, no. You crazy?" she fires back at me. "Why would I carry
on with a bunch of damn fools playin' with snakes, fallin' down on the
floor and foamin' at the mouth? I got enough to do 'round here ever'
day," she says as she plops down between two peach crates on a rickety
board that sags with her weight. She raises herself slightly and tucks
her housedress under her legs. Her ankles are swollen beyond the sides
of her shoes. "It's just too damn hot today, that's what it is. My clothes
are just a stickin' to me." She fans her chest, then dips her hand into
her dress to adjust her bra strap and her droopy left breast. She sighs,
then grumbles. "My thighs are gaulded in this heat. I'm 'bout to burn
up or have me an itchin' fit, one."

"Well," I say, "that preacher's wife is 'bout to get a lesson in
Chinese."

Flossie can't resist. At that she stands and leans over her tables
staring down the row. "Hmm. Looks to me like they's either carryin'
on a conversation or the preacher gal is speakin' in tongues." Flossie
points as if I don't know where to look.

I'll be damned if that Rosalyn isn't talking Chinese to Lin Wang.

"She must've been a missionary," Flossie says.

"Yeah, must've." I watch Lin accept Rosalyn's Bible tract. I can't imagine old Miss Wang agreeing to go to any tent revival. I mumble. "She's probably just thrilled she's got somebody can talk her language."

"Uh-huh." Flossie's response tells me she's no longer interested. I turn around. Maynard has carried in a crate full of peaches. Flossie's counting and shoving them into little bags.

Victoria is bawling and I feel bad about her full diaper. "Cm'on lil' tuba, Mamaw's gonna get that nasty thing off of ya. Where'd I put the zinc ointment?" I find I'm down to two diapers.

I kiss my granddaughter's fat cheeks, smooth her fine corn silk hair out of her baby blue eyes, and then lay her in the playpen. I change her, but she kicks and screams when I sprinkle cornstarch between her little legs. I put a fresh plastic bottle of cold milk in her mouth and cover her with a light blanket.

"Take a nap, young'un. Mamaw's gotta make you some milk money." I point to her toys. "Look at your Pooh bear, he's takin' a nap too." Victoria's playpen is under my makeshift tent. The humidity is climbing and she starts to fuss again. I sit down in my lawn chair and pat her back until she's asleep.

I could blister Vernise's butt for taking off and leaving her baby like this. I knew she was pregnant her senior year in high school. She hated school, but had just enough credits to graduate on time. A miracle. Vernise was nine months along when she walked across the stage to get her diploma. Her water broke during the Valedictorian's speech. I had to laugh when that prissy Valedictorian had all the wind knocked out of her sails and Vernise got all the attention instead.

But the next week buying groceries at Food Lion, I overheard two old biddies gossiping in the dairy aisle. "It was awful," the one said to the other. "A whore gets all the attention and a hard-working student like Debbie Fairchild cain't finish her speech."

It broke my heart. Vernise is a little misguided is all. She's no whore. I think she was looking for somebody to replace her daddy when she started dating Lenny. Unlike my youngest daughter, Vivi, Vernise remembers her daddy. She could've had her choice of men. At five foot eight, one hundred twenty pounds of legs, breasts, blonde hair down to her butt, and blue eyes that'd burn a hole through your heart, Vernise could've picked any military man from Camp LeJeune, Parris Island, and Fort Bragg. Hell, I'd have paraded her naked around the Naval Academy or The Citadel campus to keep her away from Lenny. Damn it.

But she chose that Lenny. A man ten years older than her and divorced twice; I'd heard he'd sired three of his own, and never daddy'd any of them. Then he sweet-talked Vernise into opening her legs and promised to take her away from the world I raised her in. I guess she figured she found a man to love and take care of her. It's the only way I know to explain it.

At the end of a twelve-hour day, I pack up and carry boxes of unsold bags, ashtrays, yardsticks, and my granddaughter to my Ford Fairlane by myself. Not a man around here will help me unless he's expecting an invitation to follow me home for a beer and a night of passion. Ain't interested in no passion. Not with a grandbaby in a crib by my bed and my teenager in the next room with hormones already moaning.

No man's been in my trailer since Floyd died, except Daddy. And Roger Moultrie, a handyman and long-distance truck driver who lived in the doublewide at the end of my street. Roger's gone now. Moved to Arkansas, last time I heard. Seems all the good ones are dead, married — or driving a truck in Little Rock.

I lay Victoria in her car seat; she's asleep. The trunk's full with boxes of ashtrays I can't sell. People ain't smoking much in 1985. Not like they did when I grew up. Lord, I wish I could quit. But it's the only thing I enjoy these days — besides that little girl sleeping in the back.

I see my reflection in the car window. My skin's brown from baking in the Carolina sun three days a week for the past ten years. The heat's turned my once-soft skin into a more leathery consistency, and lines from smoking two packs of Camels a day have formed around my eyes and mouth. My teeth appear white in my brown face, but I know they're really a little off color. Ain't no tar on my heel, it's all on my teeth. My hair is thin and sun-bleached, but cut off neat at my shoulders. I suppose I ain't half bad to look at. Don't weigh much. Puckered and sagging, my biceps flap a little when I wave and I sense the weight of gravity pulling on my smile. I've been feeling my face fall lately. So I fight back and try to smile all the time. Even when I'm pissed off. Maybe that's a good thing. I think it's helped me sell a lot of bags and purses.

"Good Lord, it's eight o'clock." The trailer's like an oven. I roll over and Victoria is sitting in her crib, her diaper is full and smelly — enough to knock me over. Stinks like a small animal has died and rotted in here. The night air didn't cool things off much. I let my grandbaby sleep in just a Pamper. She's holding something in her little outstretched hand and says, "Momma." My room's so small I can reach out and touch her without leaving my bed. I look at her messy little head, so beautiful. I miss Vernise and I wonder if she's missing her baby.

"What you got?" I open her tiny fist.

"Momma," she says again.

Great. A little poop ball. Must've rolled out of her diaper. She squishes it between her fingers. I grab her up fast before she puts it in her mouth, rip off her diaper, and stick her messy bottom in a warm tub. Sitting on the toilet I watch her splash. I run my hand through my hair and look at my tired face in the mirror.

It's Sunday. I gotta sell the rest of my bags today to break even.

"Damn you, Vernise. You need to be here takin' care of your own baby."

I spend the morning cleaning up and getting ready to go back to the flea market. I only work Fridays, Saturdays, and Sundays. The rest of the week I spend on my enclosed front porch where it's cooler. It's where I cut, stitch, and sew material into tote bags and purses. I've had a love affair with my Singer sewing machine the past ten years. It's all I know to do to keep us alive. I suppose I could get a part-time job serving drinks at the Crow's Nest again. But I swore to Floyd I'd never tend bar while raising the girls.

Coffee is perking on the stove. Vivi is awake and has parked our only fan on the coffee table pointed directly at her head. Like most selfish teenagers, she don't think maybe I'd like a little cool breeze blowing my way. She curls up tighter into a ball on our fat blue recliner. The one the dog chewed the stuffing out of the arms. The damn chair never did tilt back. An unwieldy floor lamp looms dangerously over her head. I walk over and shove the glass-top coffee table back with my foot, anchoring the lamp against the wall. Vivi ignores me and pulls her housecoat down around her knees and flips through the pages of her *Teen* magazine.

Sixteen, bony, and knocked-kneed, Vivi has some growing up to do. I gave her stringy brown hair a perm last week. Wants to be like Madonna, she says. "Not on my watch," I say. Floyd used to say that a lot. My Marine husband also used to shout, "Death before dishonor!" I've quoted it a time or two to the girls. From the night Vernise hightailed it out of town in Lenny's old Dodge pickup, I've been bound and determined my Vivi won't end up giving me another grandchild to raise.

Problem is, Vivi draws boys like a fresh cow patty draws flies. She inherited her chest from my momma. Viola wore a double D and Vivi is nearly there. Her face is like a young Marilyn Monroe. Flossie told her she could change her name to Norma Jean and get away with it. She's a beauty, I admit.

Vivi clenches her fist and holds her housecoat tight against her collarbone. Her hair is wet and I see goosebumps march across her arms. She turns the fan toward me now. She lets go of the collar and the fabric remains molded by her damp palm — it reminds me of how we mold our lives before we even know we've done it. Vivi tosses her magazine to the floor and smiles. Victoria has crawled to where she is.

"Hey, baby girl," she says. Vivi loves babies. It scares me to death.

I groan at the pile of dirty dishes drowning in my stainless steel sink. The kitchen counter is covered with coffee grounds, something sticky, and crumbs from the morning's breakfast of toast and scuppernong jam. The floor needs swept, and garbage cans overflow with dirty diapers. I sigh, reach for my checkbook, and pay a few past-due bills and one shut-off notice. After a cup of strong coffee, I decide to wash the dishes myself. I smoke while I do the dishes. It calms my nerves and I'm less apt to snap at Vivi again. I pinch my cigarette with sudsy hands and flick the ashes into an ashtray on the window ledge above the sink.

"Vivi, I expect this place to be spic and span by the time I get home. I mean it."

"Cain't Momma, I promised Missy I'd go to the movies with her."

"Ain't no money for you to waste on movies. Have her come here, make popcorn, there's a box of Chef Boyardee Pizza mix. But ya ain't goin' to the movies."

"You're gonna run me off like you did Vernise! Nothing changes!"

"You're right 'bout that, darlin'. Nothing changes 'round here but the size of my ass and the number of dependents I can claim on my taxes. Behave, Vivi. I'm off to work." I fill my travel mug with coffee, put a little hat on Victoria's head and hope she keeps it on.

Vivi sneers at me. I smile back and blow her a kiss goodbye. She can sass as good as Vernise, I swear. But if I go mining for the truth, I'd have to say I don't have any more to offer Vivi than I did her sister. She may take off one day too — leave me a note. I can't think about that now.

The baby's car seat gives me fits. It's second-hand from the Salvation Army. You'd think it'd be broken in by now, but it's harder than hell to buckle in a screaming twenty-five pound child without pitching my own hissy fit. Once I get her in and calmed down, I grab my Camels out of my purse, tap the bottom of the new pack, pull off the cellophane, and light up. The nicotine hits my bloodstream just in time.

I drive past old man Deeter's place. That man is as ugly as a hairless goat. He rents the trailer next to mine. His Christmas lights stay hooked to his awning all year long. Sometimes he turns them on in the summer. Keeps his dog chained to the cement block on his patio. He waves. I wave back with my cigarette in my hand. That's the extent of my neighborliness in this place.

I think about Roger Moultrie as I steer toward his abandoned trailer and exhale. He was so smart. Handsome too. I had high hopes he'd be my knight in denim armor. I heard he had a degree in Transportation — anyways, that's what Flossie said. The first time he spoke to me he said, "Ma'am, you sure have a pretty baby." I quickly corrected him, pointing out my relationship to Victoria. Don't matter now. But I think about him more lately since he's been gone.

Flicking my ashes out the window, I drive slowly past his empty trailer. I know it's empty. It's got that unmistakable way a trailer looks when nobody lives in it any more. He came to my place last winter when my pipes froze and showed me how to use my hairdryer to thaw them out. I invited him to stay for a beer and a barbeque sandwich. Of course, Vivi was there. I think she liked him but she never said. We started waving to each other after that. Then one day I heard he moved on. Some woman in Little Rock's probably making goo-goo eyes at him now.

Maneuvering through Needmore takes all of five minutes. Only a crossroads makes up this place. Calvary Baptist Church sits on the corner with their Vacation Bible School sign that reads, "Seventy-five years of celebrating Jesus." The rest of Needmore includes a one-woman beauty shop, a ceramics shop, a run-down gas station, and a few small frame houses squatting among lots of weeds. This morning I notice one house with a sign in the yard — Notary Public. I wonder if a Notary Public does much business out here and how much money I could make. I jot down a mental note to inquire in Salisbury next time I drive in for groceries and needles for my sewing machine.

I arrive at the flea market and Flossie hands me a new pile of yardsticks I'm sure she bought at an estate sale.

"Got cha' some yardsticks, 'Nel."

I shake my head. "I'll give ya a dollar for the lot. It's the best I can do."

"Sold," she says and wobbles back to sell a toilet paper doll to a customer.

"Thanks, Flossie," I yell after her, "but I still need to sell the ones I bought from ya last week."

I unpack my car and park Victoria in her playpen. It's quiet this morning, so far. A few Sunday morning customers who've skipped church wander in. For some reason, I take a hard look around me. This flea market is white boy heaven. You can buy gun racks for your truck real cheap. The man at the end of my row sells every size of Confederate flag imaginable, along with turquoise jewelry, Budweiser neon signs, belt buckles, and little homemade outhouses with half moons in the doors. When you open them, there's a little old man with his pants down reading the Sears and Roebuck catalog.

There's every kind of Nascar paraphernalia you can imagine inside the pole building. I heard they're having a drawing — if you put your name in the Dale Earnhart hat and your ticket is pulled, you win a free paint job and two tickets to Bristol Raceway. I ain't a race fan, but it'd be a way to get out of town for a day or two and have my Fairlane painted.

They sell meat on a stick here. In the food and beverage section. Nobody knows what kind of meat, but the out-of-state people love it. None of us will eat it. The stand next to it sells pork skins and lemonade. And once a month the Lexington barbeque trailer sets up and sells a large tray of chopped barbeque, slaw, and a side of hush puppies for two dollars and fifty cents. I usually get enough to take some home for supper.

The afternoon drags. I look over and Flossie is fanning herself again. This time under her triple chin. I hear her flip-flops smack the bottoms of her feet making her way to my table. Pink powder has gathered in the wrinkles of her plump face as she leans over and points like a bird dog.

"Look out Vernell; here comes Dot."

Dot Bickham is the owner of Dot's Antiques and Emporium. Most of what she sells in her store on Main Street is used furniture. Laminate kitchen tables with missing chrome chairs, or a couch with a hole chewed out of the back by somebody's dog. But if you're hard up and need to furnish your place, it's the place to shop. Dot is the woman to see when it comes to pure American junk. She even keeps boxes of overstocked and chipped tableware she buys wholesale from a once-a-year trip to factories up north.

Dot scours the papers for the best yard sales. She visits the day before they open, knocks on the door, and asks the folks if she can get first dibs. It works. Every other weekend, Dot hauls her pickup full of furniture, antique picture frames, boxes of books mixed with a few ancient magazines like *Look* and *National Geographic* to the flea market where she wheels and deals enough to make ends meet.

The old gal sleeps in the back of her store on a cot, cooks on a hot plate, and washes her clothes once a month at the Laundromat next to her store. I invite her to Thanksgiving every year. Dot has no family. She thinks I'm her family now.

I watch her cross the gravel drive, lean over the chain link fence and spit a tiny jet stream of tobacco juice into a rusted trash barrel. She taps the side of a Skoal can she's pulled from her back pocket, then tucks a fresh pinch into her lip. I can smell her. She reeks of gasoline and egg salad. She pulls her Esso ball cap down further to cover her eyes from the bright sun. I don't think the woman has any sense to buy a cheap pair of sunglasses. Her eyes are all wrinkled from squinting. I guess her to be in her fifties, but nobody knows for sure. Believe me, we all took a stab at guessing Dot's age once or twice.

Flossie shakes her head resentfully. "No wonder she ain't got any relatives, who'd claim her!" I swear, Flossie and Dot . . . they don't gee-haw very well. They're like a pit bull and a fat fluffy poodle. Get too close and somebody's going to get bit, and usually it's fluffy Flossie yelping in the end.

Flossie turns and huffs back to her tables. Her rear end sways back and forth like the rump of a Holstein heading to the barn. Her threadbare daisy print housedress does nothing for her full figure. And Flossie shouldn't talk about family. I've seen some of her unmentionable relatives. Her nephew's a bone hound that works at the Waffle House and plays Hank Williams and Porter Wagoner on the jukebox all night. Nothing to be proud of, for sure.

Thing is, Dot's not afraid to work. I heard she pumped gas at her daddy's Esso station for twenty years to buy her store in '69. She's okay in my book. Dot smiles at me with tobacco-darkened teeth. I can tell it tickles her to watch Flossie run from the confrontation she's sure to get if she sticks around.

"At least I can run better'n that Flossie Muldaney!" Dot yells. Her colonial-blue eyes and angular jaw line hint to beauty once upon a time. For an older lady, she's muscular and toned. A husky voice laden with sin, Dot takes off her ball cap and fans the summer flies away.

"Vernell, just look at my new hairdo. What in tarnation happened to it? I been a wallerin' in the bed and I guess I done wallered it to death. Your beauty shop girl fixed it real purty last week. Now look at it, what am I supposed to do with this?"

I have to admit, I'm about to bust up laughing. I smother it. Lord, my dog's hair looks better than Dot's. "When's the last time you washed it?" I ask.

"I ain't washed it since the beauty shop girl cut it."

"Dot," I say slowly, "when you go home tonight, get in the shower and wash your hair with the shampoo I bought ya, not a bar of soap. Rinse it real good then comb it with a clean comb. Let it dry before you go to bed. Wash your body while you're at it."

"That'll make my hair purty again?"

"Yes." I turn, roll my eyes, and wait on my next customer, offering to pick out a pretty bag to match her dress.

⌒⌒

That evening I drive home with my car windows rolled down. I stop at a light next to the tent revival. I can hear the faint tune of *Are You Washed In The Blood* echoing out to my car.

I never could measure up to church or to my momma and daddy. Viola and Elmer walked that sawdust aisle many times while I remained on my metal chair and ate cherry Lifesavers, or pretended to be asleep. They hauled me to revivals every summer; I refused to go after I left home.

I look over to the cars in neat rows on the blacktop. A couple stray women and children run in as the music plays. I sit at the light, the music swells and another familiar praise song floats in on a breeze. I recall the words, *Jesus on the main line, tell Him what you want.* Quite vividly, I remember the weeklong meetings where my momma would rededicate her life to holiness. Evangelists with red handkerchiefs in all-black suits or all-white suits would preach about fire and death, the book of Revelation, the judgments reserved for those who abuse their "temples of God" with cigarettes, drugs, and alcohol. They'd wage war against slow dancing, television, movies, card games, homosexuality, makeup, and rock and roll. Evangelists pounded their fists on pulpits and wailed that all liars, whoremongers, thieves, murderers, and backslidden Christians would be cast into a lake of fire. And if we didn't walk the aisle that very night, we'd surely get in a car wreck on the way home, die, and open our eyes in hell. Or worse, miss the rapture and burn forever.

The most terrible fear we knew was missing the rapture. It hung over our heads like a lit match by a gas pump and God was liable to drop the match at any minute.

I tried not to allow evangelists to heap any more fear on me than the psycho in the Alfred Hitchcock movie. I watched Momma and Daddy get saved every summer. They'd praise the Lord for about two weeks after the revival was over. The house remained peaceful for those two glorious weeks. Then, one night without warning, they wouldn't come home until early in the morning. All liquored up, they'd been out all night at the bars, road houses, and honky tonks where, in the hot, steamy Southern nights, yearning, excitement, and the desperate attempt to hold onto their secret desires for all they were worth had surfaced once again. It went thataway until the next summer when revival came back into town.

In the meantime, Momma prophesied over me plenty before she died. "Vernell, you'll end up in a trailer like me, sure as my name is Viola Pauline Truvey, with six snotty noses screamin' at yer feet, and red dust coverin' the diapers and T-shirts you hang on the line." She was wrong. Were only two baby girls in my future and Floyd bought me a Hotpoint the year before he died. I never believed in prophecy. Especially Momma's.

But the fear of hell continued to plague me with every visiting evangelist that come to town. Even as a young woman professing to be an agnostic, the terror grew stronger than ever. At night I'd think about screaming preachers, the fires of hell and the demons that meant an eternity of torment. I'd roll on my bed; confess my sins so I could sleep. And just as I'd nod off, I'd hear the archangel's trumpet to rapture the saints. My heart would race and the sweat pop as I reached for my radio to hear the news report that I'd been left behind. Then the trumpet sounded again . . . a damn blasted train whistle in the distance. After a sigh of relief, I'd leave the radio on for diversion then wish to God I'd been born in some jungle in South America and had never heard about religion.

Years later, I married Floyd and got busy having my girls. I swore I'd never put my young'uns through that nonsense. As long as I kept busy raising kids, I could focus on them and no longer fear hell. No longer lay awake wondering if some demon shared my room.

The traffic light changes and it feels like warm oil has been poured over my head. I recognize it. The feeling I heard my momma tell about. It's the sensation right before you make a decision to rededicate your life.

The side of the semi that hauled the tent and equipment into town has a sign painted on it. *Ask, and ye shall receive.* I turn into the lot and park next to the Burger King.

I find the nursery and just like a coat check, hand Victoria over to a sweet lady who sticks a ticket in my hand identifying me as the owner of the child. Victoria cries a moment then sees a trailer full of toys and children and is anxious to get down and play. I sneak out and walk to the pay phone near the gas station on the corner.

I'm tired. What am I doing here? I can hardly hold my eyes open. I call Vivi.

"Where you at, Momma?"

"I'll tell ya later, don't worry, we'll be home in a couple hours." Vivi doesn't seem to care.

I walk in and a trio is leading a song. I see Rosalyn and her husband are part of the trio. He don't look so scary. He's wearing a nice-fitting blue suit and a white shirt with a red satin tie. His hair looks stylish, much better than his wife's. From where I sit, I can see him put his arm around her. I like that. The tent is filled and eventually all the seats are taken. People start to stand around the walls of the tent and spill out onto the asphalt lot.

Between more songs I hear the rustle of fans, young'uns fussing and being told to hush, and the low talking of people in the parking lot. An occasional cough and the crackle of candy paper cuts the silence. I sit on the back row and watch Evangelist Jimmy Boudreaux step up to the microphone with a big black Bible in his hands. He begins to talk in tongues.

The congregation shouts and the organ music swells again to no song in particular. I decide to stick it out and try to concentrate on the sermon he eventually starts to preach. It's not so bad as I remember from my childhood. Brother Jimmy doesn't seem to be hard-core hell, fire, and brimstone. He's preaching about love and renewed mercies more than anything else. I like him.

But then he shouts, "Revival!" and sways from side to side, his hands raised high. The organist hits the keys again. The air is seductive. "Revival, brothers and sisters," he says, "is for those who have at one time been washed in the blood and then, through carelessness, temptation, covering their light with a bushel, and plain lack of devotion, have fallen away. Revival isn't just for those who've never been saved. Revival is for the backslider!"

He drones on, his voice gets louder and more compelling. After he's been at it for a few more minutes, the ghosts from my past loom in front of me again with special punishments reserved for those who've blasphemed. People either amen him or, like me, become agitated and shift in their seats.

The longer Brother Jimmy speaks, the louder the Holy Rollers shout and the more I feel sick. My eyes throb and by the end of the sermon, I want to crawl under piles of sawdust.

He finally gives the altar call, inviting us to receive Jesus. But I don't leave. I cave and walk the aisle, hoping it'll make a difference in my life. I walk toward redemption the same way Momma did on the same type sawdust floor. This time over asphalt instead of dirt. I see Rosalyn and she's praying with Lin Wang. I can't believe it. I kneel in the sawdust beside Rosalyn. I can tell her desire to see me get saved is a burning passion smoldering under her plain cotton dress and a pair of pointy eyeglasses.

"The wages of sin is death, Vernell," she says. *She could've said, nice to see you, Vernell, remember me?* But she looks straight into my eyes again and asks, "Are you sorry for your sins and reprobate mind? Do you want to be baptized in the Spirit?"

"Yes, I do."

She prays with me and I see the sweat beaded on her forehead and neck. I smell it. It's mixed with her perfume. She ends her prayer then looks hard at me. "The Lord loves you. Do you believe that?"

"I don't know. I've seen little evidence lately."

"Then ask Him. Ask Him to show you a sign. What is your greatest need or even your heart's desire? Jesus says, behold I stand at the door and knock. Ask Him to do more than supply your need, ask Him to grant your greatest desire." She puts her arm around my shoulders. "Oh, Vernell," there is a change in her voice, a tenderness in her words like they'd been held and rocked in a baby cradle down in her throat, "just let Jesus into your heart."

So I fold my hands and cock my head toward heaven, hoping, wishing, and praying to hear the Lord's voice.

Lord? You still up there somewhere? I'm real sorry. Sorry I dodged You all my life. I know I ain't got any right to ask, but I got me a rent payment due next week and no idea how to pay it. I cain't keep dippin' into my savings. It's 'bout gone. Unless I sell me a shit load of purses, oh sorry, a bunch of purses, I'm gonna be broke and homeless. I got a child named Vivi, she needs things. I have a little grandbaby to take care of. And my daughter, Vernise, I have no idea where . . .

I cry. Rosalyn stuffs a tissue into my hand. The congregation sings, *Just As I Am.*

True, I ain't followed You like I should have. I don't know much 'bout the Bible and religion, except that it scared me to death. Never got saved as a child. If I had walked the aisle with Momma, maybe I wouldn't be in this mess. Maybe I wouldn't have lost my husband.

I cry harder.

I miss my husband.

Anyway, dear Lord, I been stuck in a trailer park since I was four. In Needmore. Well, hell, You know where I dadgum live.

I feel the splintery sawdust dig into my knees. I sound like a hillbilly on steroids. My prayer hits a wall and I stand to my feet.

I'm not sure anybody's listening. I bend over and whisk chips of wood and dirt off my knees, wipe my eyes, and then walk out.

"Opening bottles of beer is easier'n this." An usher hears me mumble and shakes his head in disgust.

The sky is bright with stars and a full moon as I drive home. I'm in the middle of nowhere, it's rural as far as the eye can see. There's no man-made light other than my car's headlights. No traffic. I stop on the gravel road and turn off the engine. The dust from the road behind me is carried across the field on a breeze. It looks like a lone cloud sparkling in the moonlight. All is quiet. The baby is asleep in her car seat. I ease the door shut after stepping out into the night air. I hear the chuff and cough of deer in the distance, maybe a raccoon or two. The faint stench of skunk and cow manure from the plowed field reminds me of where I am, near old lady Weber's farm. Sitting on the hood of my car, feeling its warmth, I lean back on my elbows and gaze up into the vastness of space. *Where are you, God?* I'm not afraid when I hear His still, small voice. "*I can be found anywhere,*" He says. And all this time, I thought I had to go looking for Him in revival tents and buildings with steeples. The night is alive with signs and wonders that follow me, as I believe for the first time in my life. Peace floods my insides. A shooting star startles me for an instant. I wave to it passing overhead. "My turn," I say . . . amazed.

I watch a televangelist on channel seven. He drives divine words down the back of my throat and I gag on my tears again. Since visiting the revival, I seem to cry more.

"Oh sinner, reach out and touch the Lord, as he passes by, you'll find He's not too weary to hear your heart's cry. He's passing by this moment, your needs to supply. Reach out and touch the Lord, as he passes by." The tall good-looking man with slicked back hair that matches his shiny black shoes wails and sings through pearly white teeth. His white shirt is soaked in sweat and the skinny tie he wears is held fast with a tie bar that glitters in the camera.

TV cameras pan the inside of the great tent revival. The small town congregation gawks like wide-mouthed bass ready for the deep fryer. I try to guess the color of his tie on my black and white Zenith. Color TV ain't something I can afford, not this month anyway.

The healings begin. He touches people's heads and they fall to the sawdust floor. Women and children walk the makeshift aisle, just like I did a month ago, metal chairs are lined in rows. A woman looks like she's having convulsions, her hairdo shakes loose, ushers try to calm her.

The phone rings. Vivi runs to answer it. "Momma . . . for you!"

She breaks my attention. "Hush," I say. "He's 'bout to cast demons outa that woman."

The organ hymns mount. The faith healer lays his hands around the woman's neck and prays. "Come out devils!" The woman shakes harder and falls to the ground.

"Thank you, Jesus. Yes Lord! Praise Him, people!" The evangelist's chin quivers so fast you can see it on the TV. He starts hopping on one leg.

Vivi folds her arms in front of her. "They all look drunk to me."

"They are, darlin'. Drunk in the Spirit." I think about the liquored-up drunks where I used to tend bar and where I may have to go back to work to make ends meet. "Oh nuts, we're losing the signal. Need me some new rabbit ears."

Vivi giggles. "Ah shoot, Mommie, you're missin' the beggin' for money part."

"Ain't got any to send him this month, anyway," I sigh. "Shit. I'll miss out on the blessed cloth special." I smash out my cigarette butt in my favorite ashtray. "But I got my pressed flowers from Bethlehem last month. I suppose I could use them if I need to."

"Need to what?"

"Never mind." *Pray for money.* "Who called?" I ask.

"Dot. You need to go over to her store. Right away. She said it's important."

"Is she sick?"

"How would I know? I didn't ask, she didn't say."

"Watch the baby, I'll be back in an hour."

I grab my cigarettes and hope my Fairlane starts. It's been acting up the last few days. I worry about Dot. Sometimes mean people come into her store to poke fun at her. Mostly young punks. Big, unpredictable, and cruel young men. It's not Dot I should worry about, though. Last year, a young man from a neighboring high school found himself with a bottom full of buckshot for taunting her because she smelled bad. She got a week in jail. Old Dot didn't mind. She asked to stay a few more days; said the food tasted better than the slop she cooked. Lord, help us all.

When I arrive, I see Dot run toward my car. She's clenching a toothpick between her lips. I've never seen her move so fast. A half-dozen mixed breed dogs bolt out with her, barking and wagging their tails. I jump out of my car and meet her in the alley on the side of her store. Between the smell of fried okra wafting out from her kitchen window and her snuff, she can't get a decent breath.

"You . . . you, remember that box of old books you gave me to sell for ya?"

I haven't thought about that box since I gave it to Dot. "Yeah, so?"

A memory: *Rosalyn Boudreaux came to the flea market the Sunday they packed up the revival tent. She carried a box of nasty-smelling, mildewy old books and said, "Vernell, I got these books at a church yard sale in Broken Arrow, Oklahoma. We met a few local pastors for breakfast one morning before the sale, and I found these at a table marked five dollars for the box. Jimmy rummaged through and took out a few books written by Dwight Moody and John Wesley, but you can have the rest. Maybe you can sell them."*

"How much do you want for the box?" I really wasn't interested in buying old books.

Rosalyn laughed. "Heavens, I don't want any money for these. I thought maybe you could sell them for yourself. I'd like to help you, Vernell." Then she laid a twenty dollar bill in my hand. I shoved it back in her shirt pocket. Can you imagine getting an offering from a preacher? I wouldn't be able to stand myself.

"Please, Vernell, let me help you," she said.

"I'll accept that nasty box of books, but not the money. Thanks anyway," I said. That ended our conversation. The next day, I asked Dot to sell the books for me in her shop.

I heard Rosalyn and Jimmy Boudreaux pitched their revival tent in Beckley, West Virginia last week.

I repeat my question. "What about the box, Dot?"

Dot is having a tough time finding her words, which is unusual. She pulls me down on the side stoop to sit next to her on two cement blocks she uses to prop the door open on hot days.

"Vernell, you ain't a gonna believe this. But at the bottom of that box laid an aged newspaper. Dated back to 1950. Yellowed and brittle. I lifted it out thinking I might like to have it. I figured I'd pay you a dollar for it. I opened it and inside was a picture wrapped in blue tissue paper of some kind between two thick pieces of cardboard. A real purty picture of a good-lookin' cowboy. I remembered you said that preacher woman got this box in Oklahoma. I thought maybe . . . well, I thought I ought to give the whole kit n' caboodle to my friend in Greensboro. This nutty professor that likes old books. So I take the books and the cowboy picture to Professor Wendell at UNCG. My alma mater."

"What? Say that again. You went to college? Now wait . . . I cain't picture it."

"Don't tell anybody down here, it's embarrassin'. I cover it well, don't I?"

"Yeah," I say. I'm in shock.

Dot's mouth tries to keep up with her thoughts. "Middle of the night I get a phone call. 'Bout scared the fuckin' shit out of me. It's Professor Wendell askin' me to come in to talk about that damn picture." I never saw Dot so flustered.

"Dot, please don't use that language, it hurts my newly saved ears."

"Sorry." Dot stands and holds her hand out for me. "Git up Vernell, come inside."

I'm puzzled. But like a foolish puppy dog, I follow her around to the rear of her store. There's a car parked in the dirt lot beside her pickup truck. I step through the back door to her living quarters. Nothing's changed, it's still a pig sty and reeks of urine and cooking fat. I walk behind her through torn fiberglass curtains separating the back room from the front retail area. Two men are hunched over the antique pool table Dot's been trying to sell for the last five years. Warped pool sticks have been rolled into a pile in the middle of the table. A glass counter where Dot displays her junk jewelry is covered with briefcases. They're peering through a magnifying glass looking at a picture laid out on the end of the pool table.

Dot begins her introductions. "Vernell, this here's Mr. Grant Tucker from New York City. Professor Wendell asked him to come to North Carolina. Grant here wants to talk to you about your picture."

I stare at the odd-looking men. Mr. Tucker can barely take his eyes off the picture. He gives me a brief nod, then folds up the magnifying glass and sticks it in his vest pocket where I catch a glimpse of a pocket watch. He reminds me of what Sherlock Holmes must've looked like, if such a character ever existed.

I shake Mr. Tucker's hand first. Then shaking the hand of the man Dot introduces as Professor Hal Wendell, I notice Hal could pass for someone around here. He's wearing Levis, a plaid flannel shirt and boots. His salt and pepper hair match his mustache and only his wire rim glasses give him the appearance of a professor.

Mr. Tucker motions for me to take a look at the picture. "Miss Paskins, I work for a reputable auction house in New York City, called Sotheby's. Have you heard of it?"

"No, cain't say I have."

"We are experts at finding and appraising rare art. When Dot and the good Professor here tracked me down, I must say I was skeptical. But, I've known Hal Wendell a long time and he persisted. You have a rare piece of artwork here, Miss Paskins. Rare indeed."

By this time, my shock has turned to butterflies in my belly. "Well, you want to tell me about it or am I gonna have to guess?"

He clears his throat. "Charles Marion Russell was an accomplished painter, sculptor, illustrator, and a gifted storyteller. Russell was born in 1864 in St. Louis, Missouri on the edge of the flourishing Western frontier. He sketched in his free time and soon gained a local reputation as an artist. His firsthand experience as a ranch hand and his intimate knowledge of outdoor life contributed to the distinctive realism characteristic of his style. This is his *Self-Portrait*, painted in 1900."

"In when?"

"1900."

I bend over the picture. It seems to be in pretty good shape, but what do I know. The only art I have hanging in my trailer is of pretty little butterflies or bowls of fruit in cheap wooden or silver frames. I buy them at the flea market or from Dot. But, this is a cowboy. His feet are planted solid on the ground and his hat is tipped back. He wears a red sash and high-heeled riding boots.

"There's not much else to say, Miss Paskins. I am a legal representative of my company and I have reported back to them the painting is the original. I have a check here. Sotheby's has authorized me to pay you two hundred thousand dollars for this painting."

I sit down on a nearby folding chair. My legs shake and my tongue is numb.

"All I want is a finder's fee, Vernell," says Dot.

Today is Thanksgiving. I am the most thankful woman on the face of the earth.

Dot is here, bless her heart. She's had a bath and bought a new pair of blue jeans and boots for the occasion. I gave Dot a check for ten thousand dollars and told her to clean up her act. She did. She sold the store and bought a cabin with a washer and dryer in it. It sits in a meadow in the mountains where she can live how she wants, with nobody around to make fun of her. I never could figure out why she went to college. I drive up every now and then. The cabin is small, but it's nicer and somewhat cleaner than the store.

I sent twenty thousand to Brother Jimmy after I cashed the check. I figured God deserved His tithe. He and Rosalyn have decided to build a church in Raleigh and start a home for wayward girls. They're going to call it The Paskins House. Floyd would be so pleased.

I bequeathed all my handbags and sewing machine to Flossie. She's taken over my tables at the flea market, started collecting boxes of old books, and has learned to speak a few words of Chinese. Now she thinks she's an expert. We still have coffee and talk about Dot. I'm trying to quit my Camel habit, and Flossie gave up biscuits and gravy — at least for now.

I bought a house. First house I ever lived in. It's small, but it's new and it's mine. There's a park across the street, and I put some money into a college fund for Vivi. I bought a new swing set yesterday for the baby. She has her own room and I painted it blue, like her eyes. I bought some health insurance, life insurance, and a slightly used car. Now I didn't want to blow the rest on trips to Wal-Mart or Food Lion. Knowing nothing about investing money, I called the smartest man to whom I've ever been introduced. At the advice of Professor Wendell, I invested in some stock called Microsoft or some silly name like that.

I saw Roger Moultrie in town yesterday. He's moved back into his trailer in Needmore. Said he moved to Little Rock for a while to take care of his sick Momma. After her funeral, he decided to come back to North Carolina. I said, "Good, I missed you." We're going to dinner next week.

Vivi's lounging on our new recliner, watching the new color TV. The baby's asleep in her crib. I'm thinking I'll turn in early. Dot's already snoring on the couch.

The doorbell rings, the dog barks, and Vivi runs to answer it. We've already had our pumpkin pie, but there might be one piece left for a visitor, I suppose.

"Hey, Viv." I hear her voice. My eyes pool with tears and I thank the good Lord, quietly. Vernise has come home. I don't care how or why or for how long. She's here now.

God has breathed life into my past and is blowing it into the present. It feels good for a change.

There is a percentage of the female population that was not meant to bear children. Never having the slightest desire to raise offspring, they lead full and happy lives . . . childless. But when a woman decides to have a baby, nothing and nobody can stop her, not even her mate. The maternal pull to have a child is nothing short of a miracle and few men understand that urge.

The story, Punkin Head, is a spin-off of my upcoming novel, *Televenge*. Andie and Joe Oliver are the two main characters in this story and in my novel. The ignorance of blindly following a pastor, teacher, reverend, priest or even a mentor and having no mind of your own is touched on here. A few religious leaders discourage their members from having children — and in some cases, forbid it.

I explore this type of manipulation and the dark side of televangelism further in my upcoming novel.

In this story, a natural desire has been made complicated by religious legalism. Andie struggles with following "God" and listening to her heart.

I dedicate this story to my children.

Punkin Head

Andie kept her secret as long as she could.

Puking was more from fear than from her pregnancy. Joe didn't want a baby. Now or ever. A dedicated employee of the Temple of Praise television ministry, children meant less money and time Joe could devote to his job. Reverend Calvin Artury was clear in his *no children* policy for staff. An unusual request for a minister, but Artury was no ordinary preacher. He was a televangelist, in the strictest fundamental sense of the title. His ministry team had no time to raise children.

"This can't wait any longer. You need to know." She was not to bother him when he studied his Bible. Two hours of Wednesday night prayer time came before eating, watching television, or talking to his wife.

Suspicious, Joe lifted his head instead of ignoring her. His face turned as pale as school paste. He snarled. "Are you pregnant?"

She nodded and lowered her soft green eyes, whimpering a pathetic, "Yes." Andie twisted her Kleenex and dabbed at her tears. She hiccupped back her sobs into her throat.

Joe's reaction was like watching werewolf movies as a child, covering her eyes while Lon Chaney contorted into deformities of fur, fangs, and claws, mutating into a bloodthirsty werewolf. Joe ran his hand hard through his hair. Andie couldn't move. Fear and sweat trickled down her spine.

With his next breath he flung his King James Concordance at her head, missing her by a finger-width. His target hung on the wall behind her — their wedding picture. He hit his bull's-eye, knocking it to the floor, shattering the glass.

Andie gasped, clasped her hand over her mouth, and backed against the door. Joe's eyes flashed fire and daggers aimed at her heart. He sprung from the chair and lunged toward her, stopping inches from her face; bullets of spit flew into her eyes and hair.

"You promised me! You agreed, no kids! Didn't we agree, Andie? You know how important my future is on the ministry team and working in the church! How could you do this?"

Andie mulled over her reluctant *cult* membership.

"Reverend Artury told me to never get you pregnant!"

She lifted her head. Her brows formed a V and her eyes narrowed to serpent slits. She gritted her teeth. Shocked that their pastor would attempt to control their private moments together, Andie held her tongue. She had not met this side of her new husband. He'd been a gentle lover, a kind man, and a hardworking and faithful husband. Only lately had she felt him turn his attention more to church than to her. She would fight Joe's hot temper and blind allegiance he mistook for doing the Lord's work with the cool tone of common sense.

"But Joe, God has given us a gift," she said.

Panting like a rabid werewolf crazy with rage, Joe grabbed his jacket and car keys. "Get rid of it! Give it back to God!"

The Piedmont basked in an autumn sun. The late October day was bright, invigorating, and cool enough for a light jacket. The air grew crisp as breezes floated down from the north. Wine-colored crepe myrtle, pear, and dogwoods heralded the muted leaves of a North Carolina fall: colors of plum, candy apple red, nutmeg and rust — and a variety of neon yellows and peach.

Cutout jack-o'-lanterns and ghosts decorated the town's windows. A grinning cardboard skeleton with accordion-pleated legs swung from the entrance of Dr. Eshelman's office.

"I can't tell you what to do, missy. If you choose to have this baby, let me know. You two need counselin'. I can recommend somebody," he said.

Avoiding her doctor's eyes, Andie swallowed her tears and fled the exam room.

The ride home was quiet. The car radio hadn't worked in months. She missed it and the Joe she used to know.

A produce stand loomed in the distance. Indian corn, burnt orange mums and pumpkins adorned the front. The sun's rays bounced off the stand's tin roof, temporarily blinding her as her car crept into the parking lot and stopped.

Andie gazed at a line of sunny pumpkins displayed on a rickety plank of old barn siding shelved between two apple crates. Her conversation with Joe last week replayed in her head. A discussion as irritating as his scratched Reba Rambo record.

"We can't afford no jack-o'-lantern! You got no business wastin' money. Givin' to the Lord's work is more important than buyin' a pumpkin. Besides, those things are of the devil."

"Pumpkins? God made pumpkins."

"I'm talkin' 'bout the Druids, or some such nonsense people that made evil faces out of pumpkins. Remember Reverend Artury's sermon? Besides, I won't have you contributin' to a celebration of the devil."

"Oh Joe, trick-or-treat's just a fun night for kids to dress up and get candy."

"Jus' the same, evil don't need to be sittin' on my front porch!"

After counting her quarters, Andie browsed the roadside stand. Yellow and red leaves spun around her head. She took her time to pick out a large pumpkin. Daydreaming, she turned and nearly tripped over a little boy with tears lying on his plump cheeks. His skin was as black as her daddy's hunting dog, Pitch. The boy's lips were pouty pink and cracked. He wore a torn jacket that needed washing and his T-shirt appeared two sizes too small, exposing his round belly. Andie crouched down so she could look him in the eyes.

"What's wrong, Sugah? Can't you find your mama?"

He nodded his head and wiped his nose with his sleeve. "Mama's over there." He pointed to an old Volkswagen van, smashed in the front, rusted, and on its last legs. She stood and shielded her eyes from the sun with her hand. The van was crawling with kids like ants on an anthill. Andie heard the muffled yell of the extra-large woman in the driver's seat attempting to discipline her children. Pink sponge curlers sprouted from her head.

"Your Mama know you're out here?" Andie asked.

"Yes'um, sent me to get Granny. She be buyin' some beans." Another tear popped out. "I want a punkin head. Mama won't buy one. She say cost too much."

The boy's granny shuffled out the door of the produce stand with her sack of beans. She motioned for him to come. He looked up at Andie with her pumpkin in her arms then turned around and ambled back to the van, kicking at the dry leaves cartwheeling and crackling around his feet. Andie watched the little boy's granny try to pick him up and assist him into the rundown vehicle.

"Wait!" Andie shouted, hurrying toward the roar of children. "This is for you." The van full of rowdy kids hushed. She held out her pumpkin to the little boy. He took hold of it and his face beamed, exposing a bright toothy smile.

"Every child needs a punkin head at Halloween. Make a good one, okay?"

"Thanks, Ma'am."

Andie rubbed his head, then smiled and waved to his mama. She gave Andie a curious stare before the boy's granny closed the door.

Immediately, the kids returned to yelling and tussling inside the van. She heard the mother scream over the noise, "Percy, I say leave yo sistah alone! I gone beat you when we git home!"

The sun blinded Andie again, reflecting off the side mirror of the dilapidated van crawling out of the lot. She blinked.

No child should be beat.

There was only one beat that mattered to Andie. Only one beat she wanted. A beat that could stop time, or a beat to *keep* time to the tune of love songs and lullabies sung by mothers to their infants all over the world. It had rhythm and she could dance to it. A simple beat passed down for thousands of generations. A beat that was hers, inside. She could listen to the sound of it forever. A heartbeat, the most angelic sound she'd ever heard.

Wild horses from hell couldn't drag her to a clinic to "give it back to God." It was time to tell that to the other half of the heartbeat.

That evening, Joe returned home from church to a huge jack-o'-lantern smiling at him on the porch. Candlelight flickered through the devilish grin of Andie's punkin head. WE'RE HAVING A BABY was cut through the back, and glowed.

CRY is a contrast in extremes.

A young girl, living just above the poverty line, struggles with unanswered questions about her past. Running parallel to her story is the oppulent and abundent life of a televangelist, who is not only well-known, she's a woman, "God's anointed daughter."

Two different stories — two opposite women . . . merging in the most unexpected place.

The inspiration for this tale of Southern women came from the first line. I had written it weeks before all the characters revealed themselves. But also, with church being paramount in my life growing up (my religious roots go way deep), I wanted to explore what it would be like for a young girl who was not raised in church.

The characters appeared at the oddest times, visiting my mind regularly to check on my progress. Many nights they got me out of bed to finish a scene or change their dialogue. I originally intended Janey Gay to be my protagonist . . . but in the end, Essie and Loretta convinced me that they had the most important story to tell.

Cry

Essie ~ Selma, North Carolina, October 1989

Had I known my mother was going to leave me the day after I was born, I would've fought to stay inside her a while longer. My cousin, Ray Keith Bertram and his wife, Janey Gay, were my best friends. Janey, who was all of twenty-two, celebrated six months of pregnancy the same day I turned fifteen. Over time, I watched her belly inflate to the size of Ray's basketball, so perhaps it was no surprise I thought of my own mama a lot during those days.

Ray Keith had joined the Marine Corps and we were on our way to Cherry Point, Janey Gay and me, when she steered her Ford Pinto into the Wal-Mart parking lot. She said she needed to use the toilet and then get her glasses fixed. They had broken a week ago and the first aid tape she'd wrapped around the nose bridge wasn't holding. Then she mumbled something about needing makeup to cover the zit on her chin and a pair of maternity pantyhose, and said if I complained one more time she'd throw me out on the side of the road.

We planned to drive to Cherry Point and back home in three days. Janey ached to be with Ray Keith. Her baby was due in three weeks and she'd cried buckets when we heard he might be shipped to Kuwait. But, I'd not even had a boyfriend and I wasn't ready for a crash course in birth and delivery.

After she dropped off her glasses and used the ladies room, I took her by the hand on a search for the unmentionables aisle. Janey couldn't see a lick without her pop-bottle lenses, which added to the severity of her waddle. It passed like an electric current through her arm into her hand and then flowed right into me. Before I knew it, I waddled like a pregnant woman.

Janey pulled a purple hosiery package off the hook and squinted. Holding it an inch from her nose, she whispered, "Use your pretty green eyes and tell me what's it say on the package."

"Queen size, for women up to 200 pounds."

"Shhh, not so damn loud."

So I whispered back, "Sorry, queen size."

Janey leaned against an end rack of tube socks and sighed. "Well, that's me. I think I'm pregnant in both legs, too. Pull them out, let's take a look."

My eyes darted down rows of bras and underwear, searching for anyone who looked like security. I pulled the taupe meshy fabric out of the cellophane package and held it up close to her eyes. "Good God, Uncle Royal could hang a couple hams in those things."

"Shhh. Essie! Will you please keep your voice down? I can't wear this dress without hose; it wouldn't look right in front of all those officers on base." She stuffed the pantyhose back into the package, then I led her like a puppy dog to the cosmetics aisle.

After we matched a bottle of Cover Girl to her fair skin, which looked even fairer next to her coal black ringlets, we picked up her glasses and were ready for our road trip.

Almost.

Another hurried stop at a gas station so Janey could fill up her Pinto and empty her bladder — again, but the toilet was nasty. So we detoured with a quick trip to Aunt Sye's.

Although Aunt Sye's house was scrubbed clean inside, it settled unevenly onto cinderblock footings. A broken-down couch rested where the porch sagged. Getting out of the car, I wilted with the humidity like the dandelions and peonies by the porch that had gone weak-kneed. A few of the screens were missing and Sye's lace panels blew out at the front room windows. I looked around at the weed-choked yard covered with parts of things — car parts, bike parts, a warped Pepsi Cola sign, an old washing machine, and a push mower — all rusting between the prickly shrubs and patches of grass and dirt. Uncle Royal's '67 Dodge with its tires long gone corroded in the side yard. I'd played in the scruffy yard for hours as a child and had loved it.

But lately, living with Janey Gay, she'd shared with me her Dream Home Scrapbook. Pictures from magazines she'd cut out and taped to construction paper pages. Furniture, shiny kitchen appliances, curtains, china, pictures of manicured lawns, swimming pools — things she longed for, beautiful homes she daydreamed about. We spent hours driving around nicer neighborhoods at night, peeking in windows. Our Sunday entertainment was circling open houses listed in the newspaper and showing up to take a tour with the other house hunters. Janey talked to the realtor like she actually had the cash to buy the house, but I enjoyed snooping in people's closets, drawers, and refrigerators, seeing what they had that I didn't. Their houses smelled good, like furniture polish and Blue Waltz perfume, unlike Aunt Sye's house that smelled of bacon and heating oil. Janey even went to a builder once with floor plans she'd drawn of her and Ray Keith's future dream home. It was her heart's desire. Which made me wonder — what was mine?

Walking up the porch steps at Aunt Sye's, I realized the house looked just like her, worn and tired. I wondered if Sye ever had a dream house. Maybe Janey's dream house was all it was ever going to be. Just a dream. I had a cold revelation that humid afternoon, running my hand over the splintery railing of the rundown porch. We were poor as dirt and not much was bound to change that.

Janey Gay hollered for me to follow her into the bathroom. I giggled as she sat on the commode. Her belly dropped down between her legs and the whole toilet disappeared under her. I perched on the clothes hamper thinking God had stuffed two babies inside her.

She opened the package and I watched her gather the legs of the pantyhose. Janey tried to bend over, but the toilet lid squeaked and slid around on top of the seat. So as not to embarrass her, I gazed up at Aunt Sye's dotted swiss sheers on the window above the tub. A smudge of Prell had dried on the tile and I noticed the bar of Zest was about used up.

"I need you to help me get these on." She handed them to me. "Once you get them over my feet, I can get 'em up the rest of the way. Try not to snag 'em."

I took off her shoes and slid the nylons on, one leg at a time over her puffy feet, then pulled them up to her swollen ankles. Janey bent over again, groaned and grunted, and wrestled her pregnant body into her new pantyhose. It was pitiful. It reminded me of Aunt Sye squeezing into her girdle on Sunday mornings.

Janey's massive stomach filled Aunt Sye's tiny bathroom. I stood, and for a moment we were sandwiched together between the hamper and the toilet, blinking at each other.

All at once she grabbed the sink and held on. Sweat beads popped out on her upper lip and forehead, and I saw it was hard for her to catch her breath.

Watching her flinch and sweat, I hesitated. I didn't know what to do or say. Old enough to know how babies were made, it made me shiver to think about the entire process. I'd never known a pregnant woman before; she was the first. I'd watched Janey's shirt bulge and move a couple times when her baby kicked and she let me feel it. It felt like a kitten squirming under a blanket. The day she told me she was pregnant, I cried. I don't know why, I just did.

"Maybe them pantyhose are too tight," I said.

"No," she took a deep breath. "I'm fine. If you're sure about that shortcut to the base, we can be at Cherry Point in two hours." Her eyes pleaded with me through her thick glasses. I smiled and nodded, despite the creepy feeling we needed to wait.

"What's one more day; let's have supper with Aunt Sye."

"No." Tears swelled in her eyes until one rolled down each cheek. "I miss Ray Keith." She pulled a wad of toilet paper off the roll and dabbed at her eyes under her glasses. "According to last night's news, things don't look good in Iraq. Ray called and said President Bush is pretty pissed off and there's talk on base of war right soon. I remember my mama bein' pregnant with my sister when Daddy left for Vietnam. When he died over thataway, she never forgave herself for not bein' there when he shipped off. I want to spend every second I can with Ray. Let's go."

Janey blew her nose and I dutifully followed her to the car.

Atlanta, Georgia ~ October 1989

Loretta Lynette suffocated backstage. The makeup girl had plugged two fans into the wall to keep perspiration from soaking through Loretta's makeup. Her ministry team leader had been conducting praise and worship with the quartet and soloists for well over an hour, leading the congregation of over five thousand into the mood she had requested: one of heightened excitement and ready for miracles. A backstage monitor allowed her to observe the crowd and her entire ministry team. She'd been relieved after receiving the last-minute invitation to hold a weeklong revival at this mega-church in Atlanta. She needed the boost in income to cover her mounting expenses.

The *Atlanta Journal* lay at her feet. She leaned over and stared, once again, at the headlines on the Events page. LORETTA LYNETTE, PREACHING NIGHTLY AT THE CHURCH OF THE SAVIOR. The article went on —*This one-time hairdresser heads one of the world's largest television ministries. Taking Jesus To The World expects to bring in $75 million this year.* She cringed. *Why do they have to bring up money?*

For the past few months, most major newspapers reported her ministry's purchase of a one-million-dollar home in Little Rock, her one-million-dollar summerhouse on Sanibel Island, and more houses worth another two million for her staff. The articles also outlined Loretta's recent personal purchases, which included a $300,000 vacation around the world where she reportedly ministered to the nations on her *days off from relaxing in the sun.*

She'd needed that vacation. Loretta never expected to see opposition hit her to any great degree. But it was a fact: her congregations were down significantly due to last month's bad press. Evangelicals everywhere were still reeling from the Jim Bakker and Jimmy Swaggart fiascos; it had been an uphill battle the past two years to bring integrity back into televangelism. Any more bad press and her board was sure to demand cutbacks. As it was, religious leaders who made money in evangelism were now held in suspect by a world of unbelievers.

But Bakker and Swaggart's losses were Loretta's gains. Evangelicals left hanging had shifted their alliance to her. Even the fallen angels' accusers had left her alone, for reasons of chivalry or the mere fact her ministry appeared squeaky-clean and no one could prove otherwise.

Loretta had developed a fine-tuned talent of asking for money. A mass of humanity sent thousands of dollars every month so she could take Jesus to the world. She touched them all in one way or another. She televised men and women who testified they'd received blessings after sending Loretta money. Believers who claimed to have received big bonuses, unexpected checks in the mail, and healing for their children as a result of their seed-sowing, giving in faith, all to Loretta and the work of the Lord.

Making money in the crusades was like finding a treasure chest in a lonely, sunken wreck on the ocean's cold floor, there for the taking. When she walked out on the platform, her presence fell on their hearts like a ray of sun on the walls of a prison. Resembling the Apostle Peter, even her shadow was a source of comfort and healing to her followers. Cash flowed in as easy as Peter pulling tribute out of the mouth of a fish. People gave their last nickel.

Loretta's cutting-edge personality, her Southern drawl, her ability to get down on their level — a woman who had once been poor and walked in their shoes — won her the admiration and friendship of most Christian women in the country.

It didn't hurt that she was single, either. The women wanted to be like her and eligible men flocked to her crusades in record numbers. She could've had a different date every night of the week. But she turned them away, avoiding scandal, claiming she needed to spend time with the Lord.

At thirty-six, she had evolved quickly into one of the charismatic greats. Her ministry was often compared to those of Aimee Simple McPherson and the great Katherine Kuhlman. Even Billy Graham had endorsed her as, "God's anointed daughter."

Loretta stared at the monitor. Her head pounded with strange new thoughts and desires. *Evangelicals all wear the same faces, as if righteousness were nothing but a mask. None of us are better than anybody else.* She needed air.

"Tell the organist to play a little longer," she said to her assistant. Edwina had just gathered Loretta's Bible and notes for the sermon, complete with bullet points for the healing service. Reported cases of the sick and the maimed throughout the congregation: where they sat, their infirmities, weaknesses, and possible faith or resistance levels. All information gathered by "collectors." Men and women on Loretta's staff, stationed throughout the auditorium as the people entered, greeting in the name of the Lord, acting as ushers, collecting valuable pre-service information Loretta could utilize on the Lord's behalf later on in the service.

Edwina tipped her head and raised her eyebrow. "You okay?"

"Fine. Fine. I need some air, that's all. Give me another fifteen minutes. Tell Rusty and Pastor Higgins to keep singing."

"Don't be too long; I think the natives are restless."

Edwina was right. Loretta knew if she delayed much longer the congregation, despite their excitement, would end up impatient, hard to manage, and not open to the Spirit. The people came to hear her, not the praise and worship team. But she'd take her chances tonight. She wasn't ready.

Sweat had soaked through her navy blue suit. Her auburn hair, though cut short, dripped beads of perspiration down her neck and spine, which were absorbed by her bra strap. The makeup girl handed her a tissue to dab the sweat from her brow as she walked down the long concrete hallway backstage and outside into the cool evening air. She maneuvered between the buses, the tractor-trailers, the flotsam and jetsam of television equipment, power cords hooked up to the state-of-the-art traveling television studio that followed her to every city on her crusade route. The smell of diesel fuel nauseated her, and she hurried to find her private bus.

She pulled off her five-carat diamond earrings and slid them into her pocket.

Recently criticized for being fond of nice things, Loretta responded to her accusers that God had blessed her for putting Him first in her life. That she had been poor as a sinner, but as a Christian, she enjoyed spending her salary on herself. A salary her board had decided to pay her. So what if she wanted nice things? So what? She had fun buying the $11,000 marble statue of Queen Esther that greeted visitors in her ministry's Little Rock headquarters. Loretta could get away from the world in the $500,000 yacht docked behind her home in Florida. She had to take a vacation at least once a year. Everybody pulled on her. Obvious to those closest to her, and those who had the privilege of sitting in front of her carved mahogany desk with the Dresden vases displayed on top, Loretta's tastes ran more toward filet mignon than to hamburger.

"Give and it shall be given unto you." She'd preached it for years; the well-known scripture had made her a rich woman. She'd given, after all. She'd given more than any of them knew.

Loretta found her bus and motioned for her security man to open it. "You out here all alone, Ma'am?"

"I'll be fine, Sam, I need my bag off the bus. Go back inside, I'll lock up."

"You sure?"

"Yes, go, I need to pray and get a little fresh air. I won't be long."

She waved him on and watched him reluctantly return to his post, a stool just inside the back door in front of a monitor that gave him a bird's-eye view of their fleet of trucks and buses behind the mammoth church. Retrieving her travel bag, she stepped off the bus and grabbed a folding metal chair by a trash barrel that held open the church's heavy steel back door.

Her bag slung over her shoulder, she carried the chair to the edge of the parking lot, searching for seclusion behind the armada of ministry team vehicles that invaded city after city for Jesus and for her. The singers and musicians would remain on stage and continue to praise and sing their hearts and lungs out because they knew that's what she wanted. No one would miss her for at least another ten minutes.

Highway traffic rumbled in the distance. She heard a few muffled voices in the parking lot behind her, but otherwise she found herself alone next to an empty church van. It was safe to relax for a few minutes. She faced a field of weeds in a vacant lot where no one could see her unfold the chair to sit down. Loretta reached into her pocket and felt for her earrings. *Secure.* Next, she dipped her hand into her Gucci bag and pulled out a pack of Virginia Slims and a Zippo lighter.

The fingers of her right hand fondled the loose unlit cigarette. Loretta placed it in the side of her mouth, flicked the lighter, and lit up. The Zippo lid snapped shut like a pistol being cocked.

She breathed in a line of smoke that curled down her throat; the once-familiar taste warmed her inside and sent a rush of nicotine to her bloodstream. Her head bent, she stared at the cigarette in her hand as it rose to her face like a little bird. Her arm trembled and her nervous fingers fluttered, causing hot ashes to fall to her lap. They burnt a hole in her Anne Klein suit, but it didn't faze her. She continued to smoke like she was swallowing a secret.

A flood of childhood memories raced the nicotine to her brain. The October warm days and cool nights reminded her of Indian summers as a child in the South. The sun, like a bloodshot eye, sank further beyond the top of the Atlanta skyline, leaving a slight chill to the Georgia evening air. She felt the temperature drop as her world turned from the light and fell into darkness. Loretta rocked the chair back and pressed her shoulders against the van, stealing the heat it had trapped. Her head tilted back, stretching her neck taut; her eyes drifted shut.

She had picked up the lighter and cigarette pack off the floor after last night's healing crusade. The revival had reached a pitch not even the ministry team could recall. So strongly did they feel the presence of God, a stampede to the altar had interrupted the praise and worship service. People could not wait; they needed neither song nor sermon to persuade them. There were people standing and kneeling, some with hands up-lifted and others holding tight to the backs of the pew in front of them. A great number, men and women alike, were speaking in tongues.

A healing line formed that stretched from the platform to the back of the church and around the sanctuary. Old and young lined up to relay their afflictions to the woman of God and to have Loretta's anointed hands touch them. An act of faith, believing for their miracle.

A young woman, possibly fifteen or sixteen, appeared in the line. Loretta stood speechless before the girl for a moment, observing her beauty and her long auburn hair. Though her jeans were tattered and several piercings were evident in her eyebrows and nostrils, she asked for deliverance from drugs and alcohol. The congregation grew quiet, the choir sang softly in the background, every head was bowed and eye closed, believing God was speaking to Loretta about the young girl standing in front of her.

The girl's hair reminded Loretta of her own once upon a time. She told the young woman if she had any cigarettes on her to throw them to the devil. The girl reached into the back pocket of her jeans, pulled out her pack of Virginia Slims and a shiny new Zippo, then tossed them to the floor. Loretta commanded as if possessed by an archangel, "Young lady, you are delivered tonight. Let her go, Satan! Sister, never smoke again. You won't need them. In the name of Jesus, I command the demons of nicotine and of drugs and alcohol to flee from her and to never come back! Ask Jesus into your heart dear girl, ask Him to become your Savior."

Loretta laid hands on the girl's head and she fell back. Two male ushers caught her and lowered her to the floor. The wild congregation mounted to mob frenzy, shouted praises to God and they clapped without ceasing.

Loretta raised her hands and pranced around the girl, shouting, "The Holy Spirit revealed to me a black ring around her mouth, a black ring of smoking and sin, and now it's gone! Raise your hands to the Lord, Saints of God. Another soul has been saved from the flames of hell." Loretta danced on the altar in praise to the Lord. "Tonight can be your hour of deliverance. God is in this place. His angels are here, people. They're walking up and down the aisles. Jesus has entered the building. Reach out and touch the Lord as He passes by." No one but the hardest of hearts could sit in their seats. The place was ablaze with glory.

Loretta watched it all closely. Suddenly, as if bitten by a rabid dog, she let out a shrill cry, a suppressed darkness found its way out of her heart, into her mouth, spilling over in a piercing wail. A stream of tears and sobs shook her until her body threw itself to the floor. Her Assistant Evangelist, Rusty Walters, explained to the congregation the Lord was moving in His often-mysterious way through His servant, Loretta Lynette.

But Loretta knew better. Her grief and past sins had caught up with her after all these years and landed her prostrate behind the pulpit. No one knew how badly Loretta wanted her own deliverance. More than any sinner that had ever sat in her service and felt the convicting power of the Holy Ghost, Loretta longed for something she felt she could never have.

Loretta sucked hard on her cigarette one last time; the tobacco cracked and popped. Her ten minutes were up. Stretching out on the chair, her long legs found the edge of the sidewalk. She kicked off her shoes and wiggled her toes in the red dirt. She wanted to disappear like the threads of smoke that hung in the air. A long sigh escaped from her lips and ended in a deep and guttural moan.

"I can't do this any more."

Essie ~ 1983

My Aunt Sye's house was squeezed between a creek and a tiny general store she and Uncle Royal were trying to manage on the edge of town. When Granddaddy died, he left equal shares in the land and store to his children, Noble, Sye and Daddy. Uncle Royal needed income since earning his purple heart in Vietnam had landed him in a wheelchair. Minding the store was a job Royal could do from a sitting position, so Daddy and Noble sold their parts to Aunt Sye.

I spent many hot summers on their porch with a cold cola between my knees to cool off. Air conditioning was a luxury they could not afford. Every evening Uncle Royal rolled his wheelchair out onto the porch with a glass of iced tea, a damp towel to cool off the back of his neck, and his smokes to keep the bugs away. Dusk came early enough, along with mosquitoes, a dimming of the heat, and the first fireflies of the evening. But the sunset made the world soft and carefree. Strains of a country song, a fiddle and a mournful wail were tuned in on most radios in Selma. Our house was no different. Music added a cool delight to the world in which we lived. The tinny echoes of the old-timey music playing on Sye's kitchen radio identified us and gave us a sense of who we were.

I'd scoot my fanny up against the wall next to the screen door where I could hear Patsy Cline cry along with the steel guitar, and still eavesdrop on what talk there was on the porch with one passing neighbor or another.

Ray Keith was ten years older than me, a typical Southern boy who loved fast cars and pretty girls. His mullet haircut caused his daddy to have regular conniptions and instigated lewd comments from my daddy and Uncle Noble. Fag hair, they called it. Sissy hair. Pussy hair. Ray ignored them all. He wore his blue jeans as tight as he could get them and rolled up the sleeves of his white T-shirts in order to keep his arms on display. If he rolled up his sleeves twice, people could see his muscle veins just at the point where they most dramatically defined themselves from the flesh around them.

To piss off his daddy, Ray Keith liked to crank up his John Mellencamp album in his bedroom. Like clockwork, Uncle Royal would holler, "Shit-fire! Turn that devil music off!" I'd giggle because he'd say it about anything on TV or the radio that wasn't country or bluegrass. Especially rock and roll, and TV or radio preachers.

Aunt Sye said once a few years back she drove Royal home from a doctor's appointment and out of the blue, she stopped at a tent revival and wheeled him in. She said it was the last time Uncle Royal went to church, and for me to keep quiet about it.

It fascinated me to the point of making the mistake of asking him anyway.

"Danged woman evangelist, it was. They're all a bunch of looney tune, money hungry crooks . . . bah, thinkin' they know better than the good Lord Himself. I wouldn't give ya a danged dime for the whole lot of 'em!" I never brought it up again. I figured Sye had her reasons why she never pushed religion on him after that. Aunt Sye went to First Methodist, but kept evangelism out of the house.

Every night I waited on Sye's porch for Daddy to come home from the Esso station. He'd bought it before I was born. Noble rebuilt carburetors and rotated tires while Daddy pumped gas, changed his customers' oil, and sold candy bars and Cokes. Daddy was a little more polished than Noble, so he dealt mainly with the customers. At least I heard from Sye he'd finished high school, where Noble dropped out long about the eighth grade. Though half the town of Selma stepped softly around the Aikens brothers, my daddy and uncle were gentle and affectionate with my cousin Ray Keith, and me.

Daddy, Uncle Noble, and I lived in the apartment above the gas station. Daddy slept in the larger bedroom; I had a twin bed in the other. When Noble was home, he slept on the pullout couch. We ate at Aunt Sye's until I was old enough to cook. Aunt Sye and I did the family laundry in a Hotpoint wringer washer every Saturday on her back porch, saving Noble's and Daddy's grease-covered overalls for the last tub of dirty wash water.

Aunt Sye, weary and slow, protected and put up with the men in her life. She treated Daddy and Uncle Noble like little boys whose behavior was more comical than worrisome. What was worse, she encouraged it by bailing them out of unfortunate circumstances on several occasions.

Like Elvis, both Daddy and Noble kept their youthful faces. Even Noble, with two deep purple scars on his cheek from a broken beer bottle and a stacked deck in a game of strip poker. The three women he'd met at Pokey's Pool Hall had turned out to be wives of men who worked at the mill. That's all they cared to tell me about Noble's scars.

Daddy and Uncle Noble did everything they could to forget the hand that life had dealt them. Rowdy and playful, or as Sye said, "full of shit and vinegar," they'd terrorize the locals until the sheriff was called. He'd lock them up for disorderly conduct mostly. Take your pick, it was either drinking and shooting bottles off fence posts — disturbing the peace at two in the morning — or racing their pickup trucks down the middle of town at midnight, drunk as skunks. But my aunt bailed them out every time. She'd come home, yawn, kiss Ray Keith and me good night, and haul herself off to bed.

The 80s were just the tail-end of the 60s as far as Daddy, Noble, and Sye were concerned. Not much had changed in their world.

I was nine on Ray Keith's eighteenth birthday — the same night he lit out after Janey Gay and chased her to the coast following a particularly bad fight. When Aunt Sye found out, she had Uncle Royal call Daddy and Noble and they all three piled into Noble's truck and went after Ray. But it was too late. Janey Gay suspected Ray Keith loved her and she made him chase her to prove it. He chased her all right — all the way to the New Bern Justice of the Peace and into a Super 8 Motel. By the time Uncle Royal found them, naked in the sheets, Daddy and Noble were too drunk to care and found the whole thing amusing.

Daddy and my uncles rented the room next to Ray Keith and Janey Gay for the duration of their honeymoon night, and proceeded to howl and torment the newlyweds until Ray Keith punched a hole through the wall. Early the next morning, Noble and Daddy took off, leaving Ray and Janey to take Royal back home before they could continue their honeymoon in Ray Keith's bedroom at Aunt Sye's.

Some days it plain pissed me off. I'd hear about the fun after it was over. I'd sit and twist my hair into knots, wishing I'd been born a boy. But, I stayed out of the way and remained invisible. It kept my hide from being tanned. I did a good job; they ignored me most of the time.

Until the day I started asking too many questions about my mama.

I asked four different people and got four different answers. My mama's name was Elle. Not E-l-l-i-e or Elly with a "y," just Elle — one syllable, they said. Neither Sye nor Daddy would spell it for me, pretended like they didn't know how. But I'd seen it spelled E-l-l-e in one of Janey's *Glamour* magazines, and I pictured my mama as one thing only. Glamorous.

I never saw a picture of her, her handwriting, or a piece of anything that belonged to her. Only thing I had to prove she existed was myself. All evidence of Elle had been wiped clean from our apartment or Sye's house before I learned there was such a thing as a mama and that every kid in my neighborhood owned one.

I used to lay awake and pretend my mama was curled up next to Daddy in bed. That I could hear them talking through the walls. She would be whispering sweet words in his ear and he'd be trying to catch the rest of Johnny Carson. I even imagined them having sex, like most kids who hear the faint stifled moans of their parents on occasion. I tried hard to smell any perfume she might have left on Daddy's old clothes or blankets, but it was long gone by the time I thought to act like a hound dog.

My mama was a ghost who appeared, had a baby for Daddy, and then went back to her spirit world. I didn't understand why she didn't love me enough to stick around and it was evident nobody in the family would divulge that information. The family kept Daddy's secrets the best they could. But they had to give me some kind of answer when I started asking.

And asking. And didn't stop.

One day, exasperated, Aunt Sye grabbed my head and pushed my dark red hair off my face, shoving my bangs back. Then she ran her thumbs over the few freckles on my forehead. "Little girl, the moon was so damn bloated the night your mama gave birth to you, it looked infected — needed cut open and left to bleed all over God's heavens. It gave me chills, the way you're doin' now, askin' questions you'd be better off not knowin' the answers to. Why do you need to know this, child?" I didn't say a word; I just looked hard into her gray eyes that matched the streaks in her hair. I wanted to know about my mama more than I wanted to eat, or play, or sleep. And Aunt Sye knew it.

She sighed heavy and thought a moment. "Well, I suppose you're ready for the truth. She was an escaped convict, honey, and when the sheriff caught her, she bit him and gave him blood poisonin'. She's in prison now, where she belongs. Needs stuck in a nut house. Leave it alone, Essie. Quit askin' questions."

It sounded like a good enough explanation. But I knew Aunt Sye had brought me into the world and I was born in her bed. Sye said Bridie Mae, her friend from church, had worked at the courthouse when I was born. When Sye and Daddy went to report my birth, Bridie Mae recorded it as:

> Mother's First Name: *Unknown*
> Last Name: *Aikens*
> Sex Of Baby: *Girl*

Name: *Estelline Phoebe Aikens*
Born: *July 9, 1974*
Weight: *7 pounds 5 ounces*
Length: *19 inches*
Father: *Paul David Aikens*

LEGITIMATE BIRTH was stamped in bright red letters across the top of the Johnston County Record. Not long after Sye's miserable explanation, I heard Noble whisper that the car Bridie Mae bought the week I was born was still in great shape, and he was wondering how much longer they would have to give her free gas. Aunt Sye gave me my birth certificate for my ninth birthday, hoping it would shut me up.

When I confronted Uncle Royal, he wheeled his chair up to the kitchen table to peel me an apple. I figured that way he wouldn't have to look at me.

"Your mama, huh?" He started at the top of the apple and worked the knife back and forth, stripping the skin like he was skinning a squirrel. "Well, little lady, best I can say is, your daddy met the little pissant woman during a Gospel Sing in '73 at the First Baptist Church in Raleigh. She seduced him in the parking lot right after the Oak Ridge Boys sang *Jesus Is Coming Soon*. But the next year, Paul David caught her making her own fireworks following the Fourth of July picnic with some drunken salesman from Bernie's Used Car Lot. Right next to your daddy's gas station in a '70 Ford Thunderbird with dealer plates. Your mama gave birth here, at our house, five days later. Paul David sent her packing the day after. By God, it was the best thing your daddy ever did."

I liked Ray Keith's story best. I remember the cigarette flicking up and down in his teenage mouth when he spoke. He told me my mama was too young to have a baby. She cried for nine months and lost her mind. Ray said even though he was too young to remember much, he did recall she screamed for two days straight giving birth, and Royal had to close the store for fear of losing his customers.

"She's a mentally deranged woman. Ran buck naked out of the house the next day, I seen her," Ray Keith said.

I liked to think of my beautiful mama running naked through the streets of Selma. Of Daddy and Noble running after her — I imagined she was part Indian, running back to her tribe. Or that she was a mermaid and had to get back to the sea before the full moon. I'd dream up anything, imagine any kind of wild story to keep from thinking she didn't want me.

I finally got up the nerve to ask Daddy. He sat me on his knee; I was still nine. He hugged me first, like he always did. Then he cleared his throat, coughed once, and said, "Us bein' Methodist and all, we didn't see God the same way, your mama and me. She was Pentecostal Holiness, one of them Holy Roller types. She didn't like my drinkin' and carryin' on with your uncles."

Daddy said she never loved him, not in the way she should have. He revealed he'd only known her for ten months altogether. That he had met her at a revival and got saved just for her. Then he asked her to marry him two days later. She had me nine months later, and the next day, she was gone forever.

"Wasn't a forgiving woman," he said. "She called her brother, an uncle you never met, and he picked her up from Sye's the day after you was born."

Daddy never did say whether or not Mama married him. But he said she was pretty, and that's all I'll ever know for sure. Because when Uncle Noble and Daddy got drunk and flew off the bridge over the Cape Fear River in Noble's pickup truck, the mystery of who my mama was went with them. I not only lost Daddy, I lost all hope of knowing my mama. I knew Aunt Sye and Uncle Royal would take Daddy's secret to their graves.

I turned ten the same day I stood by Aunt Sye at the double funeral. Losing both brothers in one day liked to kill Sye, too. At the graveside, she folded me into her arms, left her frosted lipstick on my cheek, and said, "Damn them both."

Half the town paraded through the house that afternoon filling up on ham, black-eyed peas, corn casserole, and fruit salad. I hid in my room to avoid pitiful stares from the ladies of the Methodist church. Later, Aunt Sye opened my door and put her arms out to me. "Baby," my aunt said as I walked into her embrace. "Well girl," she sighed, "all I have left of Paul David is you. I guess that'll do me until I'm buried next to them ornery brothers of mine." Then she did the unexpected. Something I never saw her do before. She cried. I waited until she finished, and then I went into the kitchen and poured myself a bowl of Cheerios.

Essie ~ June 1989

Aunt Sye and Uncle Royal sold Daddy and Noble's gas station, paid off their debts, and the rest went into a savings account for me. All fifty dollars of it. Time stood still for the next five years, but by the time Ray Keith joined the Marines, Janey Gay was pregnant and the family, what was left of us, revived itself again. Everybody thought it'd be good for me to move in with Janey while Ray Keith finished his service to Uncle Sam. Their little apartment in town wasn't any bigger than Daddy's had been. Janey dolled up the back porch and made it my room, which she'd thought of turning into the nursery after the baby came.

The June night before Ray left for Parris Island and ten weeks of boot camp, Janey Gay cried her eyes out. Her pregnancy had recently blossomed over the edge of her pants. She begged Ray to change his mind. The rumored war in Iraq loomed large over our heads.

Ray told Janey joining up was his only way out of the poor house. The only way out of living like his parents. He wasn't going to take over his daddy's store. A store that'd be lucky to hold out until Royal retired. I had never seen Ray Keith cry. Tears dripped down his face. He said he couldn't drive a Cheerwine truck forever, and that Janey's job of waiting tables at the Hog Trough Barbeque Pit was not a career in the making.

There was no money for Ray to go to college.

"I have to find a way to go to school, make a better life for you and the family. The only way to do that is to let the government pay for it. Veteran benefits are better than ever, we have to do this, honey. I'll be back in no time."

Ray tried hard to comfort her. He said someday they could buy the dream house she'd been wanting. But it didn't ease Janey's tears; she bawled into the night.

I cried alone listening to all of it, missing my daddy, worrying about Ray Keith and Janey Gay, and wondering . . . if my mother, wherever she was, ever thought about finding me.

Atlanta, Georgia ~ October, 1989

Loretta pushed her ten minutes to twenty and lit another cigarette. She longed to talk to her brother. If Teague were alive he'd shake some sense into her. "What good is all that money when you're miserable as a pole cat?" He'd lectured her over and over the year her ministry exploded on the airwaves. "Hypocrites are like flies on a dead possum. They just reproduce more nasty flies." She hated when he said it but Teague was right: she was a fly-producing hypocrite.

She'd been horribly ashamed of her illiterate family and had all but disowned them. The Hollingsworth men had bulging foreheads, thick lips, and pale green eyes, almost yellow. The women were cursed with red hair, cowlicks, and bad skin, and there wasn't a high school graduate among them except Loretta, the tail-end of all ten Hollingsworth siblings. Each one had dropped out of school after the eighth grade to farm tobacco. All of her brothers were as crazy as dogs that had gotten a whiff of a bitch in heat but too lazy to do anything about it. And only Teague cared about her. The only person in the world she had trusted.

As a woman, she struggled to find a way out of no way. Loretta was eight when she found her parents laid out in the back yard — both shot through the head. In a jealous rage, Loretta's mother had shot her husband once in the heart and once in the head, then turned the gun on herself. Afterward, Loretta drifted from one older sister's house to another.

Her break came a few years later in the form of a grandfather she never knew she had. The old man offered money for college, and only for college, to any of his grandchildren. One grandchild took him up on the offer — Loretta. She moved to Tennessee and attended beauty school, where two of her regular customers for wash and sets were women professors at Lee College. Broke and ambitious, Loretta secured a night shift job on the janitorial staff at Lee, cleaning women's restrooms. Eventually, Loretta went to Seminary and graduated third in her class.

Her ministry grew slowly, despite her meager circumstances. Then she met Evelyn Roberts, who took one look at her and quoted the scripture in Esther Chapter Four, "And who knows but that you have come to a . . . position for such a time as this." She invited Loretta to speak at a women's prayer group on the campus of Oral Roberts

University, and the anointing of God filled the place. A word of knowledge came forth out of Loretta's lips. The evidence of that word was the miracles of barren wombs conceiving children, blind eyes opening, arthritic hands made straight, and a prosperity message for women; the news spread like an arsonist's fire through a lumberyard.

Overnight, her calendar was full of speaking engagements and invitations to preach in churches all over the country. For the first few years, she refused to risk eternal damnation by painting her face like a common floozy. She wore her hair throughout the seventies and early eighties reminiscent of a style predominant in her 1972 high school yearbook: long, straight and tucked behind her ears. She preached in starchy long-sleeved blouses buttoned to the top under her robes of white, regardless of the lack of air conditioning

Then she met Tammy Faye Bakker and her feet were set on a new path. She was set free from the bondage of dowdy-looking women. She had a complete makeover, bought a new wardrobe, learned to sing contemporary Christian music, and discovered she loved big, gaudy jewelry and designer clothes. Her ministry exploded into a mega-ministry.

By the time she appeared on Trinity Broadcasting Network, her ministry had grown to evangelistic proportions rivaling those of Lester Sumrall, R. W. Schambach, and Marilyn Hickey. God had blessed her, yet she was not fulfilled.

Now she sat years later, struggling to hear God's voice. The larger her religious empire, the bigger her problems and the more money she needed to make it all work smoothly. Her staff depended on her for their livelihood. The stress of it all woke her at night. She closed her eyes tight and tried to find peace in her prayers and in the scriptures.

In the early days she'd close her eyes and an anointed mist would fill the room. All she had to do was inhale, and strength and knowledge would fill her body. Now, the mist never came and Loretta struggled every day to get out of bed.

As she watched the moon break through the clouds over Atlanta, tears left streaks of mascara down her face. She was definitely the hypocrite her brother had called her.

For the past several weeks, Loretta found solace in a small wooden box in her dresser. *Gatlinburg, Tennessee* had been carved into the lid of the cheap souvenir made of cedar. A keepsake Teague had given her as a present the year she graduated from Lee. In the quiet of the night, she'd pull out the yellowed envelopes, read the letters, and stroke the lock of hair. Her heart would break again and again. But it was too late. She'd made a fortune, won the hearts of Christian women the world over. Thousands looked to her for a word, a miracle, a blessing, when she couldn't believe for her own. She had faith for the entire world but none for herself.

It had been said by leading evangelical ministers that Loretta's steps were ordered by the Lord. She wondered, as she climbed into the empty church van with the keys inside, was God ordering these steps?

She turned the key in the ignition, started the vehicle, pulled her sunglasses out of her bag, then drove out of the parking lot, disappearing down the highway. If she were lucky, she'd be at the beach by morning.

Essie ~ October 1989

It was a rainy Sunday afternoon in Selma the day we left in Janey's Ford Pinto and finally got on the road headed to Cherry Point. The October sky was gray and weepy, the Southern pines dripped, and raindrops dappled shimmery puddles on lawns and roads — not a pretty day by most people's standards. But the rain was gentle and well-behaved, which made it easier to drive on the wet highways. I'd traveled to Cherry Point once the year before with a friend from school and her father, who had taken a shortcut. She wrote the route number down for me in homeroom and said it would take an hour off our trip. Cherry Point was about 90 miles west-southwest of Cape Hatteras, at the foot of the Outer Banks, and I was all in favor of getting to the beach quick. I loved the beach, and Janey promised we could take a few minutes and sit with our feet in the ocean before heading back.

"Hey . . . look at that billboard. Ain't that the woman evangelist on TV? She's coming to town in January. I wonder if I should mention it to Uncle Royal?" I giggled, knowing the answer to my own question. "Loretta Lynette. I wonder if that's her real name."

"Probably not, you know them televangelists. They're like actors or Las Vegas show girls. Everything about 'em is fake."

"You think?"

"Sure. They're all in it for the money. I'm sure none of 'em make good parents."

"Why's that?"

"Can you imagine how screwed up their kids are? Always itchin' to find out what it's like to be normal. Besides, I'd heard the Methodist preacher in town can't even get to one of his son's baseball games. Too busy with one church committee or another. I want to raise my children in church, but I want Ray Keith and me to be good people first. Like Sye and Royal."

I swallowed hard. "My daddy was good people, he was just a little wild, that's all."

Janey was quiet for a moment. "Sure, Essie. That's all. Just a little wild."

We rode over an hour in silence, listening to a Randy Travis cassette tape. When I shoved in Clint Black, I noticed Janey rubbing her belly and then she'd rub her head. Whatever was happening, I hoped it'd wait two more days until we were back home and Aunt Sye could take over. Sye had nearly spit when she saw we had packed for a trip to the beach, but she knew better than to stand in Janey Gay's way.

I tried to break the silence between us. "Maybe if it's a boy, he can be the pall bearer in my wedding."

"Ring bearer."

"Oh yeah. Right."

Janey massaged her stomach again. "What road d'you say we needed to turn on?"

"Route 58, all the way to the coast. Turn right at the building that's got the big Yoo-Hoo sign on it."

"Okay, I see it. Ray's going to meet us in Morehead City if his staff sergeant will give him a pass, and then he'll take us back to the base for a tour. If he can't get a pass, we're supposed to drive to Havelock for the night and meet him on base in the morning."

"All I know is I want shrimp for dinner tonight." I looked at Janey and expected her to agree. She loved seafood as much as I did. But she looked like Aunt Sye had whitewashed her, like the oak tree in our front yard.

"I'm sick. I need to pull over."

"There, pull over there."

Janey drove the Pinto to the shoulder of the road and parked. She threw open the car door and ran behind a thicket of briars and underbrush. I could hear the low wrenching sounds of her lunch coming up. When she staggered back drained of color and sick, wiping her mouth, she reminded me of the day I had the stomach flu and Aunt Sye gave me a trash can to puke in at the same time I parked my butt on the commode with the runs.

"I wish I could drive; maybe we should turn around."

"How many times do I have to say it, Estelline? No!"

The sun came out and its rays pierced the coarsely woven tops of the pine trees as it sunk into the landscape and sparkled off Janey's tears on her cheeks. After an hour on the shortcut route the pavement ended, and a dirt road loomed ahead of us. Janey stopped.

"God, Essie, you sure this is the way? What's that sign say?"

I poked my head out the window. "Hofmann Forest. Give me the map."

She handed me the atlas. "We must've taken a wrong turn. Look, a truck!"

The asparagus-green panel truck rattled toward us slowly. A plume of red dust kicked up behind it. Janey flagged the driver down from her seat. A man with dark eyes, pitch-black hair, and a straw hat stopped and nodded politely. An old woman with no teeth, deep wrinkles, and black dots for eyes sat beside him, chewing her cud. Or so it seemed.

"Sorry to bother you," Janey said, "is this the way to Morehead City and the coast?"

"Sí. The coast. Go that way," he replied and pointed to the road behind him.

"Thank you, thank you very much." Janey smiled and watched the truck drive in the direction we had just come from.

I felt lost. My stomach filled with butterflies. "I wonder if he even knew what you said?"

"Well, we gotta assume he did, don't we? I mean, we've come this far." Janey started the car and drove in the direction the man pointed.

She weaved in and out of huge potholes filled with rainwater. For miles the dirt road had been banked with tall pines and rows of harvested fields. But suddenly we were squeezed between acres of forest and wetlands as far as we could see.

Janey turned on the car's headlights. "I haven't seen a house since we left the interstate. I need to stop and pee."

"Look out! Janey, stop!"

A deer had leaped into the road and for a moment, everything moved in slow motion. I stared into its eyes and had the feeling it knew me. The Pinto swerved sideways. The back tires slid into a deep pothole, causing the frame to hit the dirt road with a jolt strong enough to rattle our teeth. Immersed in mud and debris, the tires could only spin. We weren't going anywhere.

Janey's motherly nature kicked in as she grabbed my arm. "Are you okay?"

I nodded and started to cry. I could hear Ray Keith yelling it was my fault. We could've been eating at Crabby Mike's, had I not tried to show off and take us on a damn shortcut. Instead, we were stuck in the middle of, God only knew.

Janey let out a muffled grunt of pain between her clenched teeth. What looked like pee ran down her pantyhose to her ankles.

"Help me out."

"Are you sick again?"

"It's worse than that. And stop crying. Don't blame yourself, Essie, we shouldn't have come. This is my fault, not yours. I'm the adult here, or supposed to be. I had to try, you know? It's my fault. I had no business listening to a fifteen-year old that not only doesn't drive, but thinks she knows a shortcut. Oh God, I'm going to make a terrible mother."

"I'm so sorry." I could barely talk for the tears clogging my throat.

"Stop crying and help me out, please."

The front end of the car was tilted slightly upward. I saw one of the front tires had gone flat. When I opened Janey Gay's door, her hands wrapped around the steering wheel and squeezed for a moment then she groped her stomach, as if kneading a large pile of dough. She bit her lower lip and stifled an instinctive moan. Even if the car started, there was no way either of us could push it out of the quarry-sized mud puddle we had landed in. I pulled Janey out by her arms and she hunched over by the side of the car.

She breathed in and out hard. "Here's the situation. I'm sure I'm in labor; I think my water broke. I . . . think." She handed me some tissue. "Wipe this off my legs before the mosquitoes find me. My pains aren't too awful bad, but I've no idea how much worse they'll get and how quick it'll go. You've got to flag somebody down. We need help. I'm gonna crawl back in the car, in the back seat with my pillow and try to slow this down . . . if I can. Hell, I don't know what I'm doin', I'm goin' on pure instinct. Don't walk back the way we came, there's nothin' for miles, we know that already. Walk in the direction we were headin'. Maybe we're closer to civilization than we know. This dirt road has to lead somewhere."

"I . . . I can't leave you . . ."

"You don't have a choice . . . ohhh . . ." Janey buckled over and clutched her stomach again. "Damn, that one hurt." She inched herself down the side of the car and I tried to help her in. The back seat of the Pinto had be the most uncomfortable place in the world to give birth. I had to run for help, not walk.

"You hold on . . . I'll be back as soon as I can." My tears dripped on her arm as she reached for me.

"Essie?"

"Yes?"

"Hurry."

I nodded, handed her the car keys and her purse, then closed the door. I yanked off my sandals and threw on socks and tennis shoes. Then I grabbed the yellow plastic flashlight from the glove box. I took one last look at Janey leaning on her pillow in the back seat. Her legs were spread and her knees bent searching for a comfortable spot. I placed my entire hand on the window as if to say, *don't worry, I'll get help.* She reached up and put her hand flat against mine on the other side of the glass, then looked away. The pain on her face melted my fear. I took off running in the direction Janey told me to go.

There was nothing, nothing but insects, a dirt road, and the threat of rain.

Escape To The Beach ~ October 1989

Loretta knew by now they'd have every state police cruiser looking for her. Possibly Sam saw her take the church van out of the lot. She headed east, wanting to put her feet in the sand. But instead, the car headed due north, to North Carolina, the Outer Banks and places she grew up; faint memories of a life she wanted to relive. A life where nobody knew how important she was. A town where she could walk down the street in peace, pop in the grocery store for coffee, milk and eggs, get her hair done without incident — and not a soul ask her to pray for them.

She reached inside her bag and felt the smooth wood box that held the biggest secret of her life. A secret that could possibly destroy her as a minister of the Gospel, a secret she had kept from the world, but not from God.

Avoiding main roads, Loretta passed through small towns and obeyed the speed limits, not wanting to draw attention to herself. She observed these off-the-beaten-path areas with a more critical eye than she had in her past. They were rural communities she hadn't taken a hard look at in over fifteen years. One town after another, where people steeped like old tea bags in their humdrum lives.

"Town this deep in the shithouse has nowhere to go but to God," she mumbled, driving past roadside produce stands, flea markets, and general stores selling moon pies, three for a dollar. She'd forgotten about small town living and existing by the seat of your pants. Hanging on until payday, hoping to find a few extra quarters in the couch for a hamburger.

It all flooded back and she wanted to turn around, drive back to Atlanta, and make up a story like the one Aimee Simple McPherson had told. Maybe a story of escaping from an abductor and if she could manage a small wreck, not hurt anybody, just bruise herself up a little, maybe they'd feel sorry for her and let the whole thing go. Any way she looked at it, she knew she was in serious trouble—stealing the van, skipping out on a healing service in a mega-church like Church of the Savior.

At a stoplight, she stripped off her suit jacket and pulled on a T-shirt somebody from the church's youth group had left in the van —

Jesus Freak in big red letters. She lit another cigarette and drove by tiny Baptist, Methodist, and Nazarene churches with not even a marker out front. Some had signs with stupid quotes taken from a joke book instead of the Bible.

The next church billboard she drove by screamed at her. *The sins of the fathers are visited upon their children.* Loretta wanted to crawl out of her skin. *What about the sins of the mothers?* Sure, she wouldn't give you a nickel for most men, her old man being the biggest son of a bitch she had known. Women around him were obsessed to the point of madness. They whined like puppies to have their bellies scratched, among other things. He didn't come home much, but when he did, he'd make another baby with her mama, another red-headed child with pea green eyes. Children he didn't know what to do with. The man never cared much about anything; treated his kids like a pack of wild dogs, and his wife like a whore. Loretta couldn't blame her mother for what she did, and fantasized about killing him herself — with worse than a bullet.

But Loretta would have died for his attention. Born at the tail end of his brood, she remembered Teague said their old man probably didn't even know she was one of his; there were so many kids in the house.

Loretta learned how to channel frustration and neglect into a talent for getting everybody's attention. Even God's. Her faith unwavering, she'd flash her eyes along with her million-dollar smile and the deaf were healed, able to hear a fart in the wind. The lame jumped out of their wheelchairs and discoed on the altar. And the mute joined the choir. She raised money for ministries and missions in less time than it took any male televangelist to make a buck. The camera loved her and she freely gave Academy Award performances behind hundreds of American pulpits, prior to going international through the media of television. She was America's evangelical sweetheart, the Christian woman's idol and best friend, and the conservative voice for women of the Republican Party — a spokeswoman for the Pro-Life Coalition in Washington, D.C.

She'd been invited to nearly every event, mega-church, and woman's group from Bangor to Palm Springs and from Seattle to Miami. Her itinerary was carefully thought out and planned by a high-priced publicist and manipulated to make her a spiritual superstar. She had gained the whole world, but had lost her soul along the way. Lost it in the memory of a young lover, and a pregnancy nobody but a few poor people in North Carolina knew about. It had plagued her, night and day, for years. In the end, a gnawing guilt defined her life. She'd tried to ask for forgiveness, but the road kept leading her back. Back to a family and a moment she knew she had to face in order to stand herself one more day.

~ Essie ~

The moon was a sharp sickle, cutting in and out of bloated black clouds. I had walked for over two hours and saw nothing but darkness and shadows. My flashlight grew weak and I wanted to scream. I wanted to pray, but didn't know how.

Lightning split the dark-clouded sky next to the dry one that hung over me. I studied the storm in the distance, hoping it wasn't heading my way. Instead, I was walking toward silent streaks of silver that split the sky open.

No cars came. There were no lights from a building anywhere. I was a girl out walking in the night alone, in a forest on a dirt road with a determined gait. On a stormy night — the kind that makes most folks nervous even in the safety of their homes. The road stretched beyond the reach of my eyes. It was like some forgotten keepsake, a road leading to exhaustion, a long dark and empty road that sagged in the humid air and prickled with the coming storm.

A hoot owl, with wings spread wide, flew into a nest of low-slung trees as I trudged by. My ears closed to its frightening question, "Who, who will save you now?"

I shifted into a faster stride. Fireflies blinked their fleeting beacons in the dark, like eyes of hidden creatures opening up to see what human could possibly be walking by at this hour. At the end of a clearing were trees, tall oaks pinched together. I became hopeful when I saw the dirt road had turned into gravel. Still no car came.

By the moon's dim light and the light on my Timex, I could see it was near eleven o'clock. I had left Janey three hours ago. My legs ached,

I was cold, and my feet were wet. But I refused to stop or turn around. I kept my eyes on the road as I marched toward help or Judgment Day, watching the crackling glow of the lightning and thunder closing in.

Moments later, I rounded a bend in the road and saw headlights cutting through the thick dark night, blazing down on me. I stood in the middle of the road, took off my sweater, and waved it like a crazy person, not entertaining one thought of serial killers or a car full of drunken men. All I could think of was this is the first car I'd seen since the panel truck with the old couple pointing us in the wrong direction.

~ End Of A Long Dark Road ~

Loretta had been so careful not to be found, she'd lost herself. She thought she knew all the back roads in and out of the Carolinas — at least she used to. Especially those leading to the coast. But driving through the worst thunderstorm she'd seen up close and personal since living in the area, it was no wonder she found herself in a forest, on a road to . . . she had no clue. And she needed gas. It'd been years since she had been responsible for looking at a gas gauge. There wasn't even a service station to pull over and ask for directions.

She eased the matronly blue van to the side of the road; her radio had been tuned to the Gospel Hour supplying the perfect rapturous accompaniment for her trip to the Carolinas. Up until now it had been the perfect prison break, a breath of freedom to do and act how she wanted and nobody watching in judgment. An opportunity to right her wrongs.

But with the dark night came the fear of being discovered; she would've turned around and headed right back to Atlanta that second, except for a young girl in the middle of road waving her arms like a lunatic.

Lord, save me from calamity, or help me to save this soul from worse.

~ Essie ~

The van barely stopped and the passenger window rolled down before I jumped in, breathless, throwing all caution to the side of the road. I was shocked and relieved it was a woman, and a pretty one at that. A Jesus Freak, or so her T-shirt read.

"You got one of them new car phones? We've had an accident. My cousin's havin' a baby in our car a few miles down the road. Oh God. She's alone in the back seat!"

"What? Slow down, honey. You say you're out here all alone?" The woman driver turned off her radio and looked at me with suspicion, like I was lying — or something worse.

"Ma'am, I'm sorry, but there's no time to play twenty questions. You've got to help us. My name's Essie, my cousin's in real bad shape, she's 'bout to have a baby, if she ain't had it already."

"I'm gathering that. She's on this road? Did you say you had car trouble?"

I began to feel a larger sense of relief. "We ended up in a deep mud puddle. Janey Gay's water broke. Oh God . . ." My tears dripped down my nose, to my lips, and fell off my chin. I wiped my dirty face with the back of my hand. Mosquitoes had feasted on my legs and I began to scratch like a dog.

"Hold on, honey. We can get there fast in the van. Grab a tissue out of that box."

I had worn my shorts, tank top, and a sweater. I didn't know how chilled I was until I felt the heat inside the van. In what seemed like minutes compared to my long walk, I could see the white Pinto and Janey's head in the window. The woman nosed the coasting van over to the road's shoulder and stopped behind the car, leaving the headlights on so we could see Janey. Both of us hurried to the Pinto. Inside the back seat with her legs still bent up, Janey Gay appeared fragile-looking and barely taller than a twelve-year-old, moaning and pushing on her stomach as if she could shove the pain out if she pressed hard enough. Her thick glasses were fogged over and sweat poured off her face and down her neck, despite the cool night air. The sting of labor drank the color from her skin. Her dark hair fell oily in pain-soaked curls around her stark white face. A pale moon broke through a dark cluster of clouds and I felt raindrops on my arms and face.

"Hold on, sweetie, what's your name?" the lady asked Janey. The woman's green eyes were enormous circles; a flush deepened the dimples on her cheeks.

"I told you her name. It's Janey Bertram," I said.

"Essie! Mind your manners!" Janey pulled off her glasses and her eyes sparked at me. "It took you damn long enough. I'm sorry, Ma'am. My little cousin's worried about me."

"She should be. When did your pains start?"

"After lunch I thought we could make it to Havelock; my husband is stationed at Cherry Point. We were taking a shortcut when my car landed in this hole. Now it won't start, but I don't think we can push it out anyway. You're the first person to come down this road in hours. My doctor said I'm not due for three weeks . . ."

"If he was any kind of doctor, he would've insisted you stay off those swollen feet. Well, let's get you to a hospital. I doubt we'll see many cars on this road. At least I haven't seen any either. How'd you say you ended up here?"

I had wiped off her glasses and handed them back to her. Janey and I looked at each other and another tear ran down my cheek.

"Were my fault," I said. "I thought I knew a shortcut."

Janey drew her legs back up and clutched the back of the seat; her knuckles went white. Her faced pinched and she squeezed her eyes shut. "They're 'bout ten minutes apart, Ma'am, but they're killin' me. I don't understand it. I'm not due for another three weeks," she repeated.

"Babies come when they want," said the pretty woman. Then she looked at me. "I'm sorry, I didn't catch your name in the van."

"Essie," I said, as she turned her attention back to Janey and reached into the car with her long arms and beautiful hands. She rubbed and patted Janey's knees to comfort her. She had the prettiest red nails I'd ever seen on a woman. I knew she was a different class of people than Janey and me, or anybody I knew, for that matter.

This strange woman, now that I had a chance to look at her, no longer seemed strange. I stared at her hair, the color of red plums. I'd always hated my hair color, but this woman's hair was the color of mine, and suddenly I liked it. She looked like Reba McIntyre from the side. Her lips were thinner than paper matches, but lip lined in red, and her eyes beamed like two pencil lights through the dark. A gold cross hung around her neck and her silly T-shirt nearly covered her skirt. Mascara had run down the sides of her face, like she'd been crying. Then it hit me, she hadn't told us her name.

"We've told you who we are; what's your name?" I watched her hesitate, almost like she hadn't planned on telling us, and didn't want to say.

"Loretta. Loretta Lynette."

I touched her shoulder to get her to look at me. "Now I know why you look familiar, I seen your billboard on the interstate. You're the evangelist!"

"Yes. I'm afraid I am. I apologize for meeting you under these strange circumstances."

Janey sat up when she heard her name. "What's somebody like you doin' out here?"

"It's a long convoluted story. Right now, we need to get you some medical attention and talk about that later. Essie, go 'round to the other side of the car and get in behind her, help push her out. See if you can stand and walk, Janey. I'm going to open the back of the van and clear off a spot where you can lie down."

Janey looped her arm around my neck and we managed to scoot out and stand in the grass. We inched our way to the van. Loretta tossed boxes of Sunday school workbooks on the side of the road, along with a couple boxes of Bibles.

"Not much room in there, but you can stretch out. You think you can climb in?" Loretta asked.

"I think . . . I . . . have to," Janey said. She whipped her damp ringlets around her face as she doubled over again. Her glasses fell off and her curls stuck to her eyelashes. More water poured down her legs and into her shoes.

"Oh God, Janey, please be alright . . . please, Oh God . . ."

"Estelline! Calm down. You're no help to me like this. Find my glasses."

Loretta grabbed a roll of paper towels from the back seat. "Good Lord, get those pantyhose off her. I'll go start the van, and be back to help her in."

While I shoved Janey's glasses back on her head and worked at pulling the now ripped-to-shreds and goopy wet pantyhose off her legs, Loretta hopped into the front seat and slid the key in the ignition. The van started, coughed, then stalled. She tried again, and it started again, but soon sputtered and stopped. On her third try it clicked then — nothing. She turned around and looked at us and for a moment, I'm sure she didn't know what to say.

"It seems . . . I'm out of gas."

My face grew hot. "Out of gas? We're stuck out here with a baby on the way, and you're out of gas? How could somebody like you be out of gas?"

Janey doubled over. I think all the fear she'd felt being alone in her car hit her hard again. She couldn't speak.

Loretta shook her head and shrugged. "Look, I'm sorry. Nobody is going anywhere until morning. There's nothing around for miles. Maybe we'll see another car. Maybe by morning someone will come by. By the time I realized I was low on gas, I was on this road. I guess I'd have been stuck out here too. Even if we could push your car out of the hole, you said it won't start and if you haven't noticed, both tires in the front are flat. In the meantime, we need to get comfortable, we may be spending the night and delivering a baby before help can get to us. I see three gallons of drinking water in the van and some Styrofoam cups. I think they use this van for Sunday school field trips. There's a first aid kit under the seat. You've got a blanket in your car, I see two more in here . . . we'll pray and ask God to help us."

"You pray, you're the expert." I couldn't even look at her. I was pissed off — at myself, at God, and at this stupid red-headed woman with no gas in her van.

A half hour later, Janey Gay was laid out in the back and resting. She had a pillow and blanket and room enough to stretch out her legs. Her pains had subsided somewhat, being able to lie down flat. Loretta and I sat in the front seats. There was no need to bother Janey until she needed us. Loretta handed me a can of Diet RC and an apple. I was glad to get it. I was starved.

The night air grew cooler. My digital watch blinked the time. Two a.m. I felt Loretta staring at me. We fell into a companionable silence full of questions neither one wanted to be first to ask. She seemed distracted by the dimple on my cheek, as she rubbed the one on her own. She had a large mole on her right arm, just like mine. Her nipples came through her T-shirt like pencil erasers, hard against wide shallow breasts. I could see she was beautiful, even though she was Aunt Sye's age possibly. But she was even prettier than her billboard picture.

I looked up at the sky. "That's strange. I think the storm's blowing over."

"What did you say your name was?" she asked.

"Gosh, you don't have much of a memory for a preacher. My name's Essie, for the third time."

"No, your cousin called you something else a while ago."

"Estelline. My name is Estelline Aikens. She calls me that when she's mad at me."

I watched Loretta pull her blanket up around her neck, turn her head, and stare out the window.

"I knew some people named Aikens, once," she whispered. "Where do you live?"

"Selma. You?"

She shivered hard enough for me to notice and put her hands up to rub her eyes. Her voice cracked and she gave me a weak smile. "Well, I live all over. Evangelists travel a lot. But my home is in Little Rock, Arkansas."

"You like being a preacher?"

"Have you watched me on TV?"

I giggled. "Sorry, no. My Uncle Royal thinks you're a phony, he makes me turn it off. We don't go to church much. Just my Aunt Sye. I don't think it makes us bad people, though."

"No. Neither do I. But what do you know about televangelists, Essie? I mean, have you thought about what we do?"

"Sorry, no again. You preach a lot, I guess. You want to tell me about your job? I am kinda curious. Are you like a movie star?"

Loretta chuckled. "I suppose some evangelists would like that. But, no, the only star in my world is Jesus. We live in a time where televangelists rule the airwaves with their own networks and sometimes we're just another stop in an evening of channel surfing. People have forgotten the time of years past when revival meetings were as exciting as the circus coming to town. We used to be treated like rock stars.

The premiere woman evangelist in the old days was Aimee Semple McPherson."

"Did you know her?"

"No, but I've been told I'm a lot like her. Those days are long gone. People expect more out of me. But," she sighed and leaned her head against the back of the seat, "I think I'm gonna slow down a bit. Live in the real world for a while."

"That why you're out here all alone?" The night air blew in the cracked window of the van and across Loretta's face.

"Yes. I had to stop. I had to . . . find . . . something," she whispered and then closed her eyes. "In order to go higher with Him," she pointed to the sky, "I have to find closure about something that happened to me years ago. I was just a young girl."

"You ever been in love?" I figured it was an obvious question, with all her talk about finding closure. I guessed she meant a lost love. A romantic notion in my mind, at least.

"Yes, once. A long time ago."

"What happened?"

She sighed. "He came home one night and smelled like betrayal. Then I caught him the next night in the act."

"Most men cheat, don't they?"

"Not Ray Keith," Janey groaned from the back.

Loretta reached over the seat and stroked Janey's brow. "Hey little mama, you're supposed to be asleep. Any more pains?"

"Just twinges, nothing so severe I can't stand it."

Loretta's eyes lit up. "I forgot, I've got a box of Moon Pies in my bag."

"Oh man, I'd love one." I said.

Janey mumbled and rolled to her side. "None for me, thanks."

We ate in silence, Loretta and me. I was so tired; now that Janey was quiet and resting, my eyes were heavy. I felt warm beside Loretta. Peaceful. "Thank you, Ms. Lynette, I don't know what would've happened had you not come along, despite you runnin' out of gas." My voice had all the grace of a strangled bullfrog.

"You're welcome, but I believe you should thank Jesus, not me." Her statement struck me like an insult.

"You think I'm a sinner?"

"Have you accepted Jesus as your Savior?"

"I believe in Him. I think I got saved at Vacation Bible School once."

"If you did, then you'd know it."

"How do you know when you're a Christian?"

"You love Christ, follow Him, believe in Him, you're used according to His divine will."

"How do you know God's will?"

"For me, it was the opening of many doors, the path was made plain for me, and I walked where He said go. I can hear His voice and I relay it to those in need. He uses me because I yield to Him freely, where others do not."

I snorted so fiercely the RC Cola I'd just drank shot out my nose. "That's about the dumbest thing I ever heard. What makes you so much better than me? Hmm? Why can't God talk to me?" I laughed and wiped my nose with the sleeve of my sweater.

"He can, but most people don't have enough faith, or live in fear. Most people refuse to be open to the Holy Spirit, don't believe, refuse to listen."

"Well, I'll tell ya, Miss High and Mighty Preacher Lady, you're no better than me, or Aunt Sye, or my cousin Janey back there that got knocked up once and had an abortion when she was sixteen, before she married Ray Keith. The way I see it, we're all a bunch of no-good sinners and we do the best we can along the way. And if God wants to talk to me, I think He knows where I damn well live."

Loretta wiped her eyes. "Maybe you're right, Essie. Maybe I'm all wrong," she said hesitantly, with an apologetic ring. "Have you ever seen an evangelist? How about when your uncle isn't around, you ever turn on the TV and watch someone preach and pray for the sick?"

"Nope. Way I figure is if there really is a God who created the entire universe with all of its glories, and He decides to deliver a message to humanity, He won't use somebody on TV with a bad hairstyle."

Loretta laughed. "Now, that's one I haven't heard, but you make a good point."

I laughed too. It felt good. "Where d'you grow up?"

"Near your area, actually."

"You say you know some Aikens?"

"Yes."

"You know any of my family? Noble, Sye, or my daddy? His name was Paul David."

"Yes, I knew them. Any more questions?"

"Is that your real name? Loretta Lynette?"

"Yes, first and middle."

"You got a last name, ever been married?"

"I use Lynette as my last name; my last name was Hollingsworth. Funny, I've never told that to a soul. You're the first. And the answer is *no* to your second question. I've never been married."

I didn't ask any more questions. Her answers came to me straight and smooth. We looked into each other's eyes, and then she reached up, lightly touched my cheek, and smiled.

"You best try to sleep. We'll have to get help at first light, and it's quite possible we'll be delivering a baby if we have to."

I decided to ask one last question. "Is Janey in danger?"

"I don't know. But I'll pray God be with her and her baby."

"Thank you," I said. "I'm sorry if I insulted you."

"Not at all."

I opened my sleep-sticky eyes to light piercing through the front window of Loretta's van. She was gone, but Janey woke with a start and sat up, gasping for air.

"Janey, you okay?"

"I gotta pee, bad. And I think my pains are back and worse than last night."

"Hold on. I'll help you squat outside the van."

"Where's Loretta?"

"I don't know. I woke up and she was gone."

I stepped outside and felt like a dry little weed must feel when rain comes. A fog had settled over the road, but the dampness felt good on my body.

"Oh, Essie, this baby's coming!"

"Damn it! Where's Loretta?" I helped Janey Gay stand on the side of the road, first leaning on me, then on the van. Janey tried to pee, but there was nothing, just lots of pressure she said. She walked around a little, hoping it would help ease the labor pains that had started up again.

I slipped around the side and tried to start the van, in hopes that by some miracle gasoline had appeared in our tank. That's when I saw headlights barreling toward us through the morning fog. An ambulance and flashing lights.

She'd left me after I'd fallen asleep. Loretta walked seven miles back to a farmhouse she remembered passing in the storm. Recognizing her, the old couple allowed Loretta to use their phone. The police and ambulance picked her up first and then proceeded to find Janey and me alone and more frightened than ever. Janey's pains were down to three minutes apart.

A kind policeman filled the tank with two gallons of gas, pumped the gas pedal and started the van. The ambulance took off to the nearest hospital with Janey moaning in the back. I took all of Janey's and my luggage out of the Pinto and loaded it into the church van. Loretta and I smiled similar smiles hearing the policeman report on his radio he'd found the missing celebrity preacher and would be escorting her back to Georgia. It was then I realized she had run away from God.

The policeman allowed Loretta to take me to the hospital. They were obviously being kind to her. She was nobody's prisoner.

"Ma'am, I'll escort you to the hospital, then to the Georgia line where the state police will take you the rest of the way to Atlanta. I've been cleared to take you through South Carolina."

"Thank you, Officer." Loretta looked at me. "Ready to go?"

Janey's car, like an old sow in the mud, was behind us now. I watched it in the rear view mirror as we sped down that dirt road in the Hofmann forest, weaving in and out of potholes. I never wanted to see the Pinto or the road it sunk in again.

Loretta and I remained quiet racing to the hospital. She dropped me and all our luggage off at the front door by the emergency room.

I wanted to hug her. "Aren't you coming in?"

"No, you'll both be fine now. I have responsibilities. I need to get back."

"But, I'd like to ask you more questions . . . about God and all."

She took my hand and placed a folded piece of paper in my palm, closing my fingers around it. "Here's my personal phone number; don't give it out. Call me; let me know if it's a boy or girl, okay? And keep in touch. I'd like to get to know you better. I'll keep in touch right back, Essie, if you'll give me your phone number too. And address."

"Sure." I scribbled it down on a paper towel, and then asked the question teetering on the edge of my mind all night. "I've got one last question for you."

"Okay. Better make it quick; I think the hospital will send security after me if I don't move this van soon."

"Did you know my mama? Her name was Elle."

She smiled wide and ran her hand through her unwashed hair. "I think the press has got wind of where I am, I see a reporter making a bee line across the parking lot straight for us." She reached out and pulled me into her arms breathing in my scent, burying her face in my hair and neck. This was more than a hug, this was a lifetime of love flowing out of her arms and wrapping itself around me like a cocoon. She kissed my cheek and I could see she was crying. I wrapped my arms tight around her, not wanting to let her go.

"Yes, I knew your mama. I have something for you," she said. She opened the back of the van and slid her hand into her leather bag, then handed me a box made of wood.

"This is yours. You take it home and look at it in private. We'll meet again someday." I saw tears on her cheeks. Then she kissed my forehead one last time and rushed into the van. I felt a great loss, like I'd lost my daddy all over again. She drove away behind the police escort; her arm hung out the window, waving to me behind her. The reporter ran after the van, his strapped camera bouncing off his back.

"L! Stop! I'd like to ask you some questions. L, please stop!"

For a moment I thought I heard him wrong. The next second, I was chasing the reporter.

"Hey! Mister! What d'you call her? Hey! Stop, please . . . what, what did you call her?"

"Weren't you with her?" he asked. "Who are you?"

"Somebody she stopped to help; our car broke down. Please, what did you call her?"

"Don't you know who that was? That's Loretta Lynette. That's L."

He must have seen the confused look on my face.

"She's called L by her close friends. Okay, sure the press found out, so we all call her L. Like the letter L. Didn't you know that? Where you been, little lady?"

"In a world of sin, I guess." I held my box tight with both arms and walked on clouds into the hospital. The corners of my vision blurred. My eyes filled with tears. It all made sense. They called her L. Of course, Elle was L.

After an hour of phone calls to Cherry Point and then to Aunt Sye and Uncle Royal, I sat in the waiting room while Janey Gay gave birth to her little boy. Ray Keith arrived some time later, after Sye and Royal had been greasing up the nursery window with their noses awhile.

Everybody was thankful the "police had found us," as we told them of our rescue. Sye was too occupied with her new grandson to be mad at Janey or me. Without even discussing it, Janey and I agreed now was not the time to talk about Loretta. I bent over and kissed Janey as she held her baby boy. She waited until the family was out of the room.

"You know who she was, don't you, Essie?"

"Yes. You gonna tell Sye and Royal I know the truth about my mother?"

"No. They'll find out soon enough. You mad at them for keeping it from you?

"I don't know how I feel. I can't think any further than you, Ray, and the baby."

"You'll know how to handle it when the time comes, I think. At least now you know who your mama was."

"No, Janey. I know who she *IS*. She's not dead; she's alive. I don't know what happened, or why, but I will someday. Right now, I know she came looking for me. She loves me. I can feel it. And that's all I need to know."

Days later, after we got Janey Gay and the baby home and settled, I found the courage to open the worn wooden box. The scent of cedar and perfume floated out and I missed her for the first time. I took out the stack of letters. They were neatly arranged in order of the postmark. All letters from Daddy to her, my baby picture, and a lock of my hair attached to the picture.

I opened the first letter and began to read.

L,

I know you won't write me, but I plan to send a letter every week. I hope this one finds you well at that fancy college. I understand why you can't be with us, your grandfather being a former Governor of Tennessee and all. I know he wants more for you than I can give you. If you had just said you'd marry me, things would've been different. I wish you would've let me explain about Connie Jo. I'm sorry you caught us in Bernie's Thunderbird. Damn it, L, I wish you'd believe how sorry I am.

But, I promise, I'll be a good daddy. And if you still want to keep the baby a secret, my family won't tell it. Except for Teague, I guess your family doesn't know about little Estelline.

I'm thankful to you for a post office box to send my letters to. You said you'd come back after college, but my heart breaks when I look at our daughter. She looks so much like you.

Estelline's learned to roll over in her crib. She keeps Sye busy. I don't get to see her much, with all the work at the gas station and trying to keep Noble out of trouble with the law. You don't want hitched to no heathen, I guess. But I miss you, L.

If you're ever back in town, please call me. We can meet somewhere private. I'd love for you to meet our daughter.

All my love,
Paul David

Now I had all my answers, the second miracle of my life — the first one being found by Loretta. There was nothing left to know. God had brought her back to me. She would find a way to redeem herself and make me a part of her again. Under the stack of letters was a pair of sparkly earrings that looked like diamonds. I figured I'd keep them to wear on my wedding day.

I picked up the phone and dialed the number she'd given me. I could barely speak. I heard her voice on the answering machine and all I could do was cry.

THE HOMESTEAD lends itself to the supernatural on the page and in the writing of the story. A mystical and spiritual piece, the words leaped onto the pages during a particularly nightmarish time in my life. Needing peace, I found it in the writing of THE HOMESTEAD.

I was once close to an elderly lady named Edna, who inspired my life in many ways. Remembering her fondly, she evolved into one of the characters.

In writing and rewriting this story several times over a seven-year period, I couldn't seem to finish it. I'd put it away for weeks . . . months, dig it out again and work on it some more, but it never spoke to me and said, "done."

Not until I changed the name of a character. Not until I changed the name of Edna's husband to Leo did the story come together and finish itself quickly, within hours.

Afterward, I sat in my chair and laughed — because in real life . . . Edna's husband was named Leo.

I think she was trying to tell me something.

The Homestead

Carved out of the far most majestic region in the state of North Carolina, the homestead nestled at the foot of the Blue Ridge, near Stone Mountain. Built in 1852, seven generations of the Wenger family were born, raised children, and died on the farm. Most of them were buried in the family cemetery, resting in a meadow that dipped between a pasture and a field of winter wheat. Wenger blood and sweat built the homestead and their bond with the land gave them strength and faith — in the unbelievable.

The old farmhouse grew quiet as the grandfather clock struck eight. Outside, fireflies danced in the dusk. Noah Wenger strummed his guitar and rocked back and forth in time to his music, with his left leg resting outstretched on the swing and the other planted on the porch. Muscle-bound from years of plowing, planting, and harvesting, he could not hide the tenderness in his voice playing and singing his mama's favorite song, *Blessed Assurance*.

Edna tapped her foot and nodded her head to the beat, entertained by the dance of the fireflies. A warm breeze carried the scent of plowed dirt from the field near the house. Her mind traveled back into the dim mists of time.

Leo — she could see him there. In the field riding high on the John Deere, his overalls soaked with sweat and dirt. The stench of cow manure surrounded him. How she missed that awful aroma. Even in his old age, he had stood straight and tall. Strength abounded in his large, leathery hands. To Edna, Leo was like the landscape. He would go on forever. But his heart had exploded in his chest. At ninety, God had cheated her, rapturing Leo, leaving her behind.

"Blessed assurance, Jesus is mine . . ." Her son's baritone voice mixed with the sweet chords of his guitar. Edna's thoughts were interrupted by song as the bright orange heavens faded to glitter on dark blue velvet skies.

"Mama, let's go in. Gettin' chilly. You'll catch your death." Noah's voice trailed as he meandered inside and switched on the porch light. He listened to the sound of his mother's tiny feet shuffle down the porch.

Noah held her arm at the elbow, assisting her to the first floor bedroom. Edna's back curled like a cashew, withered and salty. She hobbled past family photographs hanging on the rose and vine-papered hallway walls.

"Mama, Dana's workin' late. Want me to fix ya a bite to eat before bed?"

"Not tonight."

"You sure?" He searched his mother's sunken lilac eyes as she laid the palm of her wrinkled hand on his cheek. "Want me to sit a spell?" he asked.

"No, you wait for your daughter to come home and fix *her* somethin' to eat."

Noah sighed and bent down to kiss her cheek lightly. "Okay. See ya in the mornin'."

Her son's patient smile warmed her. She touched his face again, then closed the bedroom door behind her. Waiting until the sound of his heavy footsteps faded away from her room, Edna shuffled to the window. The cool breeze blew the lace panels apart. A lone firefly flickered in the darkness. She blew him a kiss and turned out the light.

Weary and ready for bed, Noah flicked a match with his thumbnail and lit the gas stove for a cup of herb tea. He shook out the match and looked down at his worn overalls. Clean enough to sit on the uphostery, he sunk into his chair at the table and rested his head against the wall. Lately, he rode the worry wagon around his daughter. Tall, beautiful, and strong-willed, his only child was too much like her Grandpa Leo. Noah had hoped for a son. Instead, a daughter was left in his lap the day his wife skedaddled back to Boston.

He'd encouraged Dana to take the job at the mill, hoping she'd find any kind of life off the farm. Although he needed help, he'd hire migrants before seeing his daughter wear out before her time. But Dana had told her daddy she'd had enough of working inside a cotton mill's weave room and that she'd quit to farm full-time.

"Only thing I love more than this land is you, Daddy. And Grandma Ed."

Farming flowed in her veins as natural as the spring water spilled out of the rock by the corncrib. It was time to accept it.

Dana's last night at the mill left her tired and irritable on the drive home. Each stoplight seemed to last forever. As her Pontiac crested the hill toward home, flames licked the night sky.

Dana stared in disbelief then pressed the gas pedal to the floor. "No! God, No!"

Barreling up the gravel drive, stones pinged the underside of her car. She plowed into the side of Noah's truck. She'd barely felt the crash. It didn't matter. Dana threw open the door and flew into her daddy's sooty, black arms.

"I couldn't get her out!" Terror filled Noah's voice. "I couldn't get Mama out!" He fell to his knees. His glazed eyes mirrored the flickering flames and tears dripped down to his torn and muddy overalls. Their neighbor, Mose Johnson, directed the fire trucks into the yard and worked to move the cows to pasture as sparks drifted dangerously close to the barn.

Dana stood numb as one in a dream, watching the front porch collapse and the tinderbox old house explode into a raging inferno. She crumpled along with it, to a heap on the ground. Photographs, books, clothes . . . all lost. Seven generations of memories were now ashes. Though the deeper loss that shrouded her was the loss of Grandma Ed. *She was never meant to burn, not now, or in the hereafter.*

The empty burnt-out shell of what had been their home appeared with the first smear of foggy dawn. Noah slept under a massive hickory tree covered by a neighbor's quilt. Eyes like the blackened windows of the fire-ravaged house, Dana staggered to the smoking embers. Her heart ached and her head pounded.

She approached the porch area and stumbled through what yesterday was the front room. Amidst the debris, a tiny firefly appeared and circled her. She couldn't help but notice the beauty of it blinking in the fog and smoke, as if surveying her loss. Dana maneuvered through the rubble stepping over scorched remains of furniture, appliances, and melted memories. The smoldering ruin's stench floated into her nostrils. Rushing out the back of the farmhouse, she followed the firefly that led the way and disappeared in the mist.

Dana stood on pieces of charred boards, scorched earth and cinder block, the remaining pieces of their back porch. Her gaze and sorrow was interrupted by a woman appearing through the fog running toward a tall handsome man at the misty pasture's edge. She presumed at first they were neighbors from the next farm, but as the two embraced in the distance she stepped into the yard to observe them more closely. Suddenly, the fog thickened and she lost sight of the pair. Dana picked up her pace and jogged in the direction of the pasture, viewing them faintly through the haze atop the hill. They turned and waved to her as a field of fireflies took flight, filling the air blinking and blinking the fog away, enveloping the couple in a brilliant light. They were no longer old, but young and beautiful. Tears gathered in Dana's tired eyes.

"Grandma! Grandpa! Wait!" They didn't seem to hear. The handsome couple strolled hand in hand over the hill. When Dana reached the top where her grandparents had stood, they were nowhere in sight. She fell to her knees. Falling further into the clover, she buried her face into her hands and sobbed. *How did this happen? Why? Why did I have to see them?* In her misery, two fireflies lit on her arm and blinked. She watched them flitter to her shoulder. Rolling tears washed fresh tracks through the dirt on her face. The fireflies flew away as she heard shouts from the barn.

"Over here! I found her! Here!" Mose Johnson waved his arms and howled like a hound dog. Dana jumped up and bolted down the hill toward the barn. Noah in a sprint arrived at the site with Dana, falling to the ground beside the body both knew was the woman they loved.

"She got out, Noah," said Mose. He had crouched down over Edna's lifeless body and covered her with a blanket. Looking into Dana's swollen red eyes, he said, "She's gone."

Dana turned to Noah and threw her arms around his neck. "She's not gone, Daddy. I saw her. And Grandpa. Up there." Dana pointed to the hill in the pasture behind them. "They found a new piece of land to homestead."

In that instant, the sun's rays poured through breaking clouds illuminating the grassy knoll where eternity begins for members of the Wenger family and fireflies light the way home.

The Paper Journey Press in Wake Forest first published OLD TIME RELIGION in 2004 in the anthology, *Original Sin: The Seven Deadlies Come Home To Roost*. Under the sin category of gluttony, this story won its special place in the book.

To me, OLD TIME RELIGION touches on many sins. I performed a reading of this story in Durham at The Regulator Bookshop early in 2005. Afterward, a woman I had never met compared the story to those of the great Flannery O'Connor. Needless to say, I was humbled and honored. I still don't know who you were, but I thank you. The simple validation from your gracious comment propelled me to finish this book.

OLD TIME RELIGION has been described as funny, dark, and the most disturbing story in the collection. The stakes are high. These characters lived on my shoulder through the first draft, and then stood behind me during the rewrite. (My characters are imposing, aren't they?)

It's one of those stories you hear writers say, "it wrote itself." Few stories actually do that, but as I typed OLD TIME RELIGION it was as if my hands were not my own and the story played like a movie in my head.

It'll make you think, and it may disturb you, but remember . . . it's just a story. Isn't it?

Old Time Religion

The front porch thermometer read 102 degrees. After supper, Earl Angle maneuvered to the hammock for his customary Sunday afternoon nap. The Culvers' front porch was as good a place as any. Gastonia, North Carolina heat in the summer of 1966 was stifling, and on this day every creature moved in slow motion.

Peggy picked at the dirt between her toes and glimpsed up from time to time to watch a string of drool slide down Earl's chin and land on his bright red satin tie. Standing to cool off from her cramped toe-picking position, she fanned the flies away from Earl's sleeping body. A sweltering heap that spilled over the edges of her momma's hammock. Beads of sweat glistened on his forehead and his nonexistent upper lip.

That pig must weigh 500 pounds. Peggy sighed. She hated the way when Earl looked at her, one eye stood still while the other stared at the sky or the ground.

Earlier that morning, Peggy Louise Culver had whined to her momma. "Why's he comin' to supper again?" Peggy's friends weren't allowed to visit when Earl came to Sunday supper, and that made for a boring day as far as she was concerned.

Millie Culver tired of explaining the family's monthly ritual of playing host to Earl. "Young'un, he's our guest just one Sunday a month, you know that. Besides, Sunday is a day of rest. Don't need to be doin' nothin' but church and supper. No TV, no games, and you can't be runnin' 'round in bathin' suits when Earl comes, you 'eah?"

"But it's hot, Momma. Please let Tammy Faye come over. We like runnin' through the sprinkler."

"This ain't the day to be showin' your legs to company. You're seven years old, gal: time to grow up. Go on now and get your brother. Time for church." Millie ended the conversation by swatting her daughter's backside lightly with her hairbrush. She watched Peggy slide her hand down the hallway wall. *I am blessed to have a daughter, and cursed. She can't be a lady no matter how many whippin's she gets.*

Earl Angle managed to finagle supper each Sunday with select members of the congregation. He paid special attention to the single mothers and widows with children. Said it was his solemn duty and calling to tend to the fatherless. A member of the congregation informed him Mrs. Culver's man had left her.

"Them poor kids, all alone with no daddy. Course you know Millie's father died last year. Willed her all his money."

"No, that so?" With great interest and mounting sympathy, he'd turned his attention to Millie Culver and her children.

"Why yes, and the woman can cook. Land sakes, her pies won blue ribbons at the county fair three years in a row."

Earl's bug eyes followed Millie and her children as they exited the back of the church. He contemplated the possibilities.

Millie had indeed practiced the fine art of Southern cooking. She set the table and chuckled, flattered but surprised Earl had asked to be received at her dinner table and amused that he requested her strawberry-rhubarb pie at every opportunity, but still — she questioned his intentions.

Maybe he likes me for more than my cookin'. As much as she desired a position of importance in the church, she possessed no romantic interest toward this rotund man. A strange annoyance tugged at her. Was it her pie, or some other need that brought him to her house the second Sunday of every month?

"Peggy weren't but three when we divorced, and Kyle was nine," she told Earl the first time he sat at her supper table six months ago. Few women divorced in the South of the 60s, even though Millie's divorce was a civil one. Tom got the kids the first and third weekends each month.

"I never loved him, and he had a wanderin' eye. He was in love with Constance Littman. He dated me just to make her jealous. 'Cept I got pregnant. Poor Tom, we knew it was a mistake. But I was a sinner, and Daddy didn't want reproach on the family, so I married him. Weren't but sixteen myself."

"Missus Culver, far be it for me to cast the first stone, dear lady. Your children are blessings from Gawd. Pass them biscuits round 'eah again." Earl kept his conversation to a minimum at the table.

Millie continued to testify. "But I was lost, and now I'm found. I just want to raise my kids right. Can't fix what's past." Her eyes filled with tears and she passed him the plate of biscuits. It was obvious Earl's mind was on supper, and not on her pain, as he had nothing more to say.

Today was no different. Earl instantly began to gorge, forgetting to say grace until Millie interrupted his third bite with, "Dear Lord, we thank you for our food." She had thawed an extra pack of chicken legs, and boiled more potatoes for mashing than usual. He piled green beans next to his chicken, potatoes, and gravy, leaving just enough room for pickle relish and her bacon-grease creamed corn to spill over the sides of his plate. Peggy handed him an extra plate for his biscuits and apple butter.

The Culvers watched in amazement. Earl piled his plate twice and then a third time. After six months of Sundays, his feasting began to get on Millie's last nerve. She didn't believe her eyes when he washed the third piece of apple pie down with the last pitcher of sweet tea.

There were no leftovers when Earl came for supper.

Peggy sat on the porch steps, pulled her knees up to her chest, then wrapped her arms around her legs. Disgusted with the large sleeping lump on her momma's hammock, she knew her butt would be blistered if she woke him from his Sunday siesta.

Earl had thrown his white linen jacket over the porch railing. His white shirt, now wrinkled and wet, heaved up and down around his massive stomach while he snored. She surmised if she loosened his tie he might breathe easier. *Then again, maybe he'll strangle.* "Let him," she said.

Snoring, drooling, and an occasional fart were more than she could stand. With her shoes in hand, she ran off to find Kyle. Her brother had to see the sleeping pile of poop on their front porch. Maybe Kyle would find it as disgusting as she did.

The tool shed door was wide open. Kyle was reading his Spiderman comic. Peggy approached with her usual caution so as not to piss him off.

"Kyle, come and see. Ole' Earl's done passed out in Momma's hammock again."

"Leave me be, and who cares if he's in a food coma. Let him die. I hope he does."

"What's the matter with you, goober?"

"Nothin', let me be, and I ain't goin' back to Momma's church again. She and Daddy can whip me till I bleed, I ain't goin'. Now I told you, get out of here!"

Peggy never heard her brother talk like that. She left the toolshed and skipped to the tire swing.

Millie dried the last serving bowl and placed it in her china cupboard. She took off her apron and wiped the stray hairs that had stuck to the sweat on her face back into place. The high temperature was unbearable, and the house fans only moved the heat around instead of cooling the air. She peeked out the front door and shook her head at "comatose Earl" sweating bullets in her hammock. *I'll have to hose it down tomorrow.* Millie stepped out the back door to avoid waking Earl and stopped dead in her tracks. Had he winked at her or at Kyle during supper? At thirteen Kyle suffered from puberty and mood swings, but today he seemed more touchy than usual. She found her son where Peggy had left him earlier.

"Where's your sister?" Millie asked.

"Didn't know it was my day to watch her," he said.

"Young man, if I need to whip you on the Lord's Day, I will."

"Sorry, Momma."

Millie stared at the top of his head. *He might as well spill what's bothering him now, before it's time to go back to Sunday evening service.*

She watched her son take a deep breath. "I ain't goin' back to church."

"And why not?" Shocked, she was determined to know.

"I don't believe like you do. I think Daddy has the right idea. Love God, be a good person, and you'll still go to heaven, without having to attend church and be a hypocrite."

"Who's a hypocrite, me?"

"No, Momma. Not you."

"Who then? Who do you know that's a hypocrite?"

"Can't say."

"Why not?"

"You won't believe me."

Millie sat down on the cool tool shed floor beside her son. Her need to understand her young man swept away her anger.

"Is it Earl? What's the matter? What'd he say, Kyle? Tell Momma. I won't be mad, just tell me the truth. I'd believe you before I'd believe anyone in the wide world."

Kyle's words spilled out, along with his tears.

"Me and Earl, we was sittin' on the porch today while you and Peggy made supper. I was tryin' to be nice to him, like you told me. Earl asked me to come sit by him, said he wanted to show me a magic trick. Told me to close my eyes. So I did. He kissed me, Momma. He kissed me on the mouth. Hard. I wanted to puke my guts out."

Millie put her small hands on her son's face. The agony of his revelation tore at the core of her maternal being. Anger toward Earl mounted to fury. Tears pooled in her eyes when she spoke to her son. "Kyle, this ain't Jesus' way, baby. He don't make men do this to little boys. You don't have to worry about not goin' to church, cause I ain't goin' back there either. We'll find us a new church even if it means bein' holy at home."

Now she understood why Earl insisted on visiting only on the Sundays she had the children. It wasn't her reputation he thought about. It was her son he was after. With a mother's love, her anger grew hotter than the summer heat that oppressed them. By the time she reached her front porch, Earl had begun to stir in her hammock and had rolled onto his side. His back toward Millie, she kicked his enormous bulging butt as hard and as far as her foot would go. She pounded him with her hands, slapping and spitting in rage.

Startled, Earl rolled out of the hammock and landed on the porch floor. "What's gone on 'eah?" he yelled. "Why you do this, Missus Culver, why?"

Millie gritted her teeth. "You sonofabitch, you molested my boy! You lustful sonofabitch!" She shrieked. "You kissed him, he tole me and I want you off my property or I'm callin' the sheriff! Don't never come back 'eah! Me and mine will never step foot in that blasphemous church again!"

Earl grabbed his coat from the porch railing and ran to his Cadillac. "You tell anybody 'bout this, Missus Culver, and I'll see to it you lose those brats. You 'eah me!"

"Burn in hell, Earl Angle, you fat bastard! Burn in hell!" She screamed, chased him, and threw rocks at his car as he made his escape. Millie's legs shook, standing in her driveway. Crying and bewildered, she turned around slowly. Peggy and Kyle stood frozen on the porch, their eyes wide and mouths open like hungry pups. She stretched her arms wide and they ran to her. Wrapping herself around them, Millie and her children stumbled back to the porch, but she collapsed to the ground short of the steps. Kyle attempted to help his momma stand but they all landed back in the dirt, holding on to each other. Little Peggy had heard the whole fighting match. Her tiny arms encircled her mother's and brother's necks, attempting to comfort them.

Kyle patted Millie's hand, but could not control her sobbing convulsions. "Momma, I didn't know you could beat up a man like that. Earl weighs a ton more than you! Don't cry Momma, it's okay, I believe Jesus loves me, just like you do."

That night, the Reverend Earl Angle made his usual grand entrance into his pulpit. His congregation applauded their obese Pastor, and he began to wail, "Gimme that old time religion, it's good enough for me. Yes Gawd, I hear what you're tryin' to tell your people tonight. You reap the seeds you sow, dear people. It's time to sow your financial seeds. Who's got twenty dollars to give to Jesus tonight?"

Reverend Angle searched the congregation and found the family he'd invited to church last week sitting on the front pew. He smiled and nodded, delighted in his soul-winning ability. He had contacted the new widow after reading Tuesday's obituary. Howard Dunning had suffered a heart attack, leaving his wife, Betsy, a cook at the local diner, and their three young sons.

I t may surprise you that the main character in PIGMENT OF MY IMAGINATION is a man. But the Southern woman he loves is most definitely *fried*. Although he tries to help her in his own meager way, he is inadequate at best.

This story, another spin-off of my upcoming novel, *Televenge*, was a slice I cut from the book in the process of rewriting. Ken Kopper, though a minor and insignificant character in the novel, moved me as a soft-spoken man with a conscience. He begged me to evolve him into his own story, which resulted in PIGMENT OF MY IMAGINATION.

I love these characters, and also despise some of them. Their desires are timeless, and so are their messages — whether they are good or evil. The story deals with sensitive issues of race, regret, and longing for something you can never have.

Pigment Of My Imagination

~ November 1973 ~

Ken Kopper opened his diner for breakfast. The front door's pull shade slipped out of his hand, rolled up, and smacked the top of the window at the exact moment a ladder flew at his face from the other side. It sounded like a bomb as glass shattered on the diner's gray and white tile floor and out to the sidewalk. Startled, Ken hopped away from the door to avoid injury but fell backwards, knocking the brass coat rack behind him to the floor. Another bomb.

Corbet Butcher dropped his toolbox to the sidewalk in shock. Two men, one on each side of the busted door, stared at each other — speechless.

Corbet's runaway ladder would cost him money this time. Ken could see Corbet's embarrassment as he tiptoed to the front door of the Kopper Kettle Diner and peeked through the jagged hole. The glass cracked under his boots.

"G-Godamighty, Ken. I-I-I'm sorry. It s-slipped, I d-didn't see . . . Golly . . ."

Ken pulled himself up to the nearest booth and rubbed his bad leg. "I'll take it off what I owe ya."

"Uh . . . that'd be fine, m-m-my fault . . . got a broom?"

"I'll clean it up, just fix my damn sign." Ken picked a piece of glass out of the heel of his hand. His temper in check, as always, he limped to his supply closet for a bucket, a broom, a dustpan — and a Band-Aid.

Corbet stood five feet eleven inches with square shoulders, straight dirt brown hair, and a blue right eye. The left one was cloudy blue and blind. And he stuttered.

But people assumed Corbet and Ken were brothers, their resemblance eerie. Loyal friend and customer, Corbet arrived early each day with news and opinions of local current events. Except that chilly morning he wasn't a patron, but a hired handyman. The sign over the diner had burnt-out light bulbs under the two p's and under the coffee cup at the bottom. The only part of the sign you could see in the dark was the steam rising out of the cup. Open until one in the morning, the diner attracted the second shifts from the local newspaper and Baptist Hospital. Ken wanted his sign fixed.

After he finished duct taping thick plastic over the hole where the window had been, Ken called Eugene Guthrie at the hardware. Eugene hooted, hollered, and belly laughed into the phone. Ken held the receiver out from his ear.

"Hee hee, you hired that dim-wit? . . . Whoo wee . . . that's a good one. Sure, I'll be over after lunch to fix ya up. That redneck idiot — why the hell d'ya hire him? Blind in one eye and cain't half see outta the other. Oh — my, that's a good one — sorry, I can't . . . I can't stop laughin' . . . ole' Corbet cain't change a damn light bulb without shutin' down the electric 'round the block. Whoo, that's ripe . . . good one. Lord, Ken, he ain't no handyman . . . he's a nut! Oh — me!"

"Just come fix my damn door, Eugene!" Ken slammed down the phone.

The glass scratched at the sidewalk as Ken swept it into a pile. He ignored Corbet on the ladder, tearing his sign apart. He figured if they didn't talk, his diner's sign might get fixed without further incident.

Corbet shook his head. "You hear 'b-bout all the t-t-trouble in Brown Town on account of that c-colored man, Lighter, b-bein' elected Raleigh's mayor? First time in this s-state. Never thought I'd see it in my lifetime." He dropped a new light bulb. It popped like a firecracker when it hit the sidewalk. "Shit." Corbet fished another from his toolbox.

Ken swept it up with the rest. "Don't fall, Corbet. Don't even talk right now. Just fix the sign. And quit callin' the east side of town Brown Town. Good God, get over it. I'm sick of it."

"What?"

"Just fix the goddamn sign and get down!"

"Sorry! I'm real s-sorry; d-didn't I-I t-tell you I w-was s-sorry?"

Ken sighed. "Yes, you did." He wiped his hand on his flannel shirt; his Band-Aid rolled off. He hesitated, but he had to calm Corbet down. "Apology accepted." Examining the cut, it appeared deeper than he first thought. Blood had dripped onto his jeans, boots, and dotted the sidewalk. He needed stitches.

Ken slid the broken glass into the bucket, then cleared his throat. "There's coffee and a ham biscuit when you're done." He couldn't yell at Corbet. They were like brothers. Corbet stayed in Ken's apartment when he got evicted from his own, which was about every other month or two.

He closed the bandaged door behind him. *Glad it ain't too cold today.*

Ken hobbled into the kitchen and then stitched up his hand. Opening a new bottle of Mercurochrome, he dabbed the wound with a stinging icy swab.

His hand throbbed, but he'd wrapped it tight. Ken limped over to fire up his grill and chuckled despite the pain. "What a gimp I must look like."

He refused to yell at Corbet or anybody else. Ken's old man had yelled and screamed all his life. He wanted no part of that now, but he knew Corbet was right. Every white man he knew in Winston-Salem called the east side of town Brown Town. The term originated long before Ken was born, his dad had said. Everyone called it Brown Town, as if were its given name.

There had been some trouble near File Street at Bluey Jones' juke joint, appropriately called Bluey's. It'd been headline news for the past three days, since the state elections. The jury was still out on how the South of the 70s would continue to uphold the Civil Rights laws.

When Vince Kopper was alive, the Kopper Kettle hung a Confederate flag on the wall over the booths. It didn't matter to him what happened in Greensboro at the Woolworth counter. His diner was off limits. He kept his sign posted in the window. NO COLORED.

~ July 1962 ~

"You know I fought with Patton. Ken's goin' to Nam." Vince Kopper announced it to his customers like it was a right of passage to manhood.

"I heard things are heatin' up over there," said a customer.

"Yeah, but it'll make him a man. Teach him a few things about life. You forget the women you've bedded, all the places you been, but by God, you never forget your war. It's been the best part of my life."

"Mine too, Vince."

"Me too."

"Damn straight."

"Make him a right smart man, Vince."

Ken stood behind the kitchen door listening to their war cries. It didn't matter the military had begun shipping soldiers back in body bags or reported them missing in action. Ken picked up the phone and called Corbet. He wasn't afraid to die; he just didn't want to watch anyone else do it.

"No son of mine is a coward! No, sir. We come from a long line of patriots." Vince bragged and wiped the counter with a greasy rag. "I'm takin' him and Corbet to the Army recruiter tomorrow morning." Ken stepped behind the counter and stood beside his dad. His customers greeted Ken as if he'd already come home a war hero. The elation on Vince's face lit up the dining room.

"You must be proud, Vince."

"You bet. Wish his mother could see him." It was the last time his dad put his arm around him, hugged him — and kissed him, in front of a row of five decorated veterans sitting on bar stools, drinking cups of coffee, smoking unfiltered Camels, sharing war stories, battle scars, and old tattoos.

That was the night Ken and Corbet decided to get drunk one last time before morphing into mighty men of valor.

Ken had told his dad once he wanted to go to college, be a social worker — help people. Dreams like that struck his dad like a punch to the kidneys.

He tried to explain to his dad's stone cold face. "There's a lot of social injustice, I just want to make a difference, maybe go to law school . . ."

"Law school! Why the hell d'ya wanna be a bloodsucker? And you can forget social work. Social worker means *Communism* in my book." Vince pounded his fist on the wall. "No son of mine's gonna be some *Commie lover . . . a traitor!* Forget it!"

"But . . ."

"One more word and I'll beat it out of you with my strap!" The old razor strap hung on a nail in his dad's bedroom. He'd belt-buckled Ken's backside for less sass than this. His father's response didn't surprise him. A veteran of the "big one," Vince had fought the Nazis. Communism, Socialism, Marxism, Fascism, all meant the same thing to a man like Ken's dad. He was more scared of *catching* Communism than typhoid, the measles, or venereal disease.

Ken's mother had died when he was five. He'd lived to please his old man. And so, for his dad's sake, so he could hold up his crew cut head around his crew of regular customers, Ken agreed to join the Army right after graduation. It didn't matter what *he* wanted — Vince had planned his son's military future from the day he was born.

But the blessed event of turning Ken over to Uncle Sam never happened. The car accident had seen to that. When he woke up in Baptist Hospital, the pain of rejection and disappointment was clear in his dad's eyes. Vince Kopper would never be the same. Instead of his son coming home with war wounds, purple hearts and honor, he convalesced in shame, his leg broken in three places from a fast Chevy and four cases of Pabst Blue Ribbon.

Even though Corbet's head busted through the windshield, losing the sight in his left eye, Vince never forgave Corbet either. He swore Ken and Corbet slammed into the tree on purpose. That they'd staged the wreck so neither would have to be a soldier.

Ken recuperated in the tiny apartment above the diner. To ease some of his father's disappointment, he told his dad he wanted to learn the business. But the two barely spoke afterwards. Nobody won in the end.

Vince never got to brag about Ken shooting gooks in the trenches. Ken never went to college, never married, never saw the ocean, never did nothing after that but try to make his old man happy.

"What the hell you doin'?" Vince wrapped his leathery hand around the back of his son's neck and yanked him into the kitchen.

"Sir?"

His dad's eyes were on fire; he flashed his yellowed teeth, his mouth rigid and yelling as quietly as he could. "You heard me. We don't serve niggers in here!"

"Dad, the man just wanted a glass of water and a sandwich. He paid me and left a nice tip, for Christ sake."

"Jesus Christ ain't got nothin' to do with this, boy. Why d'you let him sit at my counter?"

"Dad, I don't get it. He's a man, just a man, like you or me."

"He's a goddamn nigger! Don't you ever, EVER, allow another nigger in this diner, you hear me? Was anybody else in here? Did anybody see him come or go?"

"No. The place was empty. Why do you care? It's skin pigment, Dad, that's the only difference between him and us. Skin pigment. Why do you imagine the worst about everybody with black skin?"

"A pigment of my imagination. Is that what you think? Bullshit." Vince plopped down at his makeshift desk in the corner of the kitchen. "I'm gonna have to make me a bigger sign!"

Ken shook his head.

"Don't you disagree with me, boy! They're more different than you know. Time you came to one of my meetings."

Ken forced a couple swallows; his throat had gone dry. *Why didn't God delete skin pigment altogether?* But he drew the line at his dad's "meetings."

"We got customers." Ken drug his bad leg out to the counter. The subject of his dad's "meetings" never came up again. Ken figured his dad was afraid he'd wreck another car to avoid becoming what he was. A proud veteran, a prominent businessman, a member of the Klan.

The day his dad died, Ken yanked the Confederate flag off the wall and replaced it with the stars and stripes handed to him at graveside. Then he limped to the diner's front window, grabbed the NO COLORED sign, and drove the ten miles back to Magnolia Acres Cemetery. It was easy to find the section of graves reserved for military. The fresh red dirt was piled on top of Vince's grave, wilted flowers in plastic baskets laid haphazardly around it. The funeral home hadn't even taken the tent down.

Ken shredded the sign over his dad's final resting place. The pieces blew into the cracks and crevices of earth, grass, flowers, and the new headstone that marked Vince Kopper's remains.

~ February 1974 ~

The Kopper Kettle sat between the Western Auto and the Glass Slipper Beauty Shop on 2nd Street. The diner was long enough to seat twelve at the counter and wide enough to fit a row of booths at the windows, which ran the entire length. A large pass-through to the kitchen allowed Ken to work at the grill and watch his help and customers at the same time.

Turning the sign from *Closed* to *Open*, Ken poked his head through the open door to catch the first warm breezes of spring, but saw Merida Holcomb in her red, white and blue voting dress instead. He'd noticed she had worn it three days in a row after the November elections, and now she had it on again. She made a beeline out of the Rexall drug store across the street and headed to the diner.

Merida lived in the apartment over the drug store and cleaned most of the stores and businesses on the block for a living. She had traveled door to door with her petitions and worked hard for black voter registration. Next to Corbet, she was Ken's best friend, if he could say he had one. He imagined Vince rolled over in his grave every time Merida waltzed into the diner.

Quite possibly she was his mother's age, though he was never quite sure and wasn't planning to ask. Her laugh was like the chiming of bells, up and down the scale, always had been. Plump and tidy, she'd taken care of him, cleaned his apartment, and washed his one load of laundry each week in exchange for a free meal now and then and on Sunday after church. When Ken's daddy died, Merida had noticed the sign was gone and toted a macaroni and cheese casserole across the street. That was the day Ken and Merida became friends.

The morning sun shone on her face as she bounded through the door.

"Kenny boy, I came home late from Bible study last night. Osa got to talkin' and you know how she do go on. Well, Osa's boy drop me off and waited 'til I got up the stairs and into my place, 'cause we had seen some white man snoopin' 'round on the street. I peeked out my front room window and seen him cross over to the diner. He was lookin' in the windows, real suspicious like. He been 'round town. I seen him before."

Ken laid a tray of mustard and ketchup bottles on the counter and nodded to Sophie, his waitress, who had walked in behind Merida. "Lots of people snoop around town after dark."

"This was different. A car pulled up fast to the curb and he hop in. A bunch of mens hid inside. The streetlight showed 'em. Be careful, Kenny. You know they still mad you didn't join up with your daddy."

Ken smiled, mildly amused at Merida's ramblings. "There's no more Klan."

"Tha's what you think. Tha's what they want everybody to think. By the way, I heard at church Mavis is comin' home. Her Aunt Lula say she be home for a while. Maybe she come sing at the church, I'll tell her to stop by and see you."

"Thanks, but I doubt Mavis remembers me."

"Sure she do. She ate at your diner every day with her friend after school." Merida slid off the stool and dashed toward the door. "Gots to run. I be deliverin' your laundry this afternoon."

Ken didn't get the chance to say thanks. She walked faster than any woman he knew. She'd always said a tribe of wild Baptists raised her, and she wasn't kidding.

His heart warmed, remembering Mavis, and he smiled. Her daddy was a white man; her mama was a Negro woman. Ken stared at the floor as if searching for a face in a dark pit below him. *So many times I wanted to ask her for a date. I would've loved to have given you some sweet brown grandchildren, you self-righteous bastard.*

The low light of early morning brought in the first customers of the day. Corbet, naturally, and Eugene Guthrie.

Eugene's craggy face and twice-broken nose became the butt of many of Corbet and Ken's jokes. Small and stocky, he was a narcissist with a spooky affinity for hardware. He seldom used it; he just liked to sell it. Sarcastic and quick-witted in a dark, sharp-edged way, he was prone to anxious twitches and restless shrugs, and his fingernails were all bitten to the quick. He was also rapidly going bald at thirty-five: his dome poked through his few comb-over strands.

With a coffee cup in one hand, his free hand fidgeted with his bow tie then palmed a greasy shock of graying hair off his forehead. His brown eyes darted around the room before he spoke, "Corbet, you been busy? You make enough money to pay your rent this month?"

"I-I'll have you know Eugene, I m-m-make out fine b-bein' a handyman. I do g-g-good work."

"Yeah. So I hear. You did a hell of job on Ken's front door."

"D-don't start with m-me, Eugene. Me and K-Ken are s-square."

Ken picked his pencil from behind his ear to take their orders and sensed Corbet's need for him to agree. But as usual, he kept his thoughts and comments to himself. His quiet nature had developed from years of refusing to be like his dad. He'd lost a few customers because of it, mostly those who knew and loved his old man.

"What'll you have, Eugene?" asked Ken.

"KKK omelet; whites only," he said.

Ken ignored him. "Ham, eggs, and biscuits, your usual."

"Right," he snickered, trying to get a reaction from Corbet.

Corbet hunkered down over his coffee and opened the newspaper. He hated Eugene.

"You guys get up on the wrong side of the bed? It's just a joke."

Ken hollered through the pass-through, "Not to you it's not."

"You're right about that, Ken, my boy. Says somewhere in the Bible, in the Book of Tribulations I do believe, 'bout the difference in the races."

"Not in my Bible," said Ken, refilling their coffee cups.

"Since when do you read the Bible?" Corbet asked.

Ken didn't feel like arguing. He left the two stooges to finish their breakfast, said he had paperwork in the back, and to check with Sophie if they needed anything.

"Thanks. Thanks a lot," Sophie whispered behind him as she cut slices of pie for lunch.

Ken had listened to Eugene and Corbet bicker back and forth enough over the years to fill a book. More recently, he'd heard Eugene had become a blatant bigot and ran blacks out of his store. Refused to wait on them. He figured one of these days Eugene was sure to bring the trouble in Brown Town to the main streets of Winston-Salem.

But Ken knew Eugene would never let up on his old friend. Simple-minded and slow, Corbet just repeated things he heard and read, not knowing what they meant. He wouldn't have made it through school if Ken hadn't helped him. Corbet poured over the newspaper, word for word. It made him feel smart, at least. He was neither friend nor foe to the black man on the street. For all the reading he did, Corbet was plain ignorant when it came to people.

Customers straggled in and out all morning. All Ken wanted to do was go back to bed, and think of Mavis. His leg gave him fits, his head pounded; his heart longed to be touched.

He could never say he had the chance to fall in love with Mavis. She had moved to New York City after graduation to become a famous singer. Besides, he was a good ten years older than her. She was worldly; he'd not traveled out of North Carolina. Her voice was angelic; his twang curled his tongue so bad no visiting Yankee could understand him. She was black but she was beautiful.

He'd not had a date since the accident. Nobody looked at him twice except for the occasional hooker running into the diner to get out of the rain. And he limped — constantly.

Ken flipped a few pancakes on his griddle when he heard a customer yell at Sophie, "Hey, you got shit on a shingle here?"

"You see it on the menu?" Sophie could sling hash better than anybody. She'd been Ken's breakfast and lunch help for the past two years. Another waitress took over the dinner and evening hours. Sophie slid the order in the window. "Eggs over easy."

Ken could see the loudmouth customer on the stool next to Eugene. He had squeezed into a forty-eight long powder blue polyester blazer, sported a blonde flat top, and a bright yellow tie. They were talking football.

"Yeah, I've crunched a lot of cartilage in my day," said the loudmouth.

Sophie had poured him another cup of coffee. She walked back to the kitchen to fill her tray with an order and said, "Yeah, and he ought to clip his nose hairs."

His deafening, non-stop, play-by-play rundown of the Super Bowl cleared the booth behind him. Two elderly ladies shot him looks of disgust, swinging their pocketbooks out the door. He lit a cigarette and pounded the counter, laughing at his own jokes. His fork fell on the floor.

He yelled at Sophie again. "Hey, sweetie, get me another fork."

She slammed one down by his plate.

"Testy little thing, ain't she?" He laughed, watching her butt walk away from him. "Damn that receiver. *I* could've caught that damn ball! It just slipped through his hands, poor bastard."

Strange enough, Ken had seen him somewhere before. The sizzle and smoke from the griddle and the noise of the diner impaired him from hearing the rest of the conversation the man had with Eugene. He noticed their conversation intensifying. They'd gone from discussing football to something much more serious.

"Ken, see you tomorrow." Eugene waved and left the loudmouth alone at the counter.

What's he up to now? Ken nodded and walked over to clear Eugene's dishes.

"You own this place, boy?"

"Yeah. And I'm not a boy."

The man's beady eyes shrunk to small dots. He pinched his cigarette, took a long drag, blew the smoke up over his face, then sipped his coffee.

"I hear you've got a checkered past."

"Who are you? What do you want?"

"They call me Bull. I hear you're a nigger lover."

"Why don't you pay your bill and leave, Bull. Now. I think that'd be a good idea."

"Fine." He stood to leave. That's when Ken noticed it, a pin in his lapel. The red circle, the white cross. "You shamed your daddy, boy. I'd be careful, if I were you."

Ken counted five new customers that day. All with red circle and white cross pins on their lapels. Merida was right. The Klan was alive and well, living in Winston-Salem, and eating in his diner.

At one a.m. he crawled up the steps and fell into bed. Eighteen-hour days, seven days a week for the past ten years, his inherited diner would kill him too, in the end.

Ken passed his hand along the other side of the bed, registering once again he was alone. Another part of his brain recognized he was an early riser and it was time to get up.

The creaks and pops of his joints threatened to drown out those of the metal spring mattress as he eased himself upright and threw his legs over the edge of the bed. He massaged the stiffness out of his knee, reached across the chair beside the bed and snagged his watch from its place. Five-thirty.

He filled the bathroom sink with steaming water and lathered Gillette Foamy on his face while examining it and his wild hair in the mirror. The dark brown strands laid at odd angles to each other after the night's sleep. Lines had formed in his cheeks, along with two-day-old razor stubble. His smile was lopsided, but irascible. His eyes had always been blue. They gleamed back at him from beneath a heavy brow; the new lines at the corners reflected his careworn life that seemed to grow deeper the past few days. A thick, muscled neck flared into broad shoulders that out-spanned the scope of the mirror, sloping down to a chest made powerful from lifting heavy trays, and using a wheelchair before physical therapy helped him to walk again. A thin tuft of hair decorated the cleft between the pectorals. He'd be thirty years old next week; he looked forty, he felt fifty.

Unfolding his tortoise shell-handled straight razor, he scraped away his night beard. Dawn crept through the curtainless window. It had rained; he could see the puddles in the street. A man walked his dog; a jogger ran past and jumped over a puddle on the sidewalk. The same sounds and sights every morning.

The emptiness of the past ten years since his dad's death had found him lacking and lonely. Though he didn't consider himself old in the sense of years, his hair showed its first signs of gray, dark shadows from little sleep circled his eyes. He had no sense of fashion or charm or knowledge of etiquette, and no concept of how to act around women. Especially one he liked.

Suddenly, he felt his life slipping away. Time hadn't stood still waiting for him to catch up, fall in love, start a family, take a vacation. He had to find himself. And it wasn't here.

Ken's hand had a slight tremble as he filled his morning cup of coffee. The pain in his leg wasn't any worse than before, just different. It was Sunday, the heathen hour. The hours between ten and noon, before the holy rollers let out of church and the restaurants fill up. A time when heathens can get a good seat — don't have to wait in line. But there was never a wait at the Kopper Kettle Diner, not any more.

The bell on the front door of the diner jingled. In walked a very pregnant Andie Oliver and Ken's secret flame, Mavis Dumass. His eyes burned a path from her big green eyes to her unbelievably full lips, down to the hollow of her neck where they rested on the see-through blouse that didn't leave much to the imagination. Mavis glowed. Her golden bronze smooth skin and delicate but tall frame was very womanly. Ken shoved his pencil into his apron and shuffled over to greet them, ignoring the pain in his leg.

He whistled when he was nervous. But then he stopped. *Girls hate old men and their vibrato whistles.* He'd heard a couple high school girls talking once when he'd served them at the counter — whistling.

He smiled wide, then led them to a booth in the back that faced the street. "Glad to see ya both, been a while — hey, Mavis."

"Hey, Ken. Good to see you, too."

The girls slid across the wooden benches opposite each other and simultaneously wiped the crumbs from their respective sides of the wooden table. It was a piece of their past and they fell into it as if it were a pair of old shoes. Worn and comfortable. They knew the menu by heart. They'd studied together there, ate cheap food, and drank fifty-cent cups of coffee. Ken recalled how Mavis always asked him to help her with math and Andie used to call him Koppy.

"Didn't know you were expecting, Andie."

"Yeah, Koppy, in a month." She patted the top of her baby-filled belly. "New menus?"

"Nah, just cleaned off the old ones. I'll get y'all some sweet tea."

"That'd be great," Andie said.

Reluctantly he walked away, but strained to listen to their conversation.

"Lawdy, Andie, ain't had me a mess of barbeque since the graduation party your mama gave me before I left town."

"Go ahead, indulge. You'll just puke it up later."

Mavis cackled, "Well in that case, I'll get the slaw and fries on the side."

He knew Andie and Mavis had been friends all their lives. That Andie had taken some heat during high school being white with a black best friend. He'd heard Andie's daddy, Bud, was one of the few white men to march on Washington with Dr. Martin Luther King. He also knew the ridicule Bud took for it. Vince Kopper had made a point of discussing it at length with his customers and had once refused to serve Bud and his family at the diner. It still embarrassed Ken. He recalled the incident like it happened yesterday.

The door's bell jingled again. Ken looked up and squinted; the sun's rays showed streams of dust particles pouring through the front windows. Two customers had strolled in, Melvin Johnson and his wife, Beulah. Sophie grabbed two plastic-covered menus and led them back to the booth opposite Andie and Mavis.

Melvin was middle-aged, slicked back his salt and pepper hair, and wore maroon double-knit polyester pants, a white leather belt and matching shoes. Ken could see his pens neatly arranged in his left white shirt pocket along with his New Testament in the right. Beulah hadn't changed since he'd seen her at his dad's funeral. Dowdy and tasteless, she wore cheap gold lamé shoes and a pink floral cotton dress way below her knees — *Church of God do-gooders.*

Ken watched them stare at Mavis. Andie was clearly a pregnant white woman, laughing and carrying on with a stunning black woman that had money and dressed like it.

Church of God man spoke up, "Was a time when they didn't allow negras and prostitutes in this diner." Ken could see Andie and Mavis had froze in their seat, not sure they had heard him correctly. But Ken heard him just fine.

He hobbled over to the back of the booth the couple sat in, dragging his right leg. The old racist's comment pissed him off. On top of being threatened the previous morning by a flatulent flattop blowhard, he wouldn't tolerate this hatred in his diner, not one more day. He'd listened to it all his life; it was time to speak up.

Ken put one arm up on the booth, leaned on it, relaxed, and said, "True enough, Melvin. Years ago when you and my dad wore bed sheets on your heads and burned crosses in folks' front yards, only white people was allowed in this here establishment."

Sophie came over to freshen their coffee, and to listen to Ken.

"But my dad's dead, and I've owned this diner for near ten years now. One day I had me a nasty car accident, you remember, I almost lost my leg. I'll be dogged if I didn't need me some blood 'cause I nearly lost all mine. Got me a rare type and only one colored man came to my rescue; gave me some of his blood. Since that day I came to understand the same color of blood flows through all people's veins, and their money spends as good as mine or yours. Besides, these two ladies have been a eatin' in here since they was too young to drive."

Ken shifted his weight off his bad leg and leaned on the other side of their booth.

"War's been over near a hundred and some years; ain't likely the South will rise again anytime soon. So if you and your Mrs. don't like the patrons in my diner, I suggest you haul yourselves to the McDonald's down the street."

He started to walk back to the kitchen but stopped, and rubbed his last comment in the old bigot's face.

"Lord, Melvin, there's black folks at McDonald's, too. Looks like you may just have to eat at home to keep away from 'em." Ken cleared his throat and motioned to his waitress, "Sophie can take your order now."

Ken turned around and winked at Mavis and Andie. Mavis stood, applauded, and whistled. Andie saluted him from her seat. Melvin Johnson hopped out of the booth and threw some change on the table for their coffee while Beulah scooted across her seat to stand. Filled with obvious indignation, they hurried out.

Mavis smiled at Andie, indicating she'd be right back. She rushed straight to the kitchen. "Ken — hey thanks. Looks like your dad died at the right time; I might never have been able to eat in here."

"True enough," he said. "But times are changin'."

"Ain't changin' fast enough." She reached out and touched him on the left side of his chest. "You've touched my heart. I've never known any white guy to do that. You're a brave soul." She smiled, then stepped back and looked around, surprised to find herself in the kitchen. She turned, then walked back to eat lunch with Andie.

He sighed. *No, not brave. If I were brave, I'd ask you out. And I'd be a lawyer, or something other than this.*

But Mavis was right about a few things. Ken had learned years ago there were rural counties and small towns in North Carolina where folks still flew Confederate flags on the steps of their courthouses and in their front yards. A scatter of trailers and single-storied houses spewed throughout the countryside, brown, gray, green, on blocks, their porches decorated with refrigerators, old couches, swings and collarless dogs, and not a soul in sight. Many black folk still refused to drive through those areas, especially at night. It was safer for Mavis in New York City. For the first time, Ken was glad she'd moved above the Mason Dixon line.

"Ken! It's Mavis Dumass on the phone." Sophie yelled back to the kitchen.

His heart raced. *Why would she call me?* "Yeah, hey Mavis," he said, resting the phone on his shoulder, wiping his hands on a towel.

"Ken, I need to ask you a favor."

"Sure. Shoot."

"I need a private booth Monday morning at nine. I'm meeting a certain man, and he won't see me unless it's in private. Can't be in the main eating area."

"I suppose you could use one of the booths in the back I usually hold for any overflow. Course, ain't been used much lately."

"Thanks. You're a doll."

Yeah, I'm a doll. I'm giving the girl of my dreams a private booth to meet another man.

Mavis arrived early, thanked him again, then stuck a twenty-dollar bill in his shirt pocket. He handed it back to her.

"Ain't something illegal going on here, is there, Mavis?"

"No," she giggled. "I'm meetin' a well-known preacher this morning, and he don't want anyone to know he's here with me. Got it?"

"You havin' an affair?"

She gave him a soft hoot. "No. Nothin' like that. We don't see eye-to-eye on a few things, that's all."

"I'll leave ya alone. Sorry, I had to ask."

"I'd ask too if this were my place. Thanks for the booth. I just want to keep it private and hope you won't say anything when you see who it is. By the way, he'll be coming to the back door. Will you let him in through the kitchen?"

"Sure. Just don't make it a habit. Meetin' men this way, I mean."

"No problem. I'm on my way back to New York City soon."

"Sorry to hear it."

"Really?"

Their eyes met and for an instant he almost said, *yes*. But he smiled instead, and set a pot of coffee on her table.

He watched her pour a cup; her hands shook. She pulled out her lipstick and a mirror from her purse and checked her face. When she worked her lipstick back into the tube, she seemed annoyed. Her mysterious preacher was late. She laid a napkin in her lap.

"You okay? Anything I can help you with?"

"No. Just . . . whatever you hear, please keep it to yourself."

"You know me, Fort Knox Ken. Andie still go to that Temple of Praise church?"

"Yeah."

"Isn't that the crazy televangelist, Reverend Artury?"

"Yeah." Mavis stared straight ahead.

"Well, let me know if you need anything else."

Ken wasn't sure Mavis heard him. She was still staring at the wall when he turned and walked back to the kitchen.

The diner had a few customers in the front. Someone dropped their fork and hollered for a clean one. The smell of bacon and sausage frying floated through the diner as Ken filled the breakfast orders. His customers seemed oblivious to Mavis in the back room. He heard the knock at the back door.

Reverend Calvin Artury stood there out of character, dressed in jeans, a ball cap, and sneakers. His plaid shirt opened down to the third button, revealing his chest hair. Expensive sunglasses covered his eyes. If it wasn't for his gold watch and pinky ring, and the gold Cadillac that waited for him in the alley, he looked like every other redneck that came into the diner.

Ken pointed to the back room. His cologne overpowered the smell of grease on the grill and lingered in the kitchen as he walked to the back of the diner. Ken watched the Reverend walk up to Mavis, startling her as he slid into the booth. *Wonder what it's all about?* He could see them talking, neither one smiling except in disgust.

Ken limped in dragging his bad foot and didn't so much as blink an eyelash at the Reverend. Mavis ordered a big breakfast for herself. Ken turned to the preacher.

"I'll just have coffee, thanks."

"It's a shame," Mavis said. "Ken here cooks a mean sausage gravy and biscuits."

"No, thanks."

Ken winked at Mavis and headed back to the kitchen. He had barely turned around when he heard, "Will he keep his mouth shut?"

"Who, Ken? He's a good ole' boy. Believe me, you can trust Ken Kopper. He hears lots of stuff in this diner, I assure you. The man's as safe as Fort Knox."

Ken told Sophie to work the counter; he'd cook, serve, and bus the tables. He kept his eyes on the back room, watching the conversation heat up between Mavis and her minister friend.

He served Mavis her breakfast, then poured the Reverend more coffee. Reverend Artury's eyes blazed hot as Mavis peppered her eggs and buttered her biscuit.

"Calm down, Cal," said Mavis. "God don't want you found out. It wouldn't sit well with all the people He's honestly tryin' to save. Lots of good folks out there, seekin' a true God. Not the kind you're sellin'."

Reverend Artury reached across the table and took hold of Mavis' wrist as she lifted a forkful of eggs up to her mouth, causing them to fling back on the table.

Ken grabbed the Reverend's arm, breaking him loose from Mavis. "Back off, mister," he said, still pretending not to know who he was. "Say what you come to say to Mavis and get out." He released his arm.

Reverend Artury took off his sunglasses and glared at Ken. Waves of terror from Artury's ice-blue eyes traveled down his spine. He turned to leave so Mavis could finish her meeting. At the same time he tried to shake the mind meld, keeping watch over Mavis in case she needed him again.

As soon as the Reverend was gone, Mavis bolted to the toilet. Ken cracked the door open; he could hear her vomiting. Slinking back to the booth, she pushed her food away and laid her head down on the table.

"You okay?" Ken cleared the table around her.

"Yeah. Just give me a minute." She pulled a twenty out of her cleavage and handed it to him.

"Keep it," he said. "Breakfast is on me."

"No, actually, it's in your toilet. Sorry. Food's great, it's the company I keep."

"I didn't hear any of it. But you looked whipped."

"Not quite. Not yet."

"You sure there's nothing I can do? Don't know what this was all about, but maybe I could help."

Mavis raised her head. "No, nothing you can do. Sorry to drag you into this. Just watch your back."

"I ain't afraid of guys like him."

"Listen to me, Ken. Obviously, I've made him angry. You saw him . . . here . . . with me. That made him nervous." Mavis wiped her mouth again with her napkin. "I know things about him. For all he knows, I've spilled my guts to you."

"Ain't he supposed to be a man of God? Why should I be afraid of him?"

"Because . . . because he's a Godfather."

Ken laughed. "In Winston?"

"Yeah. In good ole' Winston-Salem. The perfect cover. A Godfather in a Mafia of holy men."

~ May 1974 ~

Shadows from the late afternoon pushed into the diner, peach tinted, fading in and out. The only sound in the kitchen was the hum of the refrigerators. The dining room was empty. For Sale signs hung in the windows of the Kopper Kettle Diner. Summer heat brought young men to town cruising their souped-up cars down Main Street; their eight-track tapes cut mixtures of rock and country through the air.

Upstairs the sun's rays warmed Ken's apartment. The windows open, city air filtered through the screens bringing with it the smell of exhaust from the traffic below.

"Who's there? You scared the Lord Jesus out of me. Who . . . Who are you? What do you want?"

"Ken Kopper . . . thus saith the Lord, your Day of Judgment has come."

BANG!

BANG!

He lay on the floor; blood spilled from his chest wall and his mouth. It pooled around his head. His vision blurred, his speech gurgled, "B-but . . . I'm n-not Ken . . ."

There was no one there to hear him.

Merida crossed the busy street, dodging fast shiny cars — convertible Stingrays, souped-up Chargers, and throaty Camaros. The basket of Ken's clothes almost fell out of her arms. Her Baptist bun nearly came undone, shaking her head in repulsion at the young white boys wasting time and their daddy's money. "Hmmph. Gas goin' up to fifty-five cents a gallon, I swear, no respect."

Merida stuck in her key, but found the back door of the diner unlocked. *Kenny! He do live dangerously. A neighborhood full of dope pushers, muggers, and homeless folk and he leave his door open!*

She climbed the steps to Ken's apartment. Her scream was drowned out by the noise in the streets.

Ken stood with his bare feet in the ocean. He'd driven to South Carolina and Kiawah Island non-stop. His last-minute decision to leave town was the kind of spur of the moment decision he'd never made in his entire life but had always wanted to. It excited him. Leaving the state, finding the ocean, it exhilarated his soul. He was going to live again. He'd come to the Atlantic to find a new home. Start over. He'd go back, settle his affairs, and bring Corbet with him. Corbet needed taking care of. They'd buy a place near the beach, rent out boats to tourists. Find a house with a front porch.

Ken imagined he and Corbet enjoying future sunsets in rocking chairs, doing things old men do. Do something different. Corbet would like it here. All he had to do was go back to Winston-Salem and sign the papers over to the new owner. Pack his things; pack Corbet's things. And leave. Never look back.

A pretty woman walked by with her jeans rolled up, ankle deep in the salty waves.

"Hi," she said and smiled.

"Hi," said Ken.

Yeah, Corbet's gonna like it here.

The story, BEACH BABIES, began swimming around in my brain when I first met the one and only Bobbie Sue Rossi, my mother-in-law. A woman from the South of the 40s and 50s, her heart is a deep ocean of secrets and memories, and her stories only enhanced many of my own. Bobbie Sue worked in the hosiery mills and lived her childhood and early adult years in High Point, North Carolina. For me, the recollections of her life were like striking gold. As a storyteller, she became my mentor.

BEACH BABIES, though fictional, came to me a few years ago when I held a picture, now the cover of this book, and stared at it. Bobbie Sue Rossi isn't a heroine, neither will she be a legend. She's simply a woman that did what needed to be done. I understand her and identify with her in more ways than she knows. We make no excuses for our behavior or even our mistakes. But, I like to think her kind of courage will go on. And so, I dedicate this story to her.

Beach Babies

~ May 1945 ~

Bertie hated Mama. She hated her for her backhandings and beatings and allowing our boarders' sneaky nighttime raids on our sleeping bodies.

I hated her too, but not as much as my sister did.

Crawling into my bed, Bertie curled up like a cat near a fire and bawled for a good hour. "Time to get the hell out, Bertie, you with me?" I gave her my best devil-be-damned smile.

She jerked her head up and looked at me hard. Her nose dripped. Drool slid out the side of her mouth as she spit her words at me. "Hell's bells, I was ready to leave here five years ago, the day after our 12th birthday. I still got scars from that beating."

I handed her a rag to blow her nose. "Yeah, I remember. It was such a *happy* birthday. The bitch threw Daddy out of his own house not five minutes after we blew out the candles on the first birthday cake we ever had. I say he figured bein' a hobo and ridin' the rails was easier than livin' with her."

"Mama says he's in prison."

"Could be. We'll never know for sure."

I sighed and kicked the quilt off my legs.

"Why'd Daddy leave us, Bobbie? Why'd he let her run him off?"

My sister's question stung me like she'd snapped a rubber band at my head. Daddy left in a hurry, with only the clothes he had on. Erwin Doogan had hopped a train to Knoxville, we were told, and never came back.

"Men do funny things when their back's against the wall. I think the Depression broke him and Mama never loved him. Like I said, we'll never find out. Not as long as we're here."

Even at seventeen, Bertie chewed her fingernails. I watched her gnaw on her pinky. "But Mama didn't want us either. Except to cook and clean, among other things." Bertie laid her head on the pillow and turned over to her back. "The war's almost over; I hear they're hirin' at the mill."

"We gotta get far away from Mama. Hosiery mill ain't far enough. I'll find us a place." A small seed of trust slipped from her hand into mine. I watched her yawn and close her eyes.

I yawned in return then opened the windows further, hoping for a cool breeze. I put my fist into my pillow, and then pulled my nightgown off my legs. I couldn't get comfortable. Sitting up, my feet dangled over the side of the bed. The old house sighed. Apparently, Bertie had cried herself to sleep. I couldn't hear anything except the wood murmur as it settled into the night. Sometimes I thought the house held ghosts, and I imagined those creaks and moans were the whispers of our dead relatives.

For the moment I was as still as I could be, even going so far as to hold my breath. Listening to the lonesome sound of a single car on a deserted street and a train's whistle in the distance, I forgot about the ghosts. I didn't need any more spooks in my life if I could help it.

The cool floorboards felt good as I put my feet down. A shiver ran up my back, but it was a comforting feeling, this coolness. It reminded me that I was alive. I padded down the stairs and slipped out the back door. I needed the night air. My thoughts were running too wild for sleep.

Cordella Doogan, our mama, ran Doogan's Boarding House on Russell Street in High Point. A big house with lots of closets and places to hide. It had belonged to our daddy's family but they were all dead or crazy as loons, so Mama took it over after Bertie and I were born. Running the decrepit hotel got us through the worst of the Depression and it kept Mama from working in the mill.

She swore she'd not end up like Granny, trapped in a hosiery mill sewing the toes on socks. Mama didn't want anything to do with cotton and would've preferred not to wear it, except there was little else to choose from in 1945, especially when you were considered less than poor white trash. That's what Bertie heard the girls at school call us when our backs were turned.

Mama's abuse increased with our advancing teens. Like slave owners from the not-so-distant past, she unnaturally assumed it was her right to do with us as she pleased. We'd tried to run away. Twice. Sheriff Cuddy, a friend of Mama's, found us and brought us back. Each time the punishment got worse. After our last prison break, the sheriff said he'd be happy to take us to reform school. No season went by without a bruise on our faces for "sassin'."

Over the years I grew accustomed to waking in the dark and finding Bertie kneeling beside my bed, sobbing, having just been engaged in one of our boarder's invasive gropes beneath her nightgown. Mama threatened us with the strap and even harder labor if we didn't keep our mouths shut.

I smoked a cigarette outside by the trashcans and our neighbor's dog. Watching the fat mongrel chew on a ham bone, she snarled at me with each step I took toward her tar-papered dog house. The old bitch dog reminded me of Mama. Holding on to the scraps of life, showing her teeth should anyone try to take them away from her.

I scuttled back into the kitchen. Mama's roll-top desk squatted like an old wash woman in the corner. Opening the drawer where Mama kept her record books and house receipts, I rummaged through the mess until I found what I was looking for. Her address book. A few of the pages were smudged with red stain from spilled cherry pie. I

recalled the night Daddy wrote his sister's name in it. *Ruby Doogan.*
Daddy's pie had fallen off his fork; he always got nervous when he
picked up a pen. Staring at it now, I knew he recorded it because
someday Bertie and I would need to find Ruby. Our daddy didn't
write much of anything, having only a sixth-grade education. He could
barely scribble his name. But I made out Ruby's address just fine and
wrote it down, stuffed it into my nightgown pocket, and tiptoed back
upstairs.

"Bertie, you awake?"

"I am now."

I tunneled under the sheet and put my hand on her shoulder. "I'm
declaring our own private D-Day. This Sunday, after church. Viola
will drive us. She's always asking somebody to share the drive so she
can see her boyfriend at the beach. We just won't come back to High
Point with her. They won't make us. We'll be eighteen in three months.
I think we can stay with Ruby."

"Daddy's sister, Ruby?"

I stroked her dark curls and snuggled up to her back. "That's the
one. She's the only relative we got left, other than Daddy."

"Maybe she won't want us, Bob. I mean, hell, we haven't seen her
since long before Daddy skipped town."

The night air stirred the tops of the trees near our room. I could
hear Juba Lee's dog barking in her back yard.

"Think Aunt Ruby knows where Daddy is?"

"I don't care where *he* is," I said. "We need a place to stay — real
jobs. As I recall, Ruby was dumb as a tick on a toad, but sweet. She'll
let us stay if we pay our way."

Bertie blew her nose again then cuddled her pillow. "So, where
does she live?"

"Lives in the same old house near the ocean if Mama's address
book is right. She's probably still cleaning motel rooms at Carolina
Beach."

We were opposites. I was a towhead blonde with freckles, pallid and plain. Bertie had a body that caused men to walk into walls. She redefined the word "beauty." An inch taller than me, her burnt-brown locks never needed the hundred bobby pins I used every night. I had a wide nose. She had skinny arms. She'd become painfully thin over the past few months. And though I was proud of my flat stomach, I had ample hips. She was quiet. I never shut my mouth. Bertie never cussed. I said "fuck" a lot.

I loved boys, lots of boys, especially Hank Williams . . . Bertie had yet to have a crush on any movie star or famous country singer. My Dixie-cup breasts were a constant source of jokes and humiliation. Bertie's melon chest was ready to be picked. She was content to stay home, read books, and learn new recipes. Restless, I spent any time I could steal from Mama riding in cars with boys, sneaking off to picture shows with boys, and dancing until dark . . . with boys.

Bertie's lips had a natural raw redness, like she'd been chewing on them, or sucking an ice cube. Mine were plump and colorless. But our eyes were identical. Chocolate brown with yellow flecks. Daddy had said they were the color of rum. Mama laughed. "They're plain shit-brown, just like yours, Erwin."

Bertie swore she was found on our doorstep. She looked nothing like me, or Daddy, or Mama. It wasn't until we found our birth certificate that we were sure she was my twin.

She quit school in '43. Homemade hand-me-down dresses from Juba Lee Truvey's two oldest girls did Bertie in. Especially the comments in the restroom each morning as the girls at school squirmed for a spot in front of the mirror. Applying thick coats of red lipstick and pulling bobby pins out of their hair, it was a wonder the bunch of Rita Hayworth look-alikes made it to class before the second bell.

"Looks like Roberta and Alberta's mama made 'em new dresses!"

"No, Sugah, those came from the church bazaar leftover bin; I believe my cousin, Mary Margaret, threw those out two years ago."

I didn't care what the girls at school said: I was going to finish school. Be somebody. But all Bertie wanted was a man to take care of her. As much as she hated Mama, Bertie was more like her than she knew.

I graduated with the class of 1945, but we made no fuss over it. I didn't want Bertie to feel bad, and Mama . . . well, she couldn't have cared less. Bertie and I had decided to wait until our eighteenth birthday to hightail it out of High Point. Who knew God would give us a break three months ahead of schedule.

It had been twelve years since we last saw Ruby — and Bertie nearly drowned in the ocean that day. She never ventured near the water again. I loved to swim as far out as I could, until I couldn't touch bottom and the waves almost rocked me to sleep.

I swung my legs over the side of the bed, throwing the twisted sheets back and trying to shed the residue of a restless night. It was early; I'd slept maybe three hours. My turn to start breakfast for seven people required getting up at five thirty anyway. But I needed to pee first, and I didn't want to stand in line.

Our commode had been installed on the back porch and tied into the kitchen plumbing. Plywood and clapboard surrounded the two-foot square space for privacy. A sweatbox in the summer, we all but froze in the winter. Only thing that made it better than an outhouse was we didn't have as far to walk and we could flush it. Too many times, though, we waited behind one of Mama's houseguests. Mama provided a bowl and pitcher in everybody's room for washing, but we all shared the toilet.

I wiped maggots off the seat with Sears and Roebuck paper, and sat down. Just once I wished for a roll of toilet paper. I'd pestered Mama to build a bathroom, but I knew her backward frame of mind and how she clung to her old habits. Her thought was that most of the improvements in the world were frivolous, and she couldn't afford or even entertain anything more modern than the toilet she was sitting on.

Mama had made it clear that indoor toilets were nasty. Bertie and I had both discussed how tired we were of unnecessary hardships. A woman shouldn't have to freeze to death while trying to relieve herself, or wipe maggots off toilet seats in the summer. I longed to take a bubble bath in a porcelain tub with a lock on the bathroom door.

As I flushed the American Standard commode, I determined Bertie and I would someday take a step up in respectability, in being civilized, and live in houses with inside bathrooms. Have bathtubs with porcelain handles, rolls and rolls of real toilet paper, and big fluffy towels.

A fist banging on the door interrupted my daydream.

"Hey! I'm paying for use of the toilet!"

I didn't light a match. I hoped my stink would asphyxiate him.

Mama refused to take in more than three boarders at a time. Always men, she turned women away. Unless, of course, they came with a man. We provided breakfast and dinner with the cost of the room, which had to be paid for at the time of check in. She'd been stiffed too many times and learned the hard way — about everything.

Bertie and I slept in the attic but sometimes, when the weather was too hot, we slept on a cot stuck out on the screened-in back porch. It was a chance we were willing to take, depending on who the guests were for the week.

The cool air on the porch was far better than the sweat-drenched sheets of our sweltering loft. Around two in the morning we could smell Mama coming. The reek of alcohol seeped into the room before she did.

Her voice thick and slurred, she'd kick our bed. "Bobbie Sue, wake up. Somebody here wants to see how pretty my girl is . . . be nice to him." Then she'd walk off with an extra five dollars in her pocket and leave us there for whatever happened next. I learned how to shut off my mind, but Bertie . . . couldn't. She broke down, nearly twice a week.

I finished setting the table. It was Wednesday. Meat loaf, mashed potatoes, lima beans, and biscuits with peach jam. Sweet tea and coffee. Banana pudding for dessert. Bertie and I took turns serving and clearing. The guests that week had checked in on Thursday and were staying three to four days, all of them in High Point for the Southern Furniture Market. The Market had been closed since 1941 due to the war, but this year it was back in business. Mama was thrilled when Market people were in town. They were city people. Merchants who spent money, drank gallons of sloe gin and bourbon, and listened to her cackle like a love-starved hen about her few days as an actress on the Vaudeville stage.

Mama crooned to old records and pranced around the parlor with her scarf floating in and out of the air between the menfolk. Like Mae West trying to sing opera, her screechy soprano voice made Juba Lee's dog howl. I laughed until I couldn't stand up and tears came out my eyes and nose. Her mid-life thickness stuffed in her best red dress waltzed in front of men who were too drunk to care. Bertie scowled and declared she'd made a fool of herself, and of us. I agreed, but it felt good to poke fun at her. She was our only nightly form of entertainment, even if she did look like an overgrown tomato with matching red lips and a huge ass.

Mama usually picked one man and stuck to him like a bitch in heat until the end of Market week. He kept her high on Wild Turkey and love and he usually ended up staying an extra day or two, until tiring of her — or his wife called . . . whichever came first.

After supper, I often thought about hiding out for the night, sleeping outside or in Viola's car. But Mama always came looking for me. If she couldn't find me, then she'd pick on Bertie again. Bertie couldn't take much more. I'd watched her get weaker by the day knowing I had to save her. Save us.

I had managed to toughen up, refuse the latest advances on my body, and take Mama's beatings the next day. But Mama knew Bertie could not. Red welts on my legs from her switch didn't stop me from attempting to make a deal with her to lay off Bertie. "Just use me," I said. She looked at me as if I had three eyeballs. Mama refused to discuss my proposal. When Cordella Doogan was sober, she portrayed herself to the world as a loving mother, successful businesswoman, and a good Christian neighbor. The subject was closed.

I hated her, but I knew hatred was a sin. Hatred could get you sent to hell. But as our preacher had pointed out, a person had to sometimes travel over a lot of ground before getting to hell – or heaven for that matter. If hating Mama was going to send me to hell, then I had to get away from her . . . maybe I wouldn't hate her by the time I was old and ready to die.

We had declared Sunday after church our day of deliverance. Juba Lee waddled over to our kitchen Saturday afternoon and announced the new preacher for First Pentecostal had arrived. She'd heard he was young, fresh out of seminary, and not married. Mama hitched a ride into town with Juba Lee. She had to get her hair waved special for the occasion.

"You're twins?"

"Only when we're together," I said. "When you see us apart, we don't look anything alike." He glanced at my sister.

"You're right. You don't look like her. So who's Bobbie and who's Bertie?"

I stared into his Sinatra blue eyes. *He couldn't be any older than twenty-five. Twenty-seven tops.* We didn't see many good-looking young men in town. They had all been sent to Europe or the Pacific. I wondered why he wasn't married. I shook his hand and it felt like a large moist mushroom.

"She's Roberta Sue." My sister pointed at me and giggled. "I'm Alberta Lou, call me Bertie."

Reverend Ross Jenkins was a looker. As Bertie shook his mushroomy hand next, I breathed him in. He smelled of peppermint and Old Spice. The Reverend had a dimple in his chin like William Holden, and for a wild second or two I considered touching it and asking him how he shaved in there. His hair was the presence of all color, black with reflections of red, and his eyes were kind and very blue. Mama had said she'd heard he had stammering lips and supposed she'd go to church just to watch them quiver. Juba Lee agreed Reverend Jenkins was every bit as good-looking as Billy Graham. That made Mama smile. She loved having a leg up on her Baptist friends.

With a sorry shake of her head, Mama pushed us forward. "Go along, girls. Juba Lee saved us a seat on the front pew." She wanted her ten seconds with the new preacher.

"Lord, what bee's in that woman's britches this time?" Bertie whispered.

"A Bee-attitude. Blessed are the poor, for they shall inherit the kingdom, or a spot on Carolina Beach, take your pick."

Bertie smothered her laughter all the way to the altar.

Our mama was constantly pointing out something nobody cared about. The line behind her snaked out to the parking lot with church members ready to make their first impressions on the new man of God at First Pentecostal.

Mama fanned her face with her funeral home fan and winked at Reverend Jenkins. The same fan she stole the day Juba Lee's daddy died. A fan she had stuck between her thigh and the arm of the couch, and then stuffed into her purse. She waved the cardboard slowly under her chin. The funeral home advertisement side faced out. *Death, Where is thy sting? Courtesy of Bilbo-Dinkins Funeral Home.* Bertie and I caught a whiff of her whiskey breath with each twist of her wrist. A sickly sweet, hazy odor, very much like baking pies in a hot kitchen on a humid day. Such a smell also carried with it a vague threat. You could never tell what a woman with that kind of breath might decide to say at any given moment.

The First Pentecostal Church congregation hung on Reverend Jenkins' every word that morning. At some point during the sermon, I stopped staring at him and began to listen. His voice pulsed with animation and fervency.

"Exodus twenty-two tells us, thou shalt not suffer a witch to live! What is a witch today, you ask? Fortune-tellers! Psychics and Gypsies!" He preached louder than thunder, raising his arms and shaking his fists, but it wasn't convincing. A well-rehearsed and choreographed speech, in my opinion; I had the feeling he didn't believe it any more than I did.

I nudged Bertie. "Make sure we remember to get our palms read next week."

She giggled and whispered. "You think we could take Reverend Jenkins with us? He's better lookin' than Eddie Arnold. Juba Lee would be pea green with envy."

Juba Lee, our next-door neighbor, was Mama's best friend. Bookending Bertie and me in the pew, Mama on one end and Juba

Lee on the other, my sister and I were like fried peaches between two doughy crusts. Her brown-and-gray hair was pulled back in a tight bun and despite the heat, Juba Lee wrapped her shawl snug around her fleshy frame. She resembled a tightly wound serpent, coiled like a copperhead.

The organist finally sat down at the Hammond. Reverend Jenkins carried a handkerchief to wipe the sweat from his brow. Ten minutes to twelve we stood and turned our hymnals to page 54. The Reverend could not only turn a phrase — he was Bing Crosby in a minister's robe. Mesmerized by his voice, I stayed longer than I intended.

"I am bound for the Promised Land, I am bound for the Promised Land . . . oh, who will come and go with me, I am bound for the Promised Land."

Finally, I looked at Bertie. "Time to get out of Dodge."

She cut her eyes at me, nodded and smiled. "Let's go."

Mama heard us and pulled me hard back down to the pew, her hand a tight grasp on my arm. "Where the hell do you think you're goin'?"

"Oh, who will come and go with me, I am bound . . ."

"You can't stop us." I twisted my arm out of her grip. "We're packed. Viola Truvey's waiting for us outside."

She slapped my face. Some of the folks around us stopped singing to watch.

I peeled her dishwater damp hands off my arm again and gritted my teeth. "We'll be eighteen in three months. You can't bring us back this time."

Bertie grabbed my hand. Together we crossed the line of lost innocence and stepped all over Juba Lee's serpentine body getting out of the pew fast.

". . . for the promised land."

The singing had stopped, the sanctuary was dead silent — the attention . . . on us.

"Come back here Bobbie Sue, I'll snatch your arm out and beat you with the bloody stump!"

I stopped at the back of the church, turned around and screamed, "Time to find new girls for your whorehouse, Mama . . . hope you pay them more than you did us!"

The bell tower at First Pentecostal Church tolled twelve as we bounded down the front steps and into Viola's waiting Chevy. We drove north on Main Street toward Greensboro, then on to the coast and our destination — Carolina Beach.

I drove all night, after taking the wheel from Viola and then a quick stop for supper. Viola, Juba Lee's oldest daughter and our friend, was twenty-two. She worked at a furniture factory and had recently met her boyfriend, a lifeguard at Holden Beach. Viola had to go back to High Point, but helping us break out of our prison had given her the nerve to break out of her own, living with Juba Lee. I told Viola if her mama kicked her out for helping us, she could stay with Bertie and me for a while. I also supposed Mama might send the sheriff after us again, but we were both willing to risk it. Bertie and I could hide for three months if we had to.

Heading east away from the mountains and the cities, out onto the silent roads spreading out flat and dark under the bright countless stars, my excitement escalated. With one hand loose on the wheel and an elbow poking out the open window, my hair whipped around my head in a yellow swirl. I only stopped once to pee and gas up. Bertie and Viola slept all the way to the beach. I could not. The wind of freedom on my face ignited something inside of me and all I could do was sing in silence.

We dropped Viola off at her boyfriend's, who would bring her to Aunt Ruby's on Friday where she would pick up her car and head back to High Point. Without Bertie and me.

As I crossed the bridge over the Cape Fear River, I couldn't say I had a love for the sea, but I knew I was searching for something. Bertie and I were five the last time we saw the ocean. I had found God in the sea, the salt wind, and the sky that touched the water on the horizon.

I lost Him living in High Point. Maybe I was hoping to find Him again.

Around us a storm broke. Fat drops of rain splattered loudly on the roof of the car in gaining crescendo. With each gust of wind the trees swayed and shook, sounding like the cicada back home. Then the sky opened up and the heavens cried. The car provided no shelter from the torrents of rain, and I felt the lash of water that whipped through the windows. We rolled them up fast.

"Windows're fogging up, we might as well stop for the night," I said. Without Viola in the car, we each had a seat to sleep. Three in the morning — too early to barge in on Aunt Ruby. I parked behind the Five and Dime next to the birdbaths and porch swings. I sprawled out the best I could in the front seat; Bertie curled up in the back.

At seven, I woke my sister. I'd been awake to watch the sun come up. An aroma of the sea struck my nose like a soft slap and I tasted salt on my tongue. Getting out of the car, I stretched, then walked to the beach, looking out across the dunes and up and down the long sweep of sand. Blue skies, billowing clouds and the sun hot on the top of my head, I wanted to shout my freedom to the world. A stiff breeze rustled the palmettos, I was ready to work on my tan and be lulled into a stupor by the ocean's song.

"Did we bring the baby oil and iodine?" I handed Bertie a warm Coke and a pack of Saltines through the car window. It was the best breakfast I could come up with.

"We need a job, not a tan."

"I need a job, a tan, and a man. And not necessarily in that order," I said.

Bertie hopped out of the car and we walked to the Texaco station on the corner. I asked a woman who talked like Carmen Miranda for a key to the restroom and directions to Lake Park Boulevard. "Is down that way," she pointed.

It looked like any other neighborhood street, except for the palm trees and sandy soil. I drove slowly so Bertie could read the house numbers. At the end of the street it sat alone, in all its rundown glory.

Right where we had left it. On a flat treeless lot, overgrown with sea grass and dying evergreen shrubs.

Ruby's house was little more than a shack on stilts with a shaky front porch running the full length of the house. A rectangle of four small rooms laid end to end. From what I remembered, she had planned to build a bathroom off the back. I fantasized a moment and felt bubbles around my neck.

Grainy tarpaper covered the outside of the house. Colored a brick red, some of the thick sheets hung crooked. The last time we had visited Ruby, Bertie and I had just lost our first tooth and she gave us each a nickel. She spent all of her time working. Ruby took in laundry and worked at the Starfish Motor Court. When she wasn't cleaning toilets and stripping beds at the motel, she babysat for a neighbor.

A tiny woman, Ruby wore her dark brown hair braided down her back and worked in shorts and overalls. I never saw her wear a dress. But she had a pretty face, with a wide nose like mine. I wondered if she had changed much in twelve years.

A pair of beagles howled from the tops of their doghouses as soon as we came within view. I couldn't imagine why she kept hunting dogs at the beach. Years ago, Daddy had built Ruby a pit and a rack in the back yard. She made barbeque on the weekend and sold wrapped sandwiches at the beach. I had found this fascinating, and hoped she had continued her little enterprise. Maybe she could expand her operation with Bertie and me around. Mama hated barbeque. Said it was the poor Southern man's steak. I loved it.

Walking across the porch, I nearly tripped over an old kitchen chair, rusted with the vinyl seat ripped, cotton stuffing rising from it like small explosions, resting next to a leaky icebox.

Even if the place was clean inside, it was anybody's guess whether Bertie would commit her backside to any of the furniture. I, on the other hand, could make myself comfortable anywhere. Maybe living next door to Juba Lee and her filthy house had made me careless about plopping down in the mangiest-looking chair or couch stained with God-only-knew-what and smelling to high heaven. But for Bertie, cleanliness was her greatest virtue. I knew she was bound to work herself into a fit cleaning Ruby's house like she'd cleaned Mama's.

The rusty screen door was stuffed with little tufts of cotton blocking some of the holes to keep out the bugs. When I pulled it open, it fell off the hinges.

"You think she lives here? Maybe she's moved."

"She's here. I can smell bacon. Listen, Bertie." I put my ear to the window. "It's the Grand Ole Opry on the radio."

I knocked.

The front door squeaked open slowly. Ruby tossed her graying braid across her shoulder. Her skin was milk white and appeared soft as velvet. She smelled of Tabasco sauce and vinegar.

"Well, land sake, if it ain't the Bobbsey twins."

"Hey, Aunt Ruby. Can we come in?"

She gave us both a quick hug that felt like the soft nudge of a butterfly wing hitting against my breast. The odor of cigarette smoke in her hair overpowered Ruby's barbeque aroma. I knew she didn't have much life left in her; we had come just in time. After twelve years, I was startled by how small and frail she had become, even though her mental faculties did not seem diminished.

"Damned lung cancer," she said as she lit a cigarette.

When Ruby talked, every word was dragged out as if she were just waking up or falling asleep. Bertie and I figured it was the medicine. But if her speech was slow, her body was even slower. Arthritis had settled into every joint in her body. She didn't seem comfortable in an upright position. She always found some way to prop herself up. Gravity proved to be too strong for her. Layers of her had fallen away. She had curled up and retreated on herself the way a plant folds in the fall in preparation for the cold.

Ruby had no children and had spent her life savings on doctor bills. She never married. To her, love meant falling off a building and trusting a certain person would either be there to catch you at the bottom or at least possess the decency to call an ambulance. Her one and only possibility for a husband had run away before she landed and frankly, she wasn't chancing another leap of faith. She'd paid off her shack and acre of land, working endless hours for first one motel then another. In time, she retired, and then got sick.

I knew God had helped us find Ruby. Although my mortal soul was in peril due to lack of belief and knowledge of the scriptures, I had no doubt His hand was on the situation.

Turned out, we all needed each other. In the time it took to eat our first meal together, our lives changed forever. We had begun to live again, and she was completing the full circle of her life. Ruby had already returned to what she was at the beginning, a beating pulse inside a trivial human body.

~ July 1945 ~

We lived at Ruby's, except now we had five small rooms instead of ten large ones. Bertie and I cleaned, scrubbed, and made repairs to the long-neglected house. Ruby did build on a bathroom, for which Bertie and I were grateful. A tiny piece of heaven. And where a busy Russell Street ran in front of our house in High Point, here sea grass butted up against a sandy driveway, a tiny gravel road and a boardwalk that led to the beach, and then the sea.

Early one hot morning in July, Ruby found a spurt of energy. She rolled her sleeves high above her elbows and placed pots on her stove saying she had two surprises for us. First, she had bought us a palm reading. Bertie and I had giggled and talked about it from the first moment we sat at her kitchen table. Next, she announced she was making dinner. "We're having company," she said and winked. But she refused to tell us who and proceeded to kick us out of the house for the day.

"Feed my dogs on your way out. Them's good watchdogs. Lets me know when somebody's comin'." She handed us bowls of leftover breakfast scraps. "Just look for Madame Tuleh's Palm Readin's. You'll see the sign on the boardwalk," Ruby said. She shoved us out the door.

For the first time in our lives we stepped outside wearing makeup on our faces, and shorts and midriff tops, hand-me-downs from Ruby. Though Mama's wicked deeds hid behind the walls of our house, to the world she appeared as a God-fearing woman. She kept our dresses, as well as her own, respectable — shunning the very appearance of evil.

But there we were, strolling on the boardwalk without a dress to cover us — our bodies exposed. Two girls exchanging religious rags for a new look — a fresh start.

"I feel naked," Bertie said.

"You look great. Mama would die, wouldn't she?" I laughed. "No more cotton dusters, sister."

"The entire Pentecostal congregation will disown us."

"I think they already have. Who cares? Look where we are, Bertie. On Carolina Beach. We live here." I kicked off my flip-flops and ran into the sand. Twirling and kicking my feet like a child, I felt the ocean breezes whip around my legs and the sun hot on my body. Sweat dripped down my back, not the same kind of sweat that popped out of my pores in the attic in High Point. This was healthy sweat. The kind that made me feel alive, not drained of energy, but boiling over with life.

"At least you have a job!" Bertie yelled.

Out of breath, I ran back to where she stood on the boardwalk. "Do you ever look at the bright side?"

"What's a bright side?"

"Forget it."

I wanted to hit her. We had escaped the hell of our childhood, we were living in Carolina Beach, and Bertie still couldn't be happy.

"Bobbie, I'm sorry. It's better here than with Mama. But I'm tired of sitting around the house with Ruby. There's not much to do, other than wrap barbeque sandwiches twice a day. I want a life."

"I don't consider Clyde's Dry Cleaners a career in the making. They run me ragged."

"Still. It's a real job."

We stood in front of Madame Tuleh's sign, weather-beaten by the salty air. "We're here. Let's see what our future holds and have some fun for a change, alright?" I looked at Bertie with a silly grin and gave her a light punch in her arm. She hung her head, embarrassed by her complaining, then batted her lashes back up at me and smiled.

"Okay, sorry again."

"You're such a shitbucket sometimes, ya know?" I kissed her cheek.

Bertie pushed the door open and a brass bell jingled. The shop was smaller than it looked from the outside, with navy blue walls and a moon and stars painted on a black ceiling. The crude wooden floor creaked and moaned beneath us. The air was sickening sweet with a thick smell of something that burned my eyes. Behind an antique desk, the area was sectioned off with a tattered burgundy velvet material. When it flew open, I sneezed. Dust particles glittered the musty air. Then Bertie sneezed. A half-dressed older man scurried out of the back attempting to button his shirt in a hurry.

"Madame Tuleh has more customers than those wanting their fortunes told," I said. Bertie sneezed again, then wiped her nose, hiding her giggle behind her hankie.

"Hellooo, I'm Madame Tuleh, you must be . . . no don't tell me . . . you're Ruby's twins!"

Before we could open our mouths, the fortune-teller took Bertie's hand in both of hers and closed her eyes. Her black eyes were painted like a raccoon's. Heavy blue eye shadow arched over each of them — she was stunning in a strange kind of way. Like the whores on the boardwalk late at night.

"I sense peril. Your aura disturbs me," she said to Bertie. "It's illuminated." Her voice, throaty and hoarse, her accent — strange, she sounded like Greta Garbo. "Dark, very dark, and yet it sparkles with turmoil." Her earrings swinging, Tuleh motioned for us to follow her. "You must allow me to help you out of harm's way, child. Before it's too late," she added ominously. "You must make an appointment to return for more readings. I do it for half price."

I watched Bertie's eyes widen. Afraid she believed her, I interrupted. "My turn, Tuleh. My name is . . ."

"I know your name," she said. "Give me a moment to make tea. I'll be right with you."

I laughed quietly. Bertie didn't move a muscle and stared straight ahead.

I nudged her with my elbow. "I hope Ruby didn't break her bank for this," I whispered.

"She's creepy." Bertie's nervous reply made me think she was concerned about her aura.

"It's a scam, Bert. We're here to have fun, but this is just a scam. Let's play along. Okay? We've always wanted to do this."

Slow like Aunt Ruby, Tuleh had floated to the back room with a large leather book riding on her hip. I imagined it was her book of spells. I could see her filling the teapot with water. Tuleh's gauze blouse was tight across her large breasts. Her small waist accentuated large hips resembling two highly lubricated watermelons shimmying along under a skin-tight black skirt that dragged the floor. Her black hair flowed like a river down to her butt and appeared to have never been cut. Fascinated by false eyelashes as thick as spiders, I decided the effect fit her cow-brown eyes. She wore the brightest red lipstick on the biggest set of lips I'd ever seen, and the color matched nicely with her red and orange print shawl draped over her shoulders. Silver earrings dangled from her ears as she brushed back her ebony tresses with chipped-red fingernails. Tuleh reeked of garlic, onions, and Evening in Paris perfume; my stomach turned sour, and I hoped her tea tasted better than she smelled.

In minutes Bertie and I were sitting in her back room on a ratty couch. Tuleh positioned herself opposite us in a worn rocker with her teapot balanced in her lap.

All Bertie wanted was to be told good news. Tuleh gave us each a cup of tea that tasted like dishwater, and then dumped the cups upside down on a plate. "Ah," she said, poking a finger into the leaves. "Find husband and bad luck is gone."

"I don't have a boyfriend."

Tuleh shrugged. "Then you have bad luck," but Bertie didn't need a fortune-teller to tell her that.

Tuleh poked around in my cup next. "You my dear, you are star in God's heaven."

I rolled my eyes. "What does that mean, exactly?"

"It means you are stronger twin. You will lead others to righteousness. Your determination to finish school where your sister did not, it make you a great woman, loved among many."

I laughed at this, thinking about the bottle of Wild Turkey and pack of Chesterfields I had bought with my last paycheck. But Tuleh, it seemed, took her job seriously. Her face was impassive as she picked up Bertie's hand again and turned it this way and that. For some crazy reason, I felt uneasy. Like she'd seen something scary in the lines and creases.

Bertie must have felt it too. "I'm afraid we're on a time schedule, Madame Tuleh. We've got to get back to help our aunt with dinner. Thanks for the reading. It was . . . fun."

I sensed Tuleh knew that Bertie was no longer interested in seeing her future. She smiled, told us to say hello to Ruby and that she'd receive a free reading if she sent in one more customer.

"What a snake charmer," I said to break the silence walking home. But Bertie said nothing.

I made fun of Madame Tuleh, talking and moving my hips like her . . . just to make Bertie laugh. She gave me a weak smile.

"Bertie, why didn't you tell her about the young man you're dating?"

"Why? So she could tell me I'm going to lose someone I just met and like a lot? No thanks. I don't need to hear that."

I stood in front of Bertie and forced her to look into my eyes. "Everything she said was garbage. It was a quick way to make a buck. Quit bein' so damn negative all the time. Hey, maybe we should try to read tea leaves. Be her competition!"

"No thanks," Bertie said, stepping around me. "But tell me something, Bob, how did she know you graduated and I didn't? We never told Ruby. Ruby hasn't talked to Mama in years. How did Tuleh know that?"

"Good question," I said.

Ruby served sausages, which had split their casings to season fresh cabbage wedges floating in fragrant broth. A roasting chicken was browned to perfection and fell quickly into serving pieces as she wielded her knife. She checked the sideboard where an apple pie waited alongside a basket of fresh cornbread. A pitcher of lemonade sat on the table, with butter and peach preserves she'd made last fall.

"How was Tuleh?"

Bertie acted like she didn't hear her and dug into the preserves.

"Seemed fine to me. She said to say hello," I said.

"That's not what I'm askin'. How was your readin'?"

"Typical. We're both going to be millionaires and live in California. Bertie's going to marry Dean Martin and have lots of babies and I'm going to find the cure for cancer."

"Do it soon, will ya?"

My heart went out to Ruby. She finally had somebody who cared about her, and she wouldn't be around long enough to enjoy it. We'd watched her grow sicker from the time we arrived. And no matter what Tuleh the gypsy said, I didn't believe a word of it. If anyone deserved a bright future, a chance for getting the life they truly wanted, it was Bertie.

Wisps of Ruby's hair had worked loose from her braid. Short hairs clung to the sides of her damp face; her huge green eyes shone with unshed tears as she gazed up with a nervous expression.

"Okay girls, dinner's almost ready. I hear my dogs. I think you need to welcome our surprise guest." Ruby smiled, deepening the lines around her eyes and highlighting the wrinkles next to her lips.

I stepped out onto the porch and watched a car stop in the driveway. The window was rolled halfway down and a lit cigarette was tossed out. The door opened and out stepped Daddy. Tall and handsome, with a clean shirt and his hair combed. He was Jimmy Durante in tan pants wearing a pair of brown and white spectator shoes and matching argyle socks.

I screamed. "Bertie! It's Daddy!" I flew down the steps and into his arms. Bertie followed but reserved her excitement, offering only a slight hug of affection.

"Yesiree, it's my girls!" He hugged us, opened the car door, and then pulled out a birthday cake. "I figured we could try this again."

That night, lying in bed, I overheard his conversation with Ruby. Something not mentioned in the stories passed around the dinner table along with the cornbread and lemonade.

Daddy spoke softly in a deep, baritone voice; I pictured his dark razor stubble shadowing his chin, his shoeless feet parked and crossed on Ruby's coffee table, his toes wiggling in his brown and white socks.

Daddy had been in prison, that part was true. He'd come close to murdering one of Mama's drunken boarders who freely and mistakenly admitted he had taken liberty with Bertie, and that Mama had set the price at five dollars. The man turned out to be a state official, a representative from Raleigh passing through.

It took all of his self-restraint to keep from grabbing the collar of the guy's fancy shirt and twisting it tighter around his fat neck. As it was, he nearly killed the man. Daddy had put him into the hospital with a concussion and three broken bones.

I heard him cry into his hands to Ruby.

"I knew what Cordella was going to do to the twins. I couldn't stop her. I should've killed her. Hell, I ended up in prison anyway. She testified against me . . . said I was lying about what that bastard did to the girls."

"It's over, Erwin. Those years are behind you. Bobbie and Bertie are here now — with me. You come and see 'em when you want. They'll be here after I'm gone. I'm givin' them this old house. Are you goin' back to High Point?"

"The boarding house in High Point belongs to me. I plan to sell it, move to the mountains. Cordella will have to buy me out after the divorce, or move on . . . just like I've had to do. I found a little town I like, near the Blue Ridge. Sweet people. I've learned a trade."

"Naw, ya don't say?"

"Yes, Ma'am. Can ya believe it?" I heard him slap the table. "Learned how to build houses. Work with wood. I got my eye on a piece of land. Maybe later, I can send for the girls if they ain't put roots down here. They're welcome to stay with me; make sure they know that, Ruby."

He was gone in the morning. Bertie had said little at our dinner celebration. She wasn't surprised he'd not said good-bye. According to Bertie, no man had the courage to say it. And if they came back at all — it was too late.

As the wind blew in a storm off the ocean, the men from the funeral home carried Ruby's coffin and struggled to keep the flowers on top of it. Bertie and I followed behind. A few seats at the memorial service had been filled with women from the local Baptist church where Ruby was a member but never attended.

Bertie had found her. Her arthritic fist, dangled over the side of the couch, clutching a recipe for fried apple pies. Bertie placed her fist on the small mound of her chest, where it lay with the other one like two lumps of dough.

The pastor spoke very little. Just empty words over the body of someone he barely knew. No one cried. No one said they were sorry.

"At least she had us a little while," Bertie said.

"There should've been music."

"Goddam," I heard Bertie mutter.

"Goddam," I agreed.

~ August 1945 ~

In three months Bertie had fallen in love with Court Callahan, Air Force pilot.

One afternoon, she came home feeling hot and sick. She glanced into the mirror over the bathroom sink. Other than the bright flush on her narrow cheeks, she looked much as she had when she finished dressing that morning in the new pink sweater Court had bought her, a vivid contrast to her worn daisy print dress.

She stared at her image as if she'd forgotten what she looked like: glossy black curls, brown eyes, an impatient look of expectancy. With a twisting pang of recurring loss, she repeated Court's letter he'd written to her just before he left Carolina Beach for Fort Andrews.

"*I love you, Bertie. You have*" — she stopped, then wept — "*the love of adventure. You're the woman I've dreamed of falling in love with. I didn't believe you existed. Now I know you do. Someday, Bertie. We'll be together. The two of us, forever.*"

He'd kissed her, she'd said. A kiss that held a promise of unbelievable joy. "*I'll be back. Count on it.* He said that, Bob. He promised."

The light and bloom of the afternoon sun had settled in her eyes and cheeks. She looked feverish. My heart broke for her. I knew she would count the days until she heard from him again. In a way, I was jealous. I'd not found love like that, or felt the pain of missing a man.

Bertie took to her bed and told me about their first date. On a long, desolate stretch of sand, with seagulls stealing their cookies, they had kissed and their hands moved beneath each other's shirts, their hair having gone stiff with the salt in the air. They'd made love in the waves. "It was," she sucked in her breath and cried, "the most precious moment of my life."

She stood on wobbly legs and walked to the radio. Her hand rested on the dial. *"I'll be seeing you in all the old familiar places . . . "* the song echoed through the house. I wanted to absorb her pain. It was as if she were alone in the world. Instead of turning it off, she listened to the entire song. *". . . I'll be looking at the moon, but I'll be seeing you."* It ended. Bertie switched off the radio and crawled back into bed.

She fell asleep in my arms clutching his letter. The ink stained the palm of her hand like a henna tattoo. Her diary of loss, slipped from limp fingers and fluttered to the floor. I covered her with Ruby's old quilt, picked up the letter, and laid it on her dresser.

Bertie deserved him. He was her first love. I'd gone on lots of dates, but with nobody I cared to keep. I remained busy with my job at the cleaners while Bertie stayed close to home and made barbeque sandwiches. We didn't travel much past the boardwalk, the grocery stores, or the Baptist church. Bertie had settled into a routine, but I was still in search of adventure. It struck me that Court got that part wrong.

I considered a visit to Madame Tuleh again, but our money was too tight for excursions. We didn't hear from Daddy — or Mama, or Court for that matter. We had no phone, and our nearest neighbor complained if he had to deliver a message. So other than our radio, our movie magazines, and our local newspaper, we were cut off from the world.

Glancing at the newspaper before I left the house for work, I noticed the date, August 6, 1945, and realized it had been over three months since we arrived at Carolina Beach. No matter what I did to make the weeks drag on, or how hard I tried to stop time, the days disappeared in a gust. But then the headlines screamed across the paper. "U.S. DROPS ATOM BOMB; HOPE FOR EARLIER END TO WAR." Frightened at the state of the world, I thought of all the young men I'd known in school, and the few we'd met in church . . . most of them didn't come back from the war. Seemed like every family on Russell Street had lost a son, a brother, or a husband. Those who did come home were never the same. I diverted my thoughts to Court. How handsome he looked in his Air Force uniform. I prayed for his safety. I shook myself because it was the first time in years, I had prayed for anyone.

But Court never came back. We spent money we didn't have telephoning the Air Force base. In the end, we heard his plane had gone down into the Pacific.

"The densest material on earth is a broken heart," Bertie said. "People usually make do with the hand life deals them. But I've been dealt a heart of stone. I can't see or feel my future any more."

Bertie crumpled Court's letter again, shoved it into the pocket of her sweater, folded her arms, and fell into Ruby's old easy chair.

It woke her early. The sound of a low flying plane and her own voice spiraled across the room. Bertie's eyes flew open and she sat up, sucking in air between clenched teeth. She stumbled out of bed. I could see her from my room. The tendrils of the nightmare clung to her. She clamped her fingers over her lips to keep from crying out again. I ran to her and gradually, the familiar surroundings brought the world back into focus.

"It was a dream," I whispered. "Just a dream." She waited for the relief those words had brought her in years past, but this time it didn't work. Life's nightmares were Bertie's realities, and after months of struggling to put it behind her, the past haunted her even more.

For days, I sat helpless as my sister wandered through the dimness of the living room to the kitchen and back, rubbing her eyes, wishing she could sleep. She worried about everything; eventually she never left her bed. She had tried to accept Carolina Beach as her new home.

But Bertie never felt she'd had a home. She had dreams of a house and children with Court, but that's all they were — dreams. Her only happy moments were spent with the man she loved. That much, those few moments, were all he had been able to give her.

But now, the love of her life was dead. A life that had known so much loss. Bertie never again expected to be thrilled when a man walked into a room. She loved the way Court looked, the way he smiled when he said her name, his intelligence, his wry humor, his innate thoughtfulness.

She dreamed of him every night, and each dream became worse. Bertie's head was ringed in a vice of pain. I gave her aspirin every day, but it didn't help. She'd said her bowels were sick as if her very intestines were corroded and rotting. Lying in her bed, smelling of damp linen and desperation, she resigned her young life to bad luck and one nightmare after another.

One morning in late November, she peered out the window at the darkening sky over the ocean. "There must be a storm comin' in," she said. I made coffee, but she'd refused a cup or any bite of breakfast. She sat at the window and stared at the sea, as if she were waiting for Court to come walking out of the waves.

Storm clouds continued to gather. Tears fell from her face at a flash of lightning. As distant thunder rolled across the sky Bertie shivered, still fighting off the remnants of constant bad dreams.

Suddenly, she struck at her face and chest with both fists. She wanted to pummel her body, blacken eyes that had seen too much, stop a heart that had loved and hated too much. She screamed her pulse in her head beat so violently she couldn't stand it. I grabbed my sister and held her. It was all I could do. The thousands of words I'd said in the past few weeks went unheard and unchecked. I knew I had to get help. I was losing her.

When I awoke the next morning, our home was silent as a grave. Bertie was gone. I ran through the house, up and down the street, the boardwalk, and finally, to the beach. A group of locals had gathered around a body that lay still on the sand. I knew it was her. I staggered through the crowd and looked into the sorrowful eyes of a stranger who had tried to revive her. As frightened as Bertie was of water, she had walked into the sea. I fell on top of my sister, crying salty tears that mingled with the seawater beading up on her body. She was out of her pain. It was my turn to lose the love of my life.

~ July 1946 ~

Buying booze on the boardwalk was easy. The bars and stores served anyone that looked old enough. Ruby always said Carolina Beach was a drinking town with a tourist problem.

I had turned into a younger version of Aunt Ruby, working all day at Clyde's Cleaners and all night at Midtown Motor Court. I needed diversion; they needed a night clerk. Busting my butt kept me away from the house, memories of Bertie, and the vodka bottle. If I did end up with time off, I drank until I passed out in my sister's old bed. Too young to die and too pissed off to walk into the sea, I'd been cheated out of happiness and had lived a lifetime before I was twenty. The world's war was over, but mine had just begun.

Making enough money to buy a few outfits, I decided the time had come to be the whore Mama raised me to be. My new red skin-tight skirt with the kick-pleat in the back hugged my round rear and came with a matching body-hugging sweater. I dressed it up with a string of Bertie's fake pearls and matching earrings. Slipping into four-inch heels, I hung my pocketbook in the crook of my arm, painted my lips, lit my cigarette, and then swung my hips to the nearest bar.

Women rarely visited Skipper's Bar, and never on a Sunday. It was the kind of bar a woman, looking for a husband, sent her kid in to drag him home. Dozens of eyes flashed at me from the murky shadows. I walked, unconcerned, across the sticky, liquor-stained floor. The click of my heels echoed off the wood-paneled walls. A few of the men dropped their stares back into their drinks, but most kept their sloppy gazes helplessly fixed on my backside.

Determined to be a sophisticated whore, I asked for a Fuzzy Navel. "It's that peach-colored shit," I explained to the bartender.

"Oh," he nodded. "Our drinks don't come in colors or fruit flavors."

"How about a Slippery Nipple," I asked and winked.

"How about whiskey?" He suggested.

"Give her a beer," a familiar voice told him.

I turned my head to the end of the bar. The smoke-filled room made me think I was seeing ghosts.

I squinted in the darkness. "Court?"

"Skipper's house whiskey tastes like it could strip the chrome off a bumper," he said.

I froze. I *was* seeing ghosts. They'd followed me from Mama's house in High Point.

"Hey, Bobbie Sue." He moved to the stool next to mine. I nearly fainted.

"We thought you were . . ."

"Dead?"

"Yeah."

"So did Uncle Sam. It's a long story. How are you, Bobbie?"

"Fine, I guess I'm fine." In shock, I somehow managed to give him a quick hug.

I rotated my bar stool so I could watch his eyes. He spoke of being shot down into the cold water of the Pacific, being found unconscious and transported to a wounded battleship that limped into a port in Guam where he was hospitalized and remained in a coma for over two months.

"When I got out of the hospital, they flew me to D.C. I knew Bertie thought I was dead. I came back to North Carolina for her, but before I arrived, I called your neighbor to take her a message. I didn't want to scare her. That's when he told me what happened. I came anyway . . . to grieve. I've been to her grave. Then I realized I needed to see you, too. Tell you how sorry I was. I loved her, Bobbie; I really loved her. My heart was broken."

I took a sip of beer to calm my nerves. It left a little line of foam across my upper lip. He had just come in from swimming in the ocean. His hair was still wet, and there were small damp patches where his skin pinked through his cotton shirt.

We sat and talked about Bertie into the late afternoon. I agreed to meet him for drinks again the next day.

"You look good Court, for what you been through."

"Thanks, although the hearing in my left ear is shot, I'm limping like an old man, and I've put on some weight. But on the positive side, I've still got 20/20 vision."

"Here's to good vision," I said and held out my glass.

He clinked his against mine.

I took another gulp of beer.

"We're losers when it comes to finding happiness," I said.

"Here's to finding happiness."

We clinked glasses again.

I took another gulp of beer. This time he reached out and wiped the foam off my upper lip with his thumb.

He dropped a few crumpled bills on the bar, I downed the rest of my beer, and we slid off our stools. Court followed me through the bar and whispered over my shoulder. "Did Bertie ever tell you how we met?"

I uttered a slight giggle. "She said you were staring at her when we were sunbathing. She said you followed us walking home, like we were a couple of beach babes." Court opened the door and stood in a silhouette of soft daylight.

"I was following you, not Bertie."

"But . . ."

"I ran into Bertie the next day on the beach; this time she was alone. I bought one of her barbeque sandwiches. Everything happened from there. I did fall in love with her. But you were the beach baby I originally wanted to meet."

Court stamped a quick kiss on me. His hand slid into mine, pulling me behind him out of the bar. The sun was bright; I couldn't see a thing. I had to bring my free hand up to shield my eyes as he led me. I thought of the hymn, *Where He Leads Me I Will Follow* . . . I only wished he was a little more like the Lord. Secretly, I wanted to be spiritual again. And besides, I liked religious men.

We met every day after that for weeks. But guilt plagued me. I felt I was betraying Bertie. On August 1st, I stood in front of my sister's grave and asked her to forgive me for falling in love with Court. The next morning I found the letter he had written to her in a drawer of her things I couldn't part with. I showed Court the letter, and we agreed — Bertie would want us to fall in love. She would want *me* to have Court, rather than another woman. So I allowed myself to be taken over by him. Entirely.

We were married on the last day of August in 1946.

~ June 1952 ~

My life was busy the next few years. Beachfront property, unbeknownst to me, was a valuable asset. We sold Ruby's acre of land and bought a small house near Wilmington. But Court, being the good man with money that he was, took advantage of the post-war land development boom and with his degree in Business, it was a matter of months and we were sitting in a new five thousand square foot house with the biggest bathroom I ever saw.

Restless, I decided to go to college. I graduated, near the top of my class. Then I shocked my husband when I asked him to join a new church with me. Later, we both walked hand-in-hand down the aisle and dedicated our lives to the work of God.

Next, I shocked myself when I said I wanted to go to seminary. But I went, just the same, with Court's full support. He sent me to the best, to Harvard Divinity School.

The day I graduated, I recognized a familiar face smiling at me in the audience. She had cleaned herself up, lost a bunch of weight, but she was there and as bohemian as ever. *Tuleh, of all people to seek me out and attend my graduation.*

I recalled her ancient prediction — that I would lead many to righteousness. When I looked for her afterward, I was told she'd gone back to Carolina Beach. I tried to locate her days later. Her shop was locked with a sign on the door, *Out Of Business.* The merchant next door said she'd been deported.

Mama died in 1948. After the house sold, she moved in with Juba Lee, who wrote me a letter explaining Mama had caught pneumonia and died in her sleep in the hospital. That was best. I never saw her again since the day Bertie and I left her in the church, screaming after us. But I didn't hate her anymore, either.

Daddy passed on, too. He willed me a parcel of land in Sparta, North Carolina. Court and I decided to move to Sparta, to the mountains. We built a church where I could preach. Court was from

Boone originally, so it was like going home for him. Seems he had several generations of Callahan relatives buried near his old homestead on two hundred and fifty acres of mountain property near Boone.

But the best part of our life has been the birth of our son, Matthew. My son will have a blessed childhood. And my prayer for him is to someday find the love of his life.

I have come a long way. From a godless existence to one filled with the Holy Spirit. From childhood molestation to experiencing the true meaning of love. From abject poverty to the comfort of having more than enough. From the dark nights of loneliness into the light of family and friends. From the deepest of sorrows to the highest of joys. From death into life. What Satan stole from me, God restored — seven times over.

On many Sundays I have led congregations to righteousness. I have fulfilled a harlot's prophecy. I can relate to the destitute, to the homeless, to the unloved. I have taught others to give love and to receive love. I have ministered to women on the edge who have lost everything including the ability to reason, and to those who cannot forgive. And though I fall short from time to time, God has still seen fit to make my path a plain path. This is my destiny, my journey.

I carry on without her. In spite of her death, I still see her in all the old familiar places.

But through the years, nothing will take her out of my heart; she was part of me . . . every day. She still is. My Alberta Lou. My Bertie. My beach baby.

I was born a coal miner's granddaughter. That fact inspired the story COAL DUST ON MY FEET. I never dreamed one day I would write about Widen, West Virginia. The town that had so haunted my childhood was once involved in a reign of terror between labor and management that has been said to be the longest and most violent coal strike in the history of our country. As a child, I was only privy to bits and pieces of these stories.

I dug deep into the crevices of my memory. I tunneled through pages of old picture albums Daddy and Mama kept stored away for years, and found what I was looking for. My grandparent's wedding photo. Looking at it, I realized the miners of West Virginia and their children didn't romanticize their lives. They lived them, surviving the best they could. The outside world didn't exist much past an occasional radio program or newspaper article. For many years, time stood still in the hollers and mountains around Clay County. Life for my grandpa, Troy Jennings King, consisted of his wife Gussie, five children, and a job . . . mining coal for the Elk River Coal and Lumber Company.

As a writer, I returned to West Virginia, to Widen, and immediately began to develop a powerful attachment to the place. Over the next few months I learned more about the town, and discovered that my family had deep roots there. Several generations of Kings and Samples were born and lived in Clay County, all the way back to the Revolutionary War.

A short time later, I learned of the role my grandpa played in the Strike of 1952, siding with the company that had been loyal to him through the Depression. But the family was split on both sides.

COAL DUST ON MY FEET is a very real story . . . in some ways. The strike did happen. Jack Hamrick, Ed Heckelbech, Bill Blizzard, Charles Frame, John Lewis, Jennings Roscoe Bail, Governor Marland, and Joseph Bradley were real people who either lived in or near Widen, and were associated with the strike. Otherwise, the story and remaining characters are fictional, created from my imagination purely for storytelling purposes. But the violence from September 1952 to Christmas Eve of 1953 is legendary, and the men who were killed and maimed live on in the memories of their families to this day.

Families were torn apart, cousin against cousin, father against son — and the union, though it failed to break the back of the company, changed things. Eventually, the company closed its doors. In its day, 3,000 people lived in the coal camp of Widen. Today, there are less than 200. The town folded up except for the Post Office and a few that refused to leave — some of them are my relatives.

From these threads of family history, COAL DUST ON MY FEET was woven. It is a tale of love and betrayal, forbidden passions and long-buried secrets, of one woman's struggle with her heritage and with her God — and the ancient bridge where the real and the supernatural meet.

But most intriguing to me personally as I wrote this story was the possibility that I had come by my stubbornness genes honestly, and that I was more like my grandparents than I ever dared to think. I dedicate this story to them.

Coal Dust On My Feet

No one knew how long the strike would last.

Bullets whizzed past Thirl Nettles' head. Bolting for cover, he leaped into his 1940 Plymouth sedan. His right leg throbbed with a red-hot searing pain all the way up into his groin. Only moments ago he'd left the League of Widen Miners meeting, strolled past the tipple and began whistling "Walking The Floor Over You."

"Thirl! You okay?"

"I've been hit!" He slid down on the seat and pressed his hand on the wound, the inside of his car spinning around his head.

"Hold on!"

The pain was like nothing he'd experienced before. Not just a pain — an explosion like a live grenade thrown into his body. It couldn't be contained. It spread and expanded, searched for ways to escape the confinement of his skin. His flesh vibrated with it.

Hearing his heartbeat in his ears, he glanced down at his legs. Dark, warm blood soaked his pants. For a moment, he was sure they were his dad's legs, the day they carried him out of the Macbeth mine explosion — dead. Thirl remained crouched down and motionless on the seat as more rifle fire struck his car, until dark was the only hand he had to hold before he passed out.

Dawn arrived, sifting its dull light through DeDe Nettles' lace panel curtains. In the front room, the coal stove grumbled and ashes rattled into the ash pan. The morning was miserable cold, raw and damp, the kind of damp that ate into your bones and sucked out the marrow. It had rained for two weeks straight. Buffalo Creek ran high, its steep banks muddy and slick.

Thirl didn't know who had come to his rescue. He opened his dark eyes that morning to find a blurry Doctor Vance hovering over him. The other side of the bed was still made, the pillow tucked neatly under the chenille spread. Groggy, Thirl heard the doctor's voice before he passed out again.

Doctor Sherwood Vance, a wide, solid stump of a man, bald and nearsighted behind wire-rimmed glasses, worked the bulge of muscles in his jowls to and fro, all while he muttered mostly to himself, but partly to DeDe.

"Bastards . . . low lifes. Miners, they call themselves, but they have no loyalties, not to their town, not to their country, not even to each other. They call themselves godly men but they'd sell their souls for a wooden nickel and a plug of tobacco. They talk like politicians, up one side and down the other. No respect for the League tryin' to make life better for them. What do they expect when somebody like Jack Hamrick goes berserk in the mine! He deserved to be fired!"

DeDe pulled the blanket over her husband to keep him warm. She had combed back his oiled hair and washed the coal dust from his face the best she could. He'd kept a trim figure all these years despite his diet of fried potatoes, bacon, sausage, and squirrel. And daily helpings of molasses and biscuits. The man ate for enjoyment, like most men that worked in a coal mine.

DeDe watched their son, James Curtis, pull his legs up to his chest and sink into the bottom of his dad's bed. He stared at the blood on the floor. At nineteen, he stood as tall and lanky as Thirl and shared his unreadable dark blue eyes and constant smile. But where his dad's hair exuded the color of brown mountain clay, James Curtis had inherited her burnt red locks, often appearing as if they'd been dipped in honey when the sun hit at the right angle.

DeDe gave her son's shoulder a soft hug, pulled his cap off and kissed the top of his head. Until this moment, she had no strength to ask questions. Her immediate concern was to assist the doctor in keeping her husband alive. But anger bubbled just under the surface of her constraint, searching for a way out of her mouth. She wiped sweat from her forehead with the back of her hand, then followed the doctor into the kitchen to prime the pump. Tears dripped down her cheeks as she watched Doc Vance lean into the sink and wash her husband's blood off his hands.

All the nights she watched Thirl wash up after work in her tiny kitchen, stripped to the waist, mine dirt covered him like shoe polish. He'd dip his arms over and over in water up to his elbows, scrubbing with a wire brush and hard granite-like soap, turning the water black. She thought she'd never again see the true color of his skin. Black coal dust collected in the creases of his neck and in the wrinkles of his face. To DeDe, her husband's hands looked like black bear paws. She knew he was proud to never have lost a finger. Thirl had told her he regarded non-life threatening professions as jobs for women and men with too much education. She saw him as a person who'd been unknowingly thrown into a world between heaven and hell. She'd heard the Catholics had a name for it. But unlike everybody else in the coal camp, he was content in the place he stood — never expecting God to give him more. Even if he deserved it.

A sob caught in her throat. Her voice and stare were equally painful. "What happened, Doc?"

Doc Vance scrubbed then dried his hands on a clean towel. "Thirl was there when Harry Gandy fired Jack Hamrick last week. You know Jack and Opal? I believe they attend your church."

"Don't recall his face. I know his wife." She wiped her tears with the cuffs of her blouse, then motioned for him to have a seat at the kitchen table.

"The way I hear it, Hamrick went plum crazy last week when he was asked to work in a trackless section of the mine where a new machine was bein' given a tryout. Hamrick flew into a rage, shoutin' the job was unsafe and that the company was tryin' to kill its men. Damn fool, took a pop bottle, broke off the end, and slashed a gash an inch long in his supervisor's cheek. Took me an hour to stitch him up. You got any coffee?"

"I'll make some," she said. After rinsing out cups, she filled the coffee pot with water and Maxwell House, and then turned the electric stove on high. While it perked, DeDe began scrubbing found blood off the table with jagged sweeps of her arm. Her elbows pumped sharply. She sniffed more tears back in her head, but didn't speak.

Doc Vance removed his blood-spattered glasses and wiped each lens slowly. "I wasn't there when Gandy fired Hamrick. But I walked into Gandy's office tonight right after the League meeting. Thirl had just left. Nobody expected miner retaliation. After all, it'd been a week since they'd fired Hamrick — but seems Jonas Zirka, a troublemaker in my mind, got everybody all stirred up tonight. When problems come to the mine and things look bad, there's always one man who thinks he's got all the answers and is willing to take command. Usually, that individual is crazy. This time, it's Zirka. Hamrick needed firing. But Zirka's gonna use it and some other lame issues to try and bring in the union again. Lies are an infectious disease. I think Zirka contracted it from some fat cat in the UMW. Anyway, I heard the gunfire. So did Gandy."

DeDe stormed back into her husband's sick room and glared at her son. "Get a message to Mister Gandy. Make sure he knows it was your daddy that's been shot. Use the phone in his office to call the sheriff."

"Ain't no use calling the sheriff, Mama. Picket line's done been formed at the top of Widen hill. Doc's right. Zirka's behind it. All that noise last night, those car horns blowing and moving through the streets? Strike's on. I was with Savina last night. When I took her home, it was Odie who told me 'bout Daddy. I wanted to go straight to the sheriff. But her daddy said the law won't come unless somebody's dead 'cause Widen is all private property, owned by Joseph Bradley." She knew her son saw no point in holding back the truth, even from a woman.

"Odie said he's gonna strike."

"Then you get a message to Savina's daddy. Tell Odie he best remember who helped him with his farm last year when Josephine died." She gave her son a maternal once-over that made him instinctively straighten up from his slouched position on the bed.

"Yes, Ma'am. Next time I see Savina."

"Your girl, Savina, she's welcome here James, but Odie's not gonna allow your skinny company butt on his property."

"No, Ma'am."

She watched James lower his gaze to her bare feet. They were filthy and spattered with blood. A few of her pretty red toenails were chipped. They were to attend a church sing in Gassaway tomorrow. She was going to wear shoes with her toes sticking out. Two nights before she had held a bottle of red nail polish in front of Thirl, and he smiled. "Real pretty," he'd said.

Doc Vance carried two cups of coffee in from the kitchen. With his elbows fanned out and his eyes on the cups, he glided up and handed her a cup, stiffly easing himself down on the chair beside her. They continued the vigil beside Thirl's bed, watching his chest rise and fall with each breath, as if at any given moment the body would change from a wounded man to a dead corpse.

"Odie ain't too bright," said Doc. "The man has only two more years of work to gain a pension, but decides to strike. Told me he ain't gonna go on paying fifty cents a month to that no 'count company League. Damn black throat. Since the rules of pension eligibility require twenty full years of service, of which Odie already has eighteen, he's throwin' away $1,200 a year for life to save twelve dollars. The man sleeps with his head up his ass!"

James Curtis sat staring at the wall, his thoughts tumbling over one another in no particular order. He had assigned himself guard duty on his dad's bed in the middle of the night an hour after Hardrock Dodrill and Boney Butcher called Doc Vance from the Grille, drove

Thirl home, and then carried his bloody body into the house. James rose to his feet, numb and irritable. He stretched and stumbled to the front room where he fell into his dad's favorite chair, facing a magnificent ten-point buck's head hanging on the wall. A buck they'd hunted for two years, until Thirl bagged him last Thanksgiving. His dad killed it, and he sketched it. Charcoal drawings from the time he was old enough to hold a pencil collected in boxes in his mother's chifforobe. A framed sketch of the live buck hung on the wall next to its dead head. He hated hunting; killing anything that moved repulsed him.

James had ridden to work with his dad like he did every morning. It was called morning by the men who worked that shift, but to James it was still night, dark and cold and silent. He could hear his dad's muffled voice, along with his mother's, as they said their good-byes. The sound of his dad's boots pacing the kitchen floor while he waited for his lunch bucket haunted him now.

Together, he and his dad walked out of their soot-coated house. They crossed the front yard, along with dozens of other men crossing their front yards wearing hard hats with lamps attached to the front, carrying lunch buckets the size of toolboxes. A mass of men leaving in their pickup trucks and cars, their mouths already chewing plugs of tobacco to lubricate their throats against the gritty coal dust.

A first shift supervisor, his dad had worked for Elk River Coal and Lumber as long as he could remember. Mining provided a good living for his family, he'd said, and it would do the same for James. Proud to be a miner's son, James Curtis followed as expected. He'd worked the mines from the day he graduated high school, never giving his parents a notion he wanted to leave the mountains. He'd been a company man from the day he was born.

As a little boy, his mother had educated him in the importance of coal and how it kept food on their table and heated every home in the country during winter. "Why, without coal and the miners that bring it to the surface," she'd said, "America is no better than some dying country in Africa with starving children." James waved to his mother every morning, stopping at her flower garden — a giant truck tire laid flat and painted white. James had positioned it next to the dogwood tree in the front yard, a tree she'd insisted be planted the day he was born.

But it was his dad that squeezed his hand every morning without saying a word. A quick grasp just after turning the key in the ignition, keeping his eyes straight ahead. He'd never talked about their work or the dangers of it. His grip was a fast second of assuredness that everything was going to be fine — today. It was their secret, one they shared man to man.

James leaned his head back against the old chair and closed his eyes. He could smell his dad's scent of hair tonic and lye soap. Drifting between sleep and memory, he saw himself as a child being lifted onto his dad's shoulders in the Thanksgiving Barn. His dad's large leathery hand covered his entire back. He remembered being made to sit still on a hard pew in church, playing with the flexible watchband peeking out from under his dad's sleeve, how the gold had worn off, and how it pulled at the hairs on his arm. His dad sucked peppermints and whistled old country tunes when he drove the car. On his dresser, he kept a pickle jar full of change. Each night his dad emptied his pockets — nickels, dimes, and pennies into the jar, landing with tinny pings. They were the sounds James listened for as he drifted off to sleep.

Yesterday, after they'd arrived at the mine, James Curtis walked behind his dad through a few wisps of smoke left hanging in the air — the last puffs of his dad's cigarette. He turned and mumbled to his son. "Tell your mama I'll be home late; I have a League meeting after my shift."

His dad was fine then, and now he wasn't.

He couldn't recall how long he'd been sitting there. James got to his feet and walked three steps to the gun cabinet. Selecting a twelve-gauge shotgun from the rack and a box of shells from one of the bottom drawers, he shoved three shells into the magazine of the gun. Then he jacked a shell into the chamber and engaged the safety.

James Curtis paused, peeled off his Elk River Coal and Lumber Company cap, and tossed it on the buck's right antler. Grasping the shotgun in both hands, he opened the back door and slipped out, out of his mother's line of sight.

Doc Vance stood, checked Thirl's pulse one last time, then packed his medical bag. "Keep that wound clean and dressed. Send James Curtis to the office if you need me. Your lucky husband should be fine. Shove these pills down his throat for the next few weeks. We'll watch for infection. A few more inches and that bullet would've severed a main artery in his leg."

The old doctor hadn't stopped talking since he arrived minutes after Thirl was laid on his bed. "You know, the League is a legal bargaining agency for Bradley's employees. That committee was formed to create the company's welfare plan for its own workforce. I helped to put that committee together. That League's a fine a group of men as God ever made. The League of Widen Miners is company, sure, but it offers medical and retirement. Don't those fool strikers remember the mine was open two and three days a week during the Depression even when the other mines were shut down? Don't they remember that?"

"Lord, Doc, they've been trying to strike here since I was a girl. You're really worried this time, aren't you? How long do you think this one will last?"

"How long's hard to say. As long as it takes. As long as the United Mine Workers provide their strike fund. John Lewis and Bill Blizzard are behind this one again, bigger and better organized than the last strike. I'm afraid it'll get more violent before it's over, as long as their morale doesn't crack."

DeDe set her coffee cup on the table by Thirl's bed. "I believe I've told you, I'm not from Widen. My family came here from Matewan to get away from the reputation of that town, the violence — and death. Daddy died here, in Widen, from black lung back in '44. Mama . . . she passed from black lung too . . . from thirty years of washing Daddy's clothes." DeDe smoothed the front of her bloodstained blouse, her stare drifting through the windows and then back to Thirl. Her voice was strained and soft. "My daddy believed Joseph Bradley owned the safest mines in the state; that's why we moved here. But the mines will kill us all, eventually."

Every man in her life had been or was a miner, including her son. They all learned the speech patterns of the coalface. In response to the slightest tap of a pick or a shovel, the mine communicated. Sighs, hisses, pops, squeaks, groans, crackles, gurgles — each sound spoke to them and warned of underground water, a weak wall, or a methane leak. Her own father once told her if the mine choked and found itself about to crumble, it shuddered first then screamed like a woman in childbirth.

But to DeDe, a long strike was as dangerous as a cave-in. "I've seen the killing a strike will bring. I'll protect my own." Her face already beginning to sag, the carefully groomed hair already beginning to gray, the eyes already receding into a calm, dark indifference most people chose to see as insight. She never wore makeup. DeDe looked down at her bitten half-moon fingernails, then twisted her thick copper hair into a knot and anchored it at the private part of her neck with bobby pins. She picked up her pocketbook.

Everybody in town knew she kept a gun in her purse, including Doc Vance. She walked back into the kitchen, gripping it against her chest. Doc Vance followed on her heels.

"DeDe! Now you listen to me . . . I won't have you or any other woman in this town in harm's way. You let the men handle this. The company's recruited its own force. Thirteen good and loyal company men, I've heard. Sworn in as deputies by the County Sheriff to guard the town. Stay out of it, DeDe, I mean it." His stare like two grimy nickels and his tone — stern, "You tell the rest of the women in town, stay close to home and keep their young'uns in the house after school. I've always been fond of your family. Why, it was just yesterday I delivered James Curtis in this house."

"That was over nineteen years ago. I believe you stood by us when we buried a stillborn son five years later. I've had enough heartache, Doc."

Doctor Vance nodded, avoiding her eyes, then gathered his jacket and medical bag. "You know management's secret weapon when there's a strike? It's the women. Mama goes a few months with only gut paste gravy and biscuits to fix for supper, the old man's hangin' 'round the house drinkin' and yellin' because the kids're sick and cryin' and there's dirty clothes everywhere and he's gone most evenin's to a union meetin' or finishin' his shift on the picket line, comin' home tired, cold, and dirty — stinkin' of liquor. Drives every women I know crazy. They'll settle because their wives'll make them settle."

DeDe could only nod in return. She picked up his hat and led him to the door. She was the granddaughter of a much-revered Baptist minister who had also worked in West Virginia's coal mines at the turn of the century. Surely that should count for something with God. DeDe smiled deceptively and handed the doctor his hat. "Vengeance is mine, saith the Lord of hosts."

"You just remember that," he said as the screen door spanked shut behind him.

DeDe Nettles was a pistol. At thirty-nine, she carried a .38 Smith & Wesson and could shoot straight. When she slipped it into the pocket of her apron it felt heavy, like a ball and chain. Yawning, she shuffled out to the back porch for some fresh air. She stretched and leaned over the railing hearing . . . she wasn't sure. "Could be raccoons trying to get to the chickens." *Voices — someone's in the yard.* "The whole world's gone crazy."

She scurried back into the kitchen and locked the door behind her. It was the first time she'd turned that lock since she'd married Thirl and moved into the house on Nicholas Street. After pouring another cup of coffee, she walked to the front room to rest in her overstuffed chair. A chair Thirl had bought her for Christmas. He brought it in on the train from Charleston. The same year he purchased their first refrigerator and added the bathroom to the back of the house.

Before she sat down she smacked the chair. An impulse from living in a coal camp, the dust that flew out of it determined her next cleaning day. She was a small woman and felt like a child each time she sunk into her chair. The first time she took a seat and saw her reflection in the windows, she laughed and said she looked like a redheaded kewpie doll with no legs.

Life's sorrows showed in her brown eyes, Thirl had told her. DeDe had seen first hand the hardships of mining life on women, and she was no exception. Every woman she knew aged quickly. DeDe's smiles were few and far between, reserved only for special moments, and mostly for James Curtis. Up close her skin was a vague meshwork of lines and wrinkles, like the peel of an orange, only smoother. Petite, but often the largest presence in the room, her physical size often went unnoticed. She was bound to protect her own with as much commitment and passion as Joseph Bradley when he decided to build his coal empire in Widen.

Thirl teased her how she could testify about her sanctification one night and shoot a perfect game of pool the next. DeDe recruited every child on Nicholas Street for Sunday school. She never missed a church service. And everybody knew she loved her boy. James Curtis was her prize possession.

For all her religious dreams, visions, and premonitions, she headed the ladies prayer group every week, specializing in prayer for the safety of miners. Some folks said she had the "gift." Her grandma had it, and so did her mama. A sense of knowing the future, of hearing what could not be heard by normal folk. A direct line to the Almighty. She didn't gossip, but when she spoke — folks paid attention.

DeDe's hand slipped into her pocket; her fingers clasped the cold metal of her gun. With her other hand she reached out to the bookcase beside her chair and lifted the ancient picture of her grandfather, turning it in the dimly lit room, tilting it this way and that, gauging the severity of his lifeless face. He was God's minister, and yet she wondered if he heard the mine scream before his head snapped toward the explosion and the rumble of the fireball — before he was incinerated. Or maybe he never saw it coming. Maybe he was buried by tons of earth without warning. Maybe his bones were crushed, his organs split open, his senses annihilated, his life wiped out before he had a chance to understand what was happening. But she doubted it.

The coal camp sprawled over the bottom of the hollow some sixty miles northeast of Charleston, the state capital. The road to Widen was hilly, twisting and narrow. A broken road with ruined shoulders and potholes. A yellow sign at the top of the steep hill that dropped into Widen warned, HILL. Somebody scratched it into the word, HELL.

At the bottom, all along its length were small houses, occasionally a large one, set back from the road at the edge of the mountain. A twisting octopus of streets swirled through the valley, not the typical plaid grids of flatland towns. Although the valley was wide, as they typically were in that part of the country, one road and one railroad led in and out of town. Thunderous coal and passenger trains rode the rails and filled the valley with the sound of screeching brakes and shrill whistle stops. A loose-plank bridge near the Grille rumbled with a clap of thunder each time a vehicle drove over the creek below that collected beer bottles, candy bar wrappers, and cigarette butts. No streets or alleys were paved; that was only for folks in cities like Charleston and Huntington. Widen's streets were covered in slag coal or dirt.

The town was alive with coal. The Company's huge gob piles, ominous heaps of mine waste with their guts ablaze, filled a person's nostrils with the pungent odor of struck matches. Over thirty feet high, the graceful slopes of loose coal and sulfurous dirt glowed a soft orange. The tipple's steam rose like the breath of a monster. A place where coal was screened and loaded into railroad cars, the tipple demanded the town's attention and tribute. Its silo, locomotive shed and repair shops hugged the company's railroad yard.

A company town; Joseph Bradley and The Elk River Coal and Lumber Company owned it from tipple to barbershop. Despite the company store, school, post office, bank, movie house, medical dispensary, YMCA, baseball park, and 310 dwellings, Widen was first and foremost a coal mine.

The trees may not have been straighter in Widen, the grass greener, the sky bluer and the mountains more purple and majestic, but when the mine was producing, it often seemed so. On fine mornings the locals liked to tell each other that, indeed, God covered His black gold with these hills, this place — first.

But the fine mornings had ended. During the first weeks of September after the mine closed down, the town's inhabitants remained behind closed doors, clothed in fear. The school closed, the Grille closed, and even the post office closed the day after the strikers dug in and parked their cars, sons, and guns at the top of the road into Widen.

Inhaling the hills of his childhood, James Curtis watched Odie Ingram skirt the timber at the far end of the east pasture mounted on a young, edgy bay colt. Huge maples, oaks and hemlocks towered over everything, standing still in full foliage on the mountain behind his farm.

Odie worked hard in the mines and he worked his horses hard. James had been welcome once, but he had no idea what Odie would say to him now that they were on opposite sides.

James leaned his shotgun against the fence. He knew most of the younger men had sided with the strikers — he wasn't taking any chances. They were boys he'd gone to school with, like Cole Farlow. Cole was known for his hot head and short fuse. It stuck in James' memory the day Cole spouted off that if there were ever a strike, he'd shoot a kiss-ass company man faster than a nigger-lover.

If the strikers had tried to kill his dad, they'd shoot at anybody. James respected his dad's position. He'd never side with the union. Even if he did share a few union sympathies, his love and loyalty to his family far outweighed any feelings for or against the union.

But beyond his duty to honor his parents, he loved Savina with his soul, and today he wanted to explain that to her father — hoping to keep his place in Odie's house as his future son-in-law.

James Curtis suspected Odie liked him well enough, but he would not allow Savina to marry until she was eighteen. It was her daddy's stubbornness, Savina had said. James, in an attempt to be amiable, respected Odie's condition. But deep down, James believed Odie would never allow Savina to marry him. James anticipated an eventual elopement. Many couples in Clay County married early, but Odie had an innate fear of being alone since his wife died, so James agreed to wait hoping time would ease his anxiety.

Odie rode high in his saddle, appearing taller than he was. Through the mist of daybreak, the dreamy scene played like a western picture show. In the distance on his favorite colt, Odie checked the mares for signs of illness or accident. The horses fanned away from Odie and the colt. Quick in the morning chill, the mares puffed funnels of breath and shook their heads at the inconvenience.

Odie was not a company man. He worked the mine for one reason and one reason only — to pay off his farm and to raise quarter horses. Odie rode up to the barn then jumped down and hitched the colt to a post, nodding to James, acknowledging his presence. When he ambled toward the back of the house, James shivered; a chill ran the length of his body. Gazing up to the dreary sky, winter was on its way . . . the leaves were changing, like the rest of his world.

James walked toward the front of the peeling, sagging farmhouse. A pack of spittle-flinging dogs barked and paced back and forth on the porch. Chickens roamed freely. Savina had quit trying to fix up the place after her mother had died. The yard was covered with junk. Rusted bedsprings, empty Pennzoil cans, wet newspapers, bald tires, corroded truck parts . . . it looked like the house had vomited its insides.

Odie kicked open the screen door and lifted his gun from his side. Gray drizzle peppered his skin as he stomped down to the bottom broken porch step. Mud and manure covered his boots. A smile ticked briefly at the corners of his mouth like a small spasm and he pulled at his ear with his free hand. Their eyes met with awkward glances. Odie began to stare at James with the eyes of someone who thinks he's about to be told a fact he already knows. His teeth were clamped shut, his top lip drawn back in that smirking snarl.

James recalled what his daddy had said about Odie a few days ago. That he changed amazingly little over the last thirty years. Except for paunchiness around his middle and the loss of some of his hair, he was the same nice boy he'd gone to school with. James considered the fact that his daddy didn't really know Odie.

"Morning, Mister Ingram. Savina in the house?"

"I figure she's down by the crick."

James Curtis nodded and headed toward the direction of the creek.

"James Curtis!" Odie cocked his rifle.

James froze, feeling Odie's hot stare burn the back of his neck. He turned around. "Sir?"

A twelve-gauge aimed at his head revealed Odie's message before he spoke it. "I don't want you comin' 'round here any more. I don't want you seein' my Savina agin."

Up to now, James was unafraid of Odie's intimidation — it was the attempt to keep him from Savina that left him weak-kneed. "I have a right, Mister Ingram. I have a right to see her. We agreed."

Odie's blue eyes blazed, considering this. "Comp'ny men have no rights on my property."

"Mama thought you'd feel that way. Said to tell you to remember who helped you on the farm last year when Josephine died."

Odie lowered his gun, by only an inch or two. "I don't need remindin'. You tell your ma — Thirl and me are even. Ask Bonehead and Hardrock. Ask 'em who drove Thirl's car to the Grille last night. With him in it passed out and bleedin' like a stuck pig. I don't owe your daddy nothin', boy. He helped me when Jo died, and it was me that saved his life last night."

James opened his mouth but nothing came out. Except for his eyes, Odie had become a colorless man. His pale skin, gray hair, gray stubble, dirty gray pants and jacket, and gray cigarette smoke swirling between his fingers matched the shades of gray in his voice. Pockmarks and small scars marred his face. Small cauliflower ears poked out from the sides of his head. The tip of his left ear, which he tugged at whenever he felt uneasy, was cropped, and his nose lay flat against his face — the result of shoeing an uncooperative horse some years before.

Despite his unattractive features, coarse speech and rough manners, he possessed a keen intellect and a profound capacity for observing the world around him.

James stuffed his hands in his jacket pockets and shrugged. "You and my daddy been mining together since you were my age."

Odie cleared his head and throat, coughed, then spit a plug of phlegm at one of his dogs. "Boy, you ain't tellin' me what I don't know. Your daddy and me spent years together in them deep-dark-dank holes in the ground. Goin' in before sunup and comin' out after sundown . . . never saw daylight for weeks. That cage dropped us like rocks hundreds of feet into them black holes. Ever' day we'd walk toward the tipple together with our dinner buckets, givin' the comp'ny another day's labor, never knowin' if we'd come home." Odie lowered his gun further.

"Anybody ever tell you the definition of slave labor, son?" Odie flicked his cigarette to the ground. "It's coalminin'. Men that work a job where they risk their lives ever' minute and at the end of the pay period owe more to the comp'ny store than they made. Debts don't die with 'em, neither. They're passed on to their children. It's time union come in, make things better, work less hours, stricter safety rules . . . you heard Zirka . . . time to let some of the younger fellers in on them committees. You need to join us, James. Time we make some of the decisions."

"Daddy said Joseph Bradley has the highest safety standards in the state. That he kept the mine open during the Depression so the men could feed their families. Daddy said Bradley pays as high as union scale."

"Your daddy has his opinion about Bradley, I have mine. Bradley owns the damn bank. He owns us, boy. You think about that. We cain't take a shit unless Bradley approves it. Now I'm telling you to get off my land. You best hope the union gets into the comp'ny, then maybe we'll talk agin. Otherwise . . . Savina is off limits to you, son."

"Deanna? Where are you, honey?" Thirl twisted his head, his eyesight blurry in the dim light of his bedroom. He had a dream of himself in a coffin with pennies on his eyes. That the undertaker had placed the wooden box on sawhorses in their front room. He stretched his arm down to his leg — *still there* — trying to remember what happened. He felt like he'd been sawed in half. Thirl had prepared himself for a mine disaster all his life. He wasn't prepared for a bullet.

From his bed, Thirl focused on the burning coal in the stove. Like the red eyes of a black dragon squatting in the middle of the front room with its tail sticking in the chimney, it blew its hot breath into the house. Sitting defiantly on its asbestos-sheathed-in-tin mat, the cast iron dragon waited for an opportunity to strike. Thirl closed his eyes again. They felt hot. His mouth was hot. He felt sick. He sensed something staring at him and turned his head slowly. On the bed beside him laid his wife's sock monkey. It had always made him laugh. He tried to smile, but the pain wouldn't allow it.

"Deanna, you in the kitchen?"

DeDe had kept vigil for three days, more in than out of her tiny bedroom. Preparing the oven for corn bread, she'd just fried a handful of cornmeal in her iron skillet before the batter could be poured. James Curtis would be home soon to check on his daddy. No one had eaten a bite the past three days. She had pulled herself away from Thirl's bedside to cook something besides the pinto beans that simmered on the stove, a food offering from her neighbor, Pearle.

Hearing her husband stir, she crept in and turned on the light. One naked bulb overhead gave off a feverish discolored glow that failed to find the corners of the room. Daylight had faded and the room darkened into roundness. The room was like standing in the bottom of a well . . . or a mine.

Thirl's gritty face, lined with a telltale track on each cheek, gave only a hint of his agony. "You're awake." DeDe put on a smile she pulled from her sleeve and sat down on the bed's edge. She wiped his brow with a cool cloth. "Here, take this pill. Doc Vance said it'd help. You've been shot, but I suppose you know that."

Thirl fought an impulse to gag. Choking, he attempted to swallow the large pill.

"Sorry, darlin', but Doc said . . ."

"Don't care what Doc said," he gagged again. "I can't swallow pills . . . never could. You know that. And turn that damn light bulb off."

"Don't get pissy with me," she whispered. "I don't want to be a widow just yet, so if you don't mind you're gonna take the pill whenever I give it to ya."

DeDe stood and turned off the light. The glow from the front room seeped into Thirl's bedroom as she lit a kerosene lamp and sat it by his bed on a small table. Its light barely touched Thirl's head. But she sensed he preferred it.

Thirl sipped at the water glass she held at his lips, then asked, "How bad is it?"

"You'll live. But you're gonna limp a while."

"I mean the strike."

"Strikers cut off the town at the top of the hill. James Curtis says he's not sure yet if there's enough men to keep the mine open, and how many of them live out of town."

"Tell James Curtis to stay away from the line, it's dangerous."

"Shhh. You need to rest." She wiped his head again. DeDe could see his strength fading fast. "James is a man now. He knows how to take care of himself. You taught him well."

"No, honey, if he's got any good in him, it's from you."

DeDe wrung out the cloth in a chipped spatterware bowl. "Odie threw him off his farm."

"So Odie's strikin' . . . I figured as much."

"It was Odie that saved your life. Drove your car to the Grille away from the danger. Hardrock and Boney were closing the place up. They brought you home. You'd lost a lot of blood."

"Odie was my best friend, once."

"I know."

"I should've taken you and James Curtis to Oregon. We could've bought some land with my cousin after the war. I've wasted my life, DeDe." His eyes flashed with determination not to cry.

"We don't waste life. It wastes us, darlin'."

~ October 1952 ~

Finding nearly five hundred of its workmen still available, The Elk River Coal and Lumber Company, which remained completely shut down during the first week of the strike, resumed limited operations. But resumption brought Ed Heckelbech, UMW organizer, to the picket line and the violence began again. Jonas Zirka and his pickets commanded the only road into Widen and continued to cut off non-strikers who lived outside the town. All traffic in and out ceased.

As a warning to the few company men attempting to cross the picket line, the strikers yanked out the drivers and dynamited their empty cars. If a man attempted to cross the picket line again, a dozen strikers picked up the vehicle, shook it, and then rolled it with the driver inside this time, down Widen hill.

Odie spent his share of time on the picket line. Most nights were quiet. Only a couple times had they thrown rocks and bricks at cars. He'd been involved in rolling Delmar Tuller's car down the hill, but the scab had managed to limp away. Fruitless efforts to call the law proved the state troopers sided with the strikers. Each time they were notified of an incident they would arrive at the top of Widen hill, tip their hats to the picket line, shoot the breeze, and head back to Charleston, reporting no disturbance. If not for the company armed guards, it would've been a total takeover by force of the coal camp by union sympathizers.

The strikers' biggest victory was halting the train and forcing its passengers to unload. Odie wasn't near the car where he'd heard Zirka beat up a man and forced him at gunpoint to get off the train. Nevertheless, Odie stood shoulder-to-shoulder with the rest of the picketers as they dynamited the railroad trestles at Sand Fork and Robinson. He'd been part of the crew that uprooted telephone posts, cutting a quarter mile of line into short pieces. They had successfully isolated the town. He watched as the citizens of Widen went hungry for the first time in over a decade. The strikers had effectively placed a chokehold on the coal camp.

Stepping on generations of leaves, Odie perched himself on a log with a straight shot into the switch house. Guards had been posted to prevent the entry of possible saboteurs, but it was clearly a war now. A war with no help from the law for Bradley's company. The Attorney General and Governor had been voted into office with union votes, not company votes.

The switch houses controlled electric circuits into the mines. The strikers wanted to shut the mines down. Cutting the electric was Odie's idea. From the surrounding hilltops, rifle bullets went whining into the switch houses and cut power lines to the town.

Contemplating his aim, Josephine's words shot into his mind like a silver bullet meant for his heart. *She loves the boy, Odie. I weren't but her age when I married you.* He'd worked his wife into an early grave. His guilt caused him to spoil his girl and let her go off with James whenever she wanted. But he needed her at home. He wanted to keep her home. The place was falling apart without a woman's touch. Keeping Savina away from James Curtis wasn't going to be easy, and he couldn't be with her every moment.

Savina had missed plenty of school in the past year. There'd be no going back to school for her, not until the strike was over at least. Maybe not even then. She had new responsibilities now, bigger ones than going to high school.

Odie fired his last shot, taking out the electric in the mine.

Since coal could not be hauled out, the mine would close once again. Odie reached into his pocket for his tobacco pouch. He put a plug in his lower lip and hid in a grove of rhododendron until darkness would cover him going back down the mountain.

"You're from that little shithole town, Widen, right?" The man bagging groceries eyed the two men in front of him warily.

Harry Gandy, Joseph Bradley's assistant and operations boss, and Red King, loyal company man, found an old logging trail over the mountain and managed to get to Charleston to buy food, filling Harry's car to the brim.

"Yeah," said Red. "We're from Widen."

"What you doin' buyin' groceries here?"

"We're on vacation, just thought we'd stock up on the way to the beach." Harry tipped his hat and snickered as Red paid the bill.

The carload of food had to be unloaded at the first blown-out bridge by human chain like a bucket brigade passing the car's contents from hand to hand. They filled a railroad motor coach that had luckily been left in operating condition between the two blasted bridges.

At the next destroyed bridge, they repeated the same process, before the daily shipment finished its journey into Widen. At both transfer points, men worked while guarded by the protective rifles of company guards. Harry Gandy continued to sneak in carloads of food for weeks. Unloading, passing contents hand to hand, always under the watchful eyes of a man with a high-powered rifle in his hands.

Thirl stood by and grinned while the people, the non-strikers, filled their wheelbarrows and sacks with groceries. Taking nothing for himself, he thanked God for the oversized vegetable garden his wife insisted she grow every year. A garden that took up most of the back yard. And he was grateful for the fruit cellar she'd made him dig years ago. He'd been quarrelsome and nearly refused.

I've dug enough dirt for Bradley, I don't need to be doin' it in my own yard. It shamed him to think how contrary he'd been. She was always knowing things he didn't.

He was thankful for the hog she'd had butchered every year and the chickens she kept in the tiny corner of the back yard behind several feet of chicken wire. Chickens, as far as Thirl was concerned, were on a level not much higher than rats. He preferred deer meat and squirrel, but the store no longer stocked eggs. Able to collect them from her hens each morning, he'd stopped complaining.

DeDe's pantry was full of home-canned jars of raspberry and blackberry jams and jellies, pickled beans and corn. His house had turned into a small eatery. She fed those most desperate. Her breakfasts of bacon, eggs, and biscuits with sorghum molasses filled the bellies of many company men and their families over the next few months. Forks rang against plates, and the sound of glasses clinking was like angels singing in the rafters.

Every morning, the smell of bacon and coffee drifting into his bedroom, along with the mournful songs of the Carter Family on the radio, signaled to Thirl how lucky he was to have her. Even propped up against the refrigerator with her arms crossed watching people eat, she looked fetching. He sipped his coffee and gazed at the freckle on her forehead beneath the zigzag part of her hair. Her doe eyes melted him, made his chest and brain feel like corn mush. As the day wore on, the sensation hardened to a prickling along his spine, then to a low hum in his abdomen. He'd thought about her cooking and he thought about her naked — in equal amounts of time.

She was his gift from God. Because she knew things. Odd things. It wasn't the first time his wife had told him of a coming flood or the imminent death of a healthy neighbor. She'd predicted the famine a year ago. The day DeDe dropped her dusty beans on the porch because she'd 'seen' Josephine fall dead in her kitchen, gripping her heart over five miles away, Thirl never doubted her again. But he was never sure if she knew how much he loved her.

~ January 1953 ~

Winter came and stayed. Blizzard followed blizzard, each day gray with a fierce wind from the North. The hollows were deserted of man and beast, empty as any wasteland; the creeks were a perilous pile of ice. Coal trains couldn't get through, water pipes cracked; all of West Virginia was locked in, the air as brittle as kindling.

Snow fell at daybreak. Later a charcoal film would cover the day-old snow. January's drifts banked the windowpanes before it let up, the streets leveled, and the mountaintop above Widen faded like smoke. When the storm petered out at noon, the town lay steeped in fog — the ground-hugging kind that usually follows snow in valleys where coal camps nestle between the mountains. Fog by itself did not deter the citizens from carrying on with their lives, but fog with snow was something else. A person stayed inside, worn down by cold trips to the outhouse and restless sleep. Beneath this rag-and-bone sky, the only shadow cast was the violence of the strike. The snow smothered every inch of ground where the land bordered Buffalo Creek.

James Curtis followed a deer path over the mountain. Rabbits scattered into thickets of rhododendron. Bobcat tracks pocked the snow. He threaded his way over and through the mountain trails with less difficulty than a sliver of soap through his fingers. Her love pulled him like a solar eclipse — breathtakingly beautiful, spellbinding, and able to make him blind. Blessed with a young man's body, the coal dust had yet to bite at his insides. Passion and pleasure waited for him at the end of his path in a feather bed, in a secret place, a place they could be alone. A place where they'd made a pact to meet one night a week. Savina would tell Odie she was staying with Hephzibah, and Odie would never check on her for that one night, especially in Colored Holler.

The tiny cabin was warm and dark, and smelled of wood and pine. Once occupied by escaped slaves, it lay hidden under thistle brush, pine boughs, and rhododendron for the past hundred years. Jabo told stories of how it had been a small farm hidden in the hills of the federal state, long before Widen and its coal was an idea in the mind of a young man named Joseph Bradley.

Succumbing to his wife's nag, Jabo allowed the two young lovers to use it. The Kellys loved Savina. A white girl who had claimed them as her best friends. Nobody but Savina ventured into Colored Holler. Mama Ola, Jabo's mother, had tended Savina's sick bed months ago, bringing Hephzibah with her. The women became friends. An unusual relationship in Widen, which Odie Ingram tolerated and for which James Curtis was forever grateful. A relationship only a few families in Colored Holler knew about.

Savina had scrubbed the cabin until the skin on her hands bled raw. Highpockets and Percy, Jabo's sons, assisted James in making repairs to the cabin for the better part of three weeks, turning it from a shack into a one-room hideaway complete with a working fireplace, feather bed, table, oil lamp and a chair.

Careful not to be followed, James wended his way up a steep and snowy hill, eyeing the thicket of pines that held the cabin in its midst. He stood quietly for a moment, breathing deeply, his breath pluming in the frigid air. He picked up his heavy snow-covered boots, one after the other, stepping over and crunching into two feet of snow that blanketed the area. Smoke curled out of the chimney; she was already there. Savina's footprints, followed by her dog's, left a trail for him to follow. Rascal barked when James Curtis opened the door.

"Hush, boy . . . it's me . . . shut up, boy." The old beagle panted and whined; his tongue, as pink as raw bacon, hung out of his mouth.

James Curtis stomped the slush from his boots and walked over the threshold, tall and strong, like an oak tree covered with snow. Breathless, his nose dripped and ice crusted his hair. His cheeks were as red from the cold as maple leaves in autumn. James felt his chest and stomach constrict in a slow concussion of affection at the sight of her. She had told him he was always rushing her, pushing her into bed. His plans to keep the conversation light and move a little slower faded with each glance at her face.

He smiled, took off his coat and boots, laying them near the fire that warmed the room and cast a throbbing red glare on the bed. But her words fell soft on his heart like winter snowflakes.

"I hope you're hungry," she said. "There's fresh bread and butter I bought at the store this mornin'. And some candy bars . . . and I threw a couple Cokes out back in the drift."

His love for her kicked him hard in the chest. All he could utter was a squeak.

Savina stood by the fire, wearing the thin gold band she'd pulled out of its hiding place. A wedding ring he'd bought her from the Sears and Roebuck catalog. She wore it only in the cabin. Her faded dress hung below her knees and the pink of her elbow showed through the hole in her sweater. But James Curtis imagined she could wear a feed sack and be beautiful. Except most of her dresses weren't much better than the one she had on. His mother had offered to take her shopping in Summersville on more than one occasion, but Savina had always refused. It wasn't her apparel he cared about anyway. After they were married he'd make sure she had better dresses than the threadbare garments she owned.

Her face was flushed from the fire. Tears started in her eyes, but she blinked once and they were gone. Still breathless, James cupped her chin and pulled her hair back. He lifted it from her back to the top of her head and kissed her bare neck. Her face was so pretty. An angel face with a perfect nose and round cheeks, big wide blue eyes like her father's, and full lips that melted him with her kiss. Her hair was pretty, too, a light coppery brown, a shade lighter than his own, shining near the fire like a new penny.

Her head barely came to his armpit. The first time he laid her naked on a blanket in the woods, Savina's adolescent body splayed out tiny and shapeless on the ground. He had made love to her at sixteen. Her body was like a child's: no hips, bony legs, and breasts the size of fried eggs. But her breasts and hips had rounded and become ample in the two years they had been meeting secretly at the cabin. He looked forward to her eighteenth birthday. In five months he would remind Odie of his intent to marry his daughter, no matter how the strike turned out.

Savina slipped her shoes and socks off and sat on the floor. She propped her feet on a dry log, pulling her knees up to her chin. Her dress rode up, exposing her white panties. They glowed in the dim orange light of the fire. James sat down beside her crossing his legs, trying not to touch her. Suddenly, her hands were on the buttons of her dress.

Next to the heat of the blazing fire, the two wordless lovers stepped out of pools of clothes left on a makeshift wood floor, springing for the warmth of the feather bed and mounds of quilts.

James' hands skimmed over her skin. Her nails dug into his back and urged him closer. He found he could not think at all. His body, long and lean, moved over her tiny frame. This was not their first time, but his need for her was as continual as the snow falling outside the cabin's window. His touch was as light as the promises he whispered. She followed his lead through the moment when he was certain he would not stop to do what was right, and by the time their limbs were tangled together, James could not recall even one fornication scripture.

He kissed her until she was shaking for him to settle. When he did, when his mouth came over hers, she arched into him and closed her eyes. James moved as if nothing existed but the darkness of the cabin. Then, just as he could not hold on any longer, he was suddenly forcing her to look at him. "Nothing will ever keep me from you."

She smiled and he filled her.

Their bodies lay woven together, rocking to the rhythm of their own love song. Savina had lost every inhibition her world had bestowed upon her. Their world existed only in secret.

She fell asleep heavily in his arms, curled up against him. He tried to memorize the way she held her mouth, the way her dimple twitched when she slept, and the crooked part in her hair. Just like his mother's. He smelled her on his skin.

The moon rose full from behind the ridge, its light casting bright shadows of trees on the snow. He held her petite hand up to the pink sliver of moonlight that fell diagonally across the quilt, illuminating the tiny gold band. He smiled again. Someday, he could call her wife and she could wear the ring in public. He held it against his lips, forgetting everything but Savina and the path to Colored Holler.

In the early morning, the clouds broke open to clear sky and bright sun. The snow began to melt. It dropped in clumps from the bent limbs of trees; the sound of water ran in the creeks again. They lay under the warmth of quilts for some time, spooning and drowsy.

Savina inched back the covers, slid out of bed, careful to walk around the few floorboards that moaned. She laid a log on the empty grate. Pulling a quilt off the bed she curled up next to the hearth and poked at the red coals, hoping the sparks would ignite the log.

His voice was so quiet, it tipped over Savina's shoulder.

"Stop thinking, it gets your mind all tied into knots."

She jumped. "You scared me. And I ain't thinkin'."

"All liars will burn in the lake of fire . . . ain't that what Pastor Jessie says?"

"In that case, we're gonna fry."

He tried to swallow around the knot that had lodged in his throat. The truth sat in his stomach like something indigestible — a stone, a nickel. "In a couple months, this will all be over, maybe sooner. We'll be married and on our way to Ohio. I'm sure I can get a job with one of the rubber companies in Akron. We'll come back to visit, you and me and all our young'uns . . . it'll work out, wait and see."

A flicker of doubt crossed her face. Savina couldn't speak.

James crawled out of bed and stoked the fire hot so Savina could dress and not freeze. She was always cold. She hated winter. After pulling her sweater over her dress, Savina stepped into a pair of leggings made of thick wool and lined with flannel. She sat back down on the bed and smoothed her dress over the Confederate gray fabric.

"What are you laughing at?" she asked.

"Where'd you get them things?"

"They were Mommy's. Stop laughin'. They're warm."

"Sorry."

"No, you're not."

He squatted down in front of her at the edge of the bed, his limbs hinged like grasshopper legs. "They just remind me of how old-fashioned you are."

"I thought you liked that about me."

"I do. I love that about you." He took her hands and kissed them, then sang two lines of her favorite hymn, *"Some bright morning when this life is over, I'll fly away, to that home on God's celestial shore, I'll fly away . . . "*

She stood and pulled his head into her breast. "It's better when your daddy sings it."

"Lady, you ain't marrying me for my singing." He kissed her one last time. "I'm late and I have to go." He stood, pulled his jacket on and watched her take off the gold band. She hid it again, under the stone beside the hearth. It would lie there until next week.

"There's going to be a meeting at the Grille this morning and Daddy wants me to go with him. Wants to make sure I'm not being swayed by the strikers."

"When's it gonna end?" Savina tucked her scarf inside her coat and pulled another over her head as James held the cabin door open for her.

"Not soon enough. FBI says the union is violating the civil rights of miners. They say it's a federal offense to hinder anybody from going to work. I heard they been telling the strikers to get themselves a lawyer."

Savina pulled on her gloves. "Daddy said some of the men are askin' for their jobs back. But I say the strike ain't gonna end as long as the UMW gives the strikers free groceries. Only about fifty men left at the top of the hill."

"The worst fifty," James said.

"Daddy's just blind, James. He'll come around, soon as we're married. He won't want hard feelin's between the families. 'Specially with him and your daddy bein' old friends."

She giggled. "James Curtis, what are you doin'?"

"Making a snow angel. That's what you are, Savina Ingram soon-to-be Nettles. A snow angel."

He had fallen back into the drift by cabin's door, his legs and arms moving like a cartoon character in the snow.

It didn't occur to her not to get her dress wet. A second later she joined him in the snow, flapping her arms and legs up and down . . . creating her own snow angel. Her dog, Rascal, barked and jumped through the drift, enjoying the romp.

Laughing, James pulled her up. He looked down at the snow where their bodies had laid side-by-side, perfect angel depressions in the earth. Savina stepped over them with the utmost care, and seeing how careful she was, he stepped over them, too, then hugged her. Hugged her while their clothes were frozen, covered with snow up and down their bodies.

~ April 1953 ~

The sky was the color of old bones and some of the trees hadn't bloomed yet. The bare, gray maples and elms behind Widen were topped with tight red buds. From a distance they stained the hillsides a raw dark pink.

Thirl had recovered slowly over the winter, but his limp dictated his need for a cane. He'd gone back to work after Christmas as the picket line dwindled and the terror eased up, spreading itself into the surrounding countryside. When Odie's barn burned down the first week in April, Savina lit out the next morning to tell James.

"We lost two horses and our cow. The tractor was blown up. Daddy's been excused from the picket line for the week. I have to get home before he knows I'm gone. Lord, he's taken to carryin' his gun ever'where. Even to the outhouse. He's guardin' the farm, like some ole' chicken sittin' on her nest of eggs. It's doubtful he'll spend much time joinin' the strikers on the line. He's sure some poacher's gonna kill the rest of his horses and burn the house down. If I'm out of his sight for long, he comes lookin' for me."

James Curtis ran his hand through his auburn hair, tarnished from the mine's dust of working a double shift. He kissed her softly. Her mouth tasted of milk and berries. "I can't stand this any more. Why can't we be together, like we planned?"

"Won't be for a while . . . not 'til this damn strike's over." Savina said. "He knows when I leave for Colored Holler and he knows what time I'm supposed to be home."

DeDe overheard Savina's last statement from inside the house. She opened the screen door to serve her a glass of lemonade. All hugged up on the porch swing, Savina and James sat up straight as DeDe sat the glass on the railing and smiled.

"Thank ya, Missus Nettles," Savina said. She eyed the glass but pulled her heels up to rest on the swing instead, wrapping her arms over her knees and smoothing her skirt to her ankles.

"Why are you going to Colored Holler, Savina? If you don't mind me asking." DeDe noticed sadness stuck in the corners of Savina's eyes, like little bits of sleep.

Savina and James looked hard at each other, but she found her answer and quickly blurted it out. "You know old Mama Ola and her daughter-in-law, Hephzibah . . . they're my best friends." She took a sip of her lemonade and stepped over her words with caution. "Hephzibah cleans the Bradley's house over in Dundon and washes Mister Bradley's laundry. Mama Ola's son, Jabo, he fixes things 'round the house for Mister Bradley's wife. Jabo retired from the mine last year, with thirty years of service."

"How does she get over to his house? I know Jabo don't drive."

Savina scooped a mosquito off her arm and rubbed it between her palms. She hesitated, avoiding DeDe's eyes. "Ever notice how mosquitoes are like little butterflies, so dainty and easily broken?" She took a deep breath. "Mister Bradley's man picks her up. And sometimes I ride along to help her. Every other day or so. Jus' to make a few dollars and help Daddy make ends meet."

DeDe nodded then walked back into the house. She wouldn't ask how she got to be friends with Hephzibah or Mama Ola. Or why. Most folks in Widen stayed clear of Colored Holler.

~ Tuesday, April 14, 1953 ~

DeDe woke up, ran her tongue behind her teeth, and tasted bitter anguish. Unpleasant as chicory that melts on the tongue, turning it the twilight color of despair. Another storm had moved into the valley. The wind whipped pine branches back and forth, scratching across her bedroom window. Too windy to hang out clothes and sheets, her laundry would wait another day. She hated wind with no rain. At least the rain washed the air; this was wicked wind that picked up the coal splinters and hurled them at your skin. She felt an uneasiness in her spirit, and the top of her head tingled.

The scent of Thirl's Vitalis on the pillow greeted her as she stirred. Out of habit she moved her hand along the other side of the bed, feeling only the lingering warmth of the empty spot. He was always first out of bed. She hugged the abandoned pillow to her chest and inhaled the scent of his hair, letting herself drift a while longer.

Mornings like this one she was grateful for the bathroom Thirl had built. Only thing outhouses were good for was to know the bathroom habits of your neighbors. She heard Thirl maneuvering his stiff leg through the kitchen. She saw him lay his Bible on the table, limp into the tiny bathroom, then fill the basin with warm water to shave. It was time to get James out of bed or they'd both be late.

In the cold kitchen, DeDe prepared both lunch boxes for her men, filling each Thermos with boiling coffee. After stirring the coal in the stove, she glanced out the front room window at the first drops of rain pinging the panes. Her heartbeat quickened at the sight of two men rushing up to her front door.

The screen door was yanked open, causing the spring to emit a startled twang. They knocked hard and fast. Whoever it was on the other side of the door clearly wasn't worried about disturbing the household.

Thirl poked his head out of the bathroom — shirtless, wiping the remains of shaving cream off his face with his towel. DeDe could hear him pulling on his pants, his belt buckle jangling. "Who is at this time of the mornin'?"

"Company men, I'm sure." DeDe opened the door and found Dewey Wilson standing behind Jugg Pyle. The wind flung rain in their faces like cold spit.

"Morning," said DeDe.

"Thirl inside?"

"Getting ready for work. You need to talk to him now?"

"Yes, Ma'am," said Jugg. "We . . ."

Dewey interrupted with a cold stare, "We ain't got time for pleasantries. Didn't come fer no tea party . . . we gotta talk to Thirl."

"Hold on, *gentlemen*. I'll get my husband."

She opened the door and led them to the kitchen. DeDe knew Thirl was listening and probably dressed by now. James Curtis hadn't stirred from his room. She peeked her head inside his door. "Get up, son; we have visitors."

A groggy voice squeaked in the darkness. "Who is it, Mama?"

"Company men here to see your daddy. Get up now. You're both gonna be late as it is."

Thirl had walked into the kitchen to find the men standing by the stove with their hats in their hands. "You fellas want some coffee?"

"Ain't got time for coffee," said Dewey.

Jugg stared at Thirl's clean face, rubbing the stubble on his own. "Some of the men had a meetin' at the church early this mornin'. We knew you wouldn't want to be a part of this, but me and Dewey thought we'd at least let you know, on account of you bein' shot and for all your misery."

"Just tell him, for Christ sake." Dewey blew a wrathful breath from his nostrils, while his huge brown hand came thundering down on the table. "It's like this. From the start, the comp'ny has admonished us to avoid any action that might be construed as retaliation against the strikers. But we're tired, Thirl, tired of turnin' the other cheek. You know it weren't comp'ny men that burned Odie Ingram's barn. Strikers did it to their own to make us look like a bunch of vigilantes. Here's the deal. Bosses don't know yet, 'cept you. A group of the men are takin' a bulldozer up to the head of the Widen road. They plan to plow the striker's headquarters off the hill. We're through with 'em. We want to get back to work. Comp'ny's losin' money, and it might destroy the town if the strike goes on any longer. We ain't safe in our own homes. Time we did somethin' beside sit by and let them take pot shots at our cars and our families. Tub Perry's got a dozer he used when he worked on the roads. He's on his way now."

James Curtis bounded out of his room, his shirttail hanging, one boot on and holding the other. "Y'all cain't do that! Somebody's gonna get killed!"

"Son! Calm down. Get yourself some breakfast." Thirl threw a glance at DeDe to keep James Curtis out of the conversation.

She laid her hand on James' shoulder. "You men ever lost a loved one? Other than your parents, have either of you laid a dear soul into the ground? I'm not prepared to lose my husband or my son because you boys want to act like a bunch of John Waynes and plow the strikers into the dirt."

Dewey Wilson spit a stream of tobacco juice into the pop bottle he pulled out of his pocket. A steel-eyed glare was his only response.

Jugg, the town's undertaker for the past ten years, quoted from the book of Job, "The Lord gave and the Lord hath taken away."

"I prefer Deuteronomy," she said and looked hard at the men. "I will render vengeance to mine enemies. Vengeance is the Lord's work . . . not ours!"

Suddenly, Dewey pulled an ancient gun out of his side pocket and spun the barrel like John Wayne in Red River, making a crooked aim out the window. His eyes were loose-closed; a trembling rim of white showed between his lashes. The tip of his tongue stuck out of the corner of his mouth. His red finger tightened on the trigger. "I'm ready to help the Lord out, what about you, Jugg? I think you need to calm your wife down, Thirl, this here talk is between the men."

DeDe picked up a dishtowel and pretended to clean off the table. "And who do you think suffers the most? The men?"

"Dewey, put your gun away. My wife is privy to all I know. She has a say in what goes on in this house, gentlemen. I believe she's fixed breakfast for your families a time or two. And if you want to discuss business in my wife's kitchen, you're gonna have to listen to her."

Jugg nudged Dewey toward the door. "We're sorry, Ma'am." He nodded to all three of the Nettles family. "We just wanted to let you know what happened at the meetin'. But ya cain't stop it, Thirl. It's already started."

Dewey slipped his gun back in his coat pocket, spit in his bottle again, shoved his hat on his head and stormed out the door.

"Good thing he ain't a union man." Jugg's nervous chuckle brought no reaction from DeDe or Thirl. "I apologize for Dewey; he ain't been himself lately. Strikers rolled his car down the hill last week. He'll settle down. I don't see this as an act of violence, just us peaceful men bein' fed up. That's all. Rest easy, Ma'am. Ain't gonna be any killin'."

"And a cat's butt ain't puckered," said DeDe, throwing her kitchen towel on the table and leaving the room.

Off the state highway, in the middle of the company road at the top of Widen hill, the strikers had set up their field station. Benches and old automobile seats ringed a cluster of fifty-gallon drums. James Curtis had heard Odie refer to them as fire barrels.

As men for the union scattered right and left to safety, the bulldozer tracked into their camp, pushing barrels, benches, lunch boxes and accumulated trash across the road and over the lip of a deep gully.

Whooping and hollering, Dewey, Jugg, and a hundred company men drove back into town, honking their car horns and lighting firecrackers as if they deserved a parade. Their celebration could be heard from one end of town to the other.

"They're rejoicing for the wrong reason," said DeDe. "Strike's not over, the battle's just begun." She rocked back and forth on her porch swing.

Her neighbor Pearle squatted on an apple crate and broke pole beans. "If ya ask me, I'm hopin' that's the end of it. I ain't been to Strange Creek to see my grandbabies since this thing started last year."

The people of Widen walked out of their homes that evening, gathered on porches talking and feeling free to move about. They allowed their children to roam the streets once again. A few young boys carried baseball bats and gloves toward the baseball park. A young girl rode her bike toward the Grille.

DeDe sensed the tingling in her head again . . . and thunder rolled in the distance.

~ Saturday, April 18, 1953 ~

"Can we come in?" the woman said, with a sheepish smile. "It's rainin' fit to start the second flood out heah."

DeDe recognized Hephzibah Kelly and her husband Jabo. "Of course, where are my manners? I wasn't expecting guests. Today being Saturday, the men are out doing whatever it is men do on Saturdays." She smiled.

Jabo returned her smile, but Hephzibah held a steady gaze into the house.

DeDe opened the front door wide, while her unexpected guests pulled open the screen door.

Jabo was so tall, he stooped when he walked in. DeDe could see his eyes register everything immediately.

"Sho is uh nice place y'all got heah."

"It'll do until we get our mansion up yonder." Neither Hephzibah nor Jabo registered a grin, or acknowledged they'd heard her. They stared at her furniture, the buck head on the wall, and the linoleum on her kitchen floor. "Well, please, come sit at the table. Would you like anything cold to drink? It's gettin' warmer. Summer's 'round the corner."

DeDe's instant politeness smoke-screened her quest to find out about a person. The minute she talked to anyone her eyes were everywhere — glaring into their soul. Within seconds she had strangers pegged. It scared the hell out of James Curtis, but fascinated Thirl.

She led them to her kitchen table and motioned for them to have a seat. DeDe didn't remember Hephzibah being so pretty. Her hair was dark as a crow's wing, smoothed back, but frizzed out around her forehead. Her licorice smooth skin contributed to her looking younger than her years. A blue cotton waistless dress hung from her shoulders to her knees. Her stockings were rolled down to her ankles.

"We came heah, Missus Nettles . . ."

"Oh please, call me DeDe."

"Miz DeDe, we came heah 'cause we good friends of Savina. Your James and Savina aimin' to marry. I knows that ain't no secret."

"No, but I believe it'll happen later than sooner, with the strike and all."

"True, Miz DeDe. Tha's fuh sho."

Jabo dropped his head wearily. His gray hair curled in tight clumps around his ears. A frost of unshaven stubble smudged his chin, and his eyes were light blue to the point of grayness. Veins ran along the top of each thick bicep. His pants hung loose and rumpled.

Hephzibah eyed her husband and continued. "You knows I work for Mist' Bradley."

"Yes, I heard that."

"I try to stay outa the white man's business. I do. But Jabo and me, we love Savina like our own. And we love your boy, too, Miz DeDe. He's a good boy. Savina say we can trust you."

"Thank you, Hephzibah." DeDe smiled. "How long have you known James Curtis?"

Jabo stared at his wife. "Oh . . . well, me and James Curtis shoot da breeze sometimes when da women folk visit . . . after they finish work over at da Bradley house."

"Oh."

"I'll state the reason for our call. Jabo do it better though. You tell her. You tell Miz DeDe what you heah."

Jabo slid down in his seat, steepled his fingers and looked across the table to the wall.

"When ah retired last year from da mine, Mist' Bradley offer me a handyman job at his house. Fixin' whatnot 'round his place. Big place, you ever seen it?"

"No, I've heard it's lovely."

"Yes'um. Anyway. Ah was layin' a new rug in they dinin' room two days ago and ah heah Mist' Bradley talkin' on da phone. Comp'ny men ought not to make da strikers mad. They gone start a war, Miz DeDe. It gone be a bad one. Strikers took over da garage in Dille as a new headquarters and made it a cook shack too."

DeDe grabbed her throat, and her eyes filled. "What else do you know, Mr. Kelly?"

"Only reason Ah'm stickin' my ole' neck out, is 'cause Savina love James Curtis. She loves her daddy, too. Hephzibah and me jus' want yo family to be safe. Tha's all."

"Anything else?"

"Someone at da FBI owes Mist' Bradley a favor. He calls Mist' Bradley from time to time. Sent two deputies — askin' da strikers lots of questions. Pretty rough stuff, what they say to each other." Jabo paused and lowered his voice.

"Mist' Bradley say, iffen he could fine a way to split 'em, to make all Widen men see that da UMW's jus' a bunch of lef-wing troublemakers, don't have their best interests at heart, well, then, this strike be over in a week." Jabo paused again and stared out the window this time. "Ain't gone happen, tho'."

"He say, the UMW sees Elk River Coal and Lumber as a test case. Win heah, they win da whole state. They dug in for da duration. As long as it takes. Now, 'cause of da comp'ny men shovin' pickets off da hill, the union is cocky as hell. 'Cause of they threats, they think Mist' Bradley gone throw in da towel, jus' give dem whatever they damn

want. Mist' Bradley say it'll go on for a while, and probably be some
men gettin' hurt or worse."

"Later, ah heard two of dem union fellas walkin' in da woods near
my place. They been collectin' lots of guns. They laugh and say they
gone shoot the first man drivin' in the comp'ny convoy one mornin'
this week. Don't know what mornin'. Could be this town be havin' a
few funerals next week, he say."

"Why didn't you tell this to Mister Bradley?"

"Ah jus' a handyman, Miz DeDe. We don't speak much. Like ah
say, ah don't stick this ole' neck out for jus' anybody. Still, it gone on
too long. Dem comp'ny mens, they cain't take they family in and out
of Widen. Been months for mos' of 'em, 'ceptin on Election Day. Da
only day they able to get out of Widen. Thank da Lawd, nobody got
killed."

"Worse part, Savina's daddy, Mist' Odie, he sent word to Mist'
Bradley at da house today. He say he die before he work in non-union
mine, and he say he take a few Comp'ny men wid him."

DeDe straightened in her chair. "I've been sitting here thinking,
I'm going to have a special women's prayer meeting at my house this
Wednesday evening. I'm inviting every woman in this town. Hephzibah,
you and Mama Ola are more than welcome to join us."

Hephzibah crossed her arms in front of her. "That'd be nice, but I
don't know how the white ladies in your church take to coloreds invadin'
they prayer meetin'."

"You have as much right to divine protection as the rest of us. I
want you here, praying with us."

Jabo chuckled. "Oh we protected. We do like da Hebrews. We
sprinkle da blood over our door, tell da Angel of Death to Passover
this house. It work too. You should try it." He pushed his chair back
from the table and grinned as one does when disclosing an unsettling
secret.

"Da rich man thinks we's all niggers, Miz DeDe. They call my
home nigger holler. But all Widen is nigger holler. You and yo' kind
well as me and mine. You jus' got a little more jiggle room, tha's all."

DeDe caught Hephzibah's eyes roaming around her kitchen. "We're
not rich, Mister Kelly. Nobody in this town is rich, except Mister
Gandy and, of course, Mister Bradley."

Hephzibah stood and pushed her chair into the table. "Jabo don't see what I see. They's not rich, neither. I sees they socks, they underwear. I wash they clothes and I sees how Mist' Bradley worry over his bills. Some days don't even get home 'til way late at night. And his wife is sick. Always a guard there protectin' his home with a gun. Nah, he ain' no rich man."

Jabo held out his hand. "Was nice talkin' to you today. Ah hope we didn't put yuh out none."

DeDe smiled. "I enjoyed the company." His touch was warm, firm, and yet gentle. A double-handed shake. Preachers always grabbed you with both hands, one squeezing your palm and the other squeezing your wrist. "You're a minister of the gospel?"

"Yes'um. How you know that, Miz DeDe? Lawsamercy," Jabo chuckled. "Ah preach every Sunday in our church up da holler. Come visit sometime?"

DeDe's eyes opened wide, her mouth quivered for words. She'd never received an open invitation from a colored church, nor had anticipated attending a service surrounded by Negros. But there was always a first time. "Yes, when the strike is over, I'll be glad to visit. Thank you for your kind comments about my son, and thank you for warning us. I hope my emergency prayer meeting will reach God's ear."

"Ah be bringin' Hephzibah and my mama by Wednesday long 'bout seven. They's prayin' women. Prayer warriors. It be after dark, that way nobody sees. That be fine wid you?"

"Yes, of course." Her eyes met Hephzibah's and the two women embraced. Another first.

~ Wednesday, April 22, 1953 ~

Opposing sides filled DeDe's house quickly. Women sympathetic to the union and company women, who wanted the strike to end, managed to exchange a few polite nods, stares and smiles. The ladies, lacking for words, gathered in opposite rooms of DeDe's house — company women in the kitchen and union women in the front room. Despite the heat, tension chilled the air. Some hadn't seen or spoken to each other in months. It wasn't until a tiny old lady named Ossie Casto, whose flesh was the color of toadstools and whose memory was so eroded she thought they'd come to pray for President Roosevelt, stood and sang the wedding song, *Oh Promise Me,* that giggles erupted throughout the house.

Stifled words longing to be said spilled out of their mouths and the rooms converged on one another. Long hugs, apologies, and passing the tissue box — DeDe heaved a sigh of relief and put her purse away. The healing was long overdue.

Opal Hamrick arrived late. A wide-bottomed, pale, hard-looking woman of forty-five or so, she carried a Jello mold in her hand. Her husband, Jack, had remained on the strike line despite being fired by the company. Opal hugged DeDe so hard her hair had to be combed again.

"DeDe, you're so skinny, I'll bet you have to squat to fart."

Tessa Butcher, Bonehead's wife, was nine months pregnant with her fourth child. Her swollen bare legs above tight ankle socks held the interest of every woman in the room. A topic of conversation, along with possible remedies, it was a welcome diversion from the strike.

Each woman searched for conversation to divert themselves from the past months of living in a war-torn town. Sylvia Dodrill complained she'd lost her shape with her last child. But Fleeta Thigpen disagreed, stating the only thing wrong with Sylvia was her faded yellow hair clung too close to her skull like some giant ear of corn with not enough silk.

The Digg sisters, Lottie and Goose, busied themselves in DeDe's kitchen, making lemonade and cutting the crust off cheese sandwiches. Tootsie Barrow, Imogene Sanders, and Edith Holcomb, a heavyset woman with thin legs and wide feet, exchanged recipes. Pearle Gibson arrived late with her Bible-toting Aunt Hattie Mae from Summersville.

The old woman walked over to DeDe and immediately knit her brows together. She gave DeDe's hand a gentle squeeze. "The Lord holds a flashlight as we walk through the valley of the shadow of death, dear. He helps us find new life in the midst of the valley."

Embarrassed, Pearle grabbed her arm and pulled her to a seat in the corner. She mouthed "sorry" to DeDe. But DeDe smiled. She smiled because it was all she could do; she chilled for a moment as Hattie Mae's words shook her to the core. Immediately, DeDe turned her attention to the other women in an attempt to rid her mind of the old lady's words and to remind herself that the room wasn't cold. In fact, she had opened all the windows. The temperatures had broken records that early May evening. The heat and humidity in the room was stifling. Some stood to catch a breeze while their dress hems lifted in the hot air and moved around their legs like a sigh in church.

When DeDe answered the door, and Hephzibah and Mama Ola stepped into the house wearing their church dresses and holding their Bibles in the crooks of their arms, the room shut down. Not one woman's chin quivered. A dozen pairs of inquisitive eyes glared at them.

DeDe spoke aloud, in a commanding voice. "I invited Hephzibah Kelly and her mother-in-law to visit with us this evening. You all know Mama Ola. I prayed hard about it. And I believe God laid it on my heart for them to be here. We are all women, women of faith, women who want an end to the strike, but above that, we are women who know how to love. Women who want our families safe. These women do too. And they have voiced their love for my family. I am proud to have them in my home tonight. I want you all to welcome them."

The words dashed against her teeth, the wave of emotion unable to carry them farther.

Mama Ola's wide smile showed a mixture of gaps and brown teeth. Her white hair glistened against her dark brown skin.

DeDe's pleading glance fell on Opal, who chewed her gum in short, irregular snaps. If Opal would accept them, the rest would follow. Opal stood and walked over to Hephzibah. "Your boy, Highpockets. He did a fine job buildin' my hog pen last summer. Got good manners. It's nice to meet ya both. Cm'on ladies, meet DeDe's guests."

DeDe breathed deeply. A breeze moved against her sweaty back. She pulled her sticky blouse from against her skin and decided to stand where she was and let the air dry her clothes while the rest of the women surrounded her two new friends from Colored Holler, welcoming them in the name of the Lord.

The social hour had passed. DeDe intended to devote the next hour to the scriptures, reading and praying. She scarcely found her voice as she preached. "I'm going to read the scripture Pastor Jessie read last week in service. I believe it's appropriate for this evening."

"Finally, my brethren, be strong in the Lord, and in the power of his might. Put on the whole armour of God, that ye may be able to stand against the wiles of the devil. For we wrestle not against flesh and blood, but against principalities, against powers, against the rulers of the darkness of this world, against spiritual wickedness in high places. Wherefore take unto you the whole armour of God that ye may be able to withstand in the evil day, and having done all, to stand. Stand therefore, having your loins girt about with truth, and having on the breastplate of righteousness; And your feet shod with the preparation of the gospel of peace; Above all, taking the shield of faith, wherewith ye shall be able to quench all the fiery darts of the wicked. And take the helmet of salvation, and the sword of the Spirit, which is the word of God."

The darkness from the outside permeated the room, even with DeDe's single lamp that sat on her bookcase. The night sounds of frogs and crickets, and an occasional dog's bark were the only noise. Then, as if on cue from God, these sounds also ceased.

There was no breeze to speak of. The air around them felt heavy and dead. The screen door to the porch was open and DeDe's white chiffon curtains at the windows suddenly blew gently inward, billowing like angel's wings, as if some supernatural being was coming into the room for a landing. Lottie put a hand to her mouth. The breeze stopped, the women froze, and their fanning ceased. Nothing moved, not even the wind.

The singing came from outside. As if a choir were floating up Nicholas Street. A soft carol of voices. The song escalated in strength, grew stronger, louder, and became recognizable — a chorus. A mass of voices singing in a heavenly language. The sound grew as if someone had turned up the volume on a radio. It floated through the doorway and as it did, a light came with it, filling the room. It expanded and appeared to seep into every mind and heart. And then, just as it came, it descended out the west window, as if someone opened a vacuum and the singing was sucked out.

No one could speak for a period of unknown time, as every watch on every wrist had stopped. Even the mantel clock on DeDe's bookcase ceased to chime the hour. Sounds of murmured praise came first from their lips. Hephzibah whispered to Opal that she saw tongues of fire over each woman in the room. Opal reached for her hand and smiled. "I see 'em too."

Questions oozed from every mouth . . . "Did you hear it?" "Yes, what did you hear?" "What was it? A choir?" "Angels, yes it was angels singing."

Sylvia and Tessa believed it was the radio next door and an electric surge. Lottie and Goose cried. Ossie, Opal, Tootsie, Imogene, Fleeta and Edith sang, *"Praise Him, Praise Him, Praise Him in the mornin', Praise Him in the noontime, Praise Him when the sun goes down . . ."*

One by one, the ladies bid their teary good-byes. Pearle pulled DeDe aside after most had gone and a few waited for their rides. "Was it a sign? A good sign or a bad sign? What'd it mean?"

Hattie Mae couldn't hold back any longer. "It was a sign of the second comin'."

"Oh, hush, Hattie Mae! You don't know that." Pearle shook her head at her elderly aunt.

"I know somebody's comin'," she said.

Hephzibah looked at Mama Ola. "What you think, Mama?"

The old black woman stared at DeDe and grinned. "She know. She know what it was."

Pearle's hand, still on DeDe's arm, trembled. She asked her again. "What do you know, DeDe?"

"I know it's late. Thank you all for coming."

~ **Thursday, April 23, 1953** ~

"He must be a new hire!"

"Let's roll him!"

"Teach him not to take our jobs!"

The 1947 Ford truck bounced and crashed down through a different grove of trees and brush this time. Having been removed from their previous headquarters, the striking men found a steeper embankment than the Widen hill to roll cars. Each company man rolled narrowly escaped with his life; many nursed wounds months later. Scars and broken bones were not an uncommon sight in Widen. Doctor Vance had a new patient in his office nearly every week from a fight or a car having been shoved to the bottom of a gully.

Jonas Zirka bounded toward the truck, to scare the man inside with a few pot shots and laugh while he watched him run like a coward into town — same as he'd done with the rest of the men they had rolled.

He yelled to the men back up the hill, "You see this feller get out of his truck?"

"No, where'd he go?"

"Nobody here. Not a trace of him. Nothin' in the truck to say who he was."

The air was agitated and humid, rough as sandpaper in the lungs. Coal dust filled the afternoon sky. Static disrupted the gospel songs of Mom and Dad Speer on the radio. An early afternoon storm rumbled in the distance. Inside, the house became dark. DeDe lit two kerosene lamps that held their flames like shivering butterflies. She thought of Savina.

Last night's prayer meeting phenomenon had kept her awake until morning. Drowsy, she rested her head against the back of her chair. Dreamy and drifting into slumber, DeDe jerked awake in the midst of a strange dream when she heard the knock. She moved in slow motion as if wading through waist-deep water. Thunder rolled again, nudging the storm closer to the valley.

When she opened the door, it sounded as if a seal had been broken.

"May I help you?" DeDe attempted to smother her yawn.

"Howdy-do, Ma'am. I'm looking for Odie Ingram's place. Do you know Savina Ingram and where I might find her?"

Despite the smell of the oncoming storm, DeDe inhaled the woodsmoke of his voice followed by the fragrance of apple blossoms floating through the screen door.

Her tone was soft and clear, with a slight touch of fascination. "I know her, yes. May I ask who you are?"

He grabbed the rim of his black felt hat and tipped it. Nodding his head curtly, he said in a rugged voice, "Sorry, Ma'am."

His apology drew a small smile from DeDe.

"My name's Herald. Herald Wingate."

He was an odd-looking man, thin, tall, and handsome in an out-of-the-ordinary way. His colorless eyes, long elfin nose, unshaven face, and powerful hands were pale against his ragged and dirty clothes. His tattered pants ended at scuffed leather boots. High cheekbones suggested Cherokee blood, but his presence was like an offensive profanity against the backdrop of pink impatience in her flowerbed behind him. It was comparable to finding lice on a little girl's head.

"I'm an old friend of her mother's. I wanted to check on the child and see how she was doing."

"So you're from . . ."

"Bethlehem, Ma'am."

"Oh, yes. I remember now. Jo lived in Pennsylvania before she moved here with Odie. 'Bout the same time Thirl and I moved to Nicholas Street in Widen."

"That's right. I promised her mother I'd check on her now and then. I knew Missus Ingram was dying and I'd had a few conversations with her. She really didn't want to leave Savina alone to take care of Mister Ingram. But these things can't be helped sometimes."

The brim of his hat was pulled down low enough to hide his strange-looking eyes again. Long dark hair grazed the shoulders of his blue wool jacket with holes in both elbows.

DeDe recalled the Depression years when her mother befriended many a man walking through Matewan with his family, or alone. Ragged men, poor men — her mother had fed them and sent them on their way with a sack of salt pork and biscuits.

All of a sudden she found herself standing in the middle of her front room with a stranger.

"Would you like a bite to eat? I have some leftover ham from breakfast. I could fry you a couple eggs."

"That'd be nice, Ma'am. I thank ye kindly."

"You can wash up in there." She pointed to the bathroom.

DeDe cracked two eggs in the skillet and listened for her guest to return to the kitchen again. She propped her purse on her cutting board, just in case. When he emerged, his hands glowed raw and pink from the scrubbing he had given them, and he smelled like lye soap mixed with apple blossoms. He nodded and took a seat at the table. His left hand rested against his leg with the palm turned out and a New Testament held loosely between his thumb and two fingers.

"Smells mighty good, Ma'am." He ate slowly and articulated words that sounded like music, his voice echoing through the house. For the next hour Herald Wingate pulled topics of religious conversation from thin air and made DeDe a verbal bouquet of Biblical subjects irresistible to her. She'd never met a man with knowledge of the scriptures like this man.

DeDe stood near the stove, looking down at the dusty, bedraggled stranger. The first stranger she couldn't peg. Her back remained gracefully straight, but the loose knot of hair at her nape quivered with her indecision. Was he who he said he was and should she tell him where Savina lived?

~ Sunday, May 3, 1953 ~

As night faded and the morning sky drowned the stars, Thirl heard the screen door stretch on its rusted spring.

"DeDe home Thirl?"

"No, Pearle . . . she leaves early on Sunday. Teachin' Sunday School this mornin'."

"Oh, right. I suppose she told you about our prayer meetin' last week?"

"Sure did."

Pearle walked back out the door. "Guess you know then, it's the women in this town that God talks to."

Thirl and James Curtis smiled at each other across the table. "Your mama tell you anything about this strange new fella, Herald Wingate? I heard he been spotted several times around town the past week. But seems only the women have met him. Word has it he's a guest at the Ingram farm. An old friend of Josephine's. You meet him?"

"No, ain't met him, but I'm sure Odie wouldn't let him stay there unless he knew him. Kind've makes me a little uneasy though."

"Why's that?"

"Savina says he's been preaching to the women. Even been up to Colored Holler. Telling them to pray for the peace and safety of the town. To reach out to God, trust and obey Jesus. That this town is on the verge of destruction unless the women pray harder because the men, with the exception of Pastor Jessie, don't pray at all. Just make a mess of things."

"Next time this Herald fella comes to the house, I want to meet him."

"If you can see him. Hardrock said Sylvia was talking to the air out in the yard a day ago, and he asked her what she was doing. She said, 'I was talking to Herald Wingate. What — you think I talk to the trees?'"

~ Thursday, May 7, 1953 ~

Savina stood with her colorless lips apart, while a shudder ran through her frame. "What?"

Herald Wingate sat on the steps that led up to her porch. He held his Bible in his hand and pointed in the direction of Dille. "I said your daddy's in danger. The next shift of men driving into Widen for work, they're all in danger. There's a group of pickets at the cook shack, laying in wait. Your daddy's one of them. This violence must stop, Savina. God is not pleased."

"How can I stop it? Why don't you stop them? How do you know?"

"Heard voices while I was praying in the woods yesterday. I came here, to Widen, for three reasons: to preach to those with open hearts and minds — turns out that's the women, to check on *you* for your mama, and to warn your father. My work is done; it's time for me to take leave." He closed his Bible and stuffed it into his coat pocket. "I advised your father not to go to the cook shack today. He told me to mind my own business and that it was time I vacate his farm. Savina, all you can do is gather with the women in town and pray."

"But you just got here. Is it too cold in the barn for ya? It's not as good as the old one that burned down. What we have now is just temporary 'til we can afford to build a new one. Daddy won't let strangers in the house. He always sends drifters in need of a meal to the barn to sleep."

"No, the barn was fine. The horses were pleasant company. I thank ye both for your hospitality."

"I want to talk to you more about Mommy. Please stay a few more days."

"Can't. I told you everything I know about your mama. She's in heaven now — you'll have to be satisfied with that.

"But you knew her from the time she was born, didn't you? How old are you?"

"Old enough. Too old." He smiled. His voice was like music.

"You sure don't look it." A bittersweet smile eased across her lips. Lightening flashed in the distance. Savina pulled her sweater closer to her neck and shifted her gaze to the lowering sky. "I think another storm is comin' over the mountains. I need to bring daddy home. I can take you as far as the cook shack, Mister Wingate."

"You shouldn't go. Go to town and pray with the women instead. My talking to your father hasn't done any good. You'll not bring him home, Savina. Men are creatures of free will. But these men won't stop until innocent blood is shed — the town will not recover from it. I'm going into Widen to say goodbye to Missus Nettles and a few other ladies gathering for a prayer meeting this morning."

"Maybe you should meet some of the other men in town. Try to convince them."

"Like I said, my business here is done."

Savina hugged him quickly, ran up the porch and into the house to grab her purse and her daddy's car keys. When she came back out she wanted to ask him to please stay for church on Sunday. But he was gone.

"Signs and wonders follow them that believe," Pearle raised her hand. "I believe I have a testimony."

The ladies that gathered in DeDe's front room shouted, "Bless God, tell us, Sister Gibson." "Yes, speak to us, Sister Gibson. Go on and testify, Sister."

"I believe in miracles. I believe God is going to end this strike soon. I believe he's given me the strength to endure until the end. Union or non-union. We're all God's children. I want to testify to the strength I've felt since the night we all heard the angels sing . . ."

"We don't know for sure what that was, Pearle!" Sylvia Dodrill shook her head.

"Oh ye of little faith." The voice startled the women, causing them to jump and turn their heads to the screen door. Herald Wingate stood on the other side, curling the brim of his hat in his hands. No one had heard the usual sound of footsteps stomp up the clapboard porch.

DeDe stood. "Mister Wingate, you shouldn't walk up on people like that. Would you like to come in and join us?"

"No, thank ye. But keep praying ladies; my time here is up, I have to get back home. I came to say good-bye and that there's a storm coming. And to pray for Savina Ingram."

DeDe felt her insides turn to mush. "Why? Herald, is Savina alright?"

"She's gone to warn her father. There's danger on the roads this morning, ladies. Remain here and pray through to victory. Call on the forces of heaven to hold back the darkness that's coming."

"Don't! Don't scare us like this anymore, Mister Wingate!" Sylvia stood and stomped to the door. "He's an old beggar that's waltzed into town and you ladies think he's the voice of God!" Sylvia glared at him on the other side of the screen. "Stop it! Stop scaring us. Go home to wherever you're from. Leave us alone!"

"Sylvia!" DeDe shrieked. "Sit down!"

The sky had grown dark, until it was the color of a bruise beneath the skin. Lightning flashed in a dry sky and thunder rolled through the hollow.

"Sorry to bother you, ladies. Good-bye again."

"Wait, Mister Wingate!" DeDe ran out the screen door and down the porch following him into the street. "Please forgive Sister Sylvia. Her husband's been sick and . . ."

"He has black lung. I know Missus Nettles. Mister Dodrill is dying. Somebody has to have faith for him. His wife does not."

"Won't you stay a while longer?"

"Actually, Ma'am, I've got coal dust on my feet. It's time to shake it off. You've been kind to me. I thank ye. Good-bye, now." He tipped his hat one last time, walked down Nicholas Street and disappeared around the corner.

DeDe stood in a solemn gaze, watching Herald Wingate walk away carrying no pack, sack, or piece of luggage. Only the top of his Bible stuck out of his pocket. Her mouth moved whispering the scripture that flowed off her tongue. *And whosoever shall not receive you, nor hear you, when ye depart thence, shake off the dust under your feet for a testimony against them. Verily I say unto you, It shall be more tolerable for Sodom and Gomorrah in the Day of Judgment, than for that city.*

As the convoy of miners on their way to work passed the striker's headquarters in the pouring rain, a blaze of rifle and shotgun fire hit the lead car. Next to Odie, Jennings Roscoe Bail fired his .35 caliber steel jacketed rifle. In the dull gray light of the cook shack, Jennings' complexion was pitted and pocked like an old bone. Odie's stomach soured and bile came up in his throat. He swallowed it back down.

"You hit him!"

"Son of a bitch! I sure did! Maybe I can get me another . . ." Jennings shot again. "Hey, where you goin'? This's jus' like ole' times, shootin' at the Germans! Stay and have some fun!"

"You're crazy!"

Jennings crouched by an open window, his coat flapping, his face pinched, mouth a tight, thin line. "Don't stand there like a damn idiot, Odie. You're a union man, don't tell me you're goin' scared on us! Here." He held up another rifle, his knuckles white, and pushed it at Odie. "Use one of mine!"

It was on Odie's tongue to say that he was a coal miner, and miners didn't shoot at people, when he realized it was not only irrelevant, it was untrue. He'd done plenty of shooting the past few months, and every time he used his gun, it could've easily killed somebody he knew . . . old friends . . . family.

"I think I hit me another comp'ny bastard! Don't run off, Odie. This's what we been waitin' for!"

Odie tossed Jennings's rifle to the floor of the cook shack and ran in the direction of the gully. Panic vibrated in his head, shouting and chaos echoed in his ears. His gut hurt. The killing wasn't what he wanted. Not really. He'd talked a big talk but when it came down to it, he ran — a coward. He couldn't see for all the smoke and men bolting for cover. It wasn't until the smoke cleared that he glimpsed the lead car. It belonged to Charles Frame, a miner he had played a few games of pool with at the Grille only last year. The car had plowed head-on into the deep ravine. Odie charged down the hill, tripping over tree roots and sticker bushes. Taking cover behind a thicket of pines, he hid as close as he could to Charlie's car.

A bullet hit the chrome bumper with a sharp clang, making his pulse leap and his breath catch in his throat. Odie steadied his hand deliberately and shot back. He'd left the shelter of the cook shack knowing ricocheting bullets could accidentally hit him from his own men, who were firing rapidly again. He had about ten feet to go. Another shot whizzed past and hit the pine tree beside him. He tripped and half fell just short of the car. Looking up he saw blood on the broken windshield. He crawled the last yard.

"It's all right," he said urgently. "I'll get you to Doc's." From his crouched position, he had no idea whether Charles could hear him. Odie glanced up — Charles' face was pasty white and his eyes were closed. He looked about thirty. Odie knew he had three kids, remembering Savina had babysat for his wife last year. There was blood on his mouth. "You'll be all right," he said again, more to himself than anyone else. He opened the car door but shots rang out from above him again, shouting ensued, then more shots fired in the distance from the road and the cook shack. He remained hunkered down beside the car until the shooting stopped.

Finally, Odie stood and felt Charles' pulse. The miner's thick, dark brown hair was matted with blood — he didn't move. Charles was dead at the wheel. There was more blood on the floor. A single shot had killed him. It had gone in the back of his skull and emerged at the front, destroying the left side of his face. The right side recalled he had been handsome in life. There was no expression left but the leftovers of surprise.

Odie surmised the only decent thing about Charlie's death was that it must have been instant. Still, he felt his stomach tighten and he swallowed to keep from getting sick. *Please God, let it not be one of my bullets that has done this.*

Another volley of shots rang out from the road above, cracking and ricocheting above his head, embedding bullets in the trees around him. Odie felt a stunning sense of failure. Ignoring the gunfire he shivered staring down at the dead man — a miner just trying to get to work. Odie only looked back once as he climbed out of the ravine.

Rain drummed down in opaque sheets. Savina squinted to see beyond the steady sweep of windshield wipers that barely kept up with the downpour. The Widen road ran alongside the creek, as crooked as a snake's back. She had to keep reminding herself to use the clutch. She would catch hell if the car slid down the muddy bank into the creek. Herald Wingate's words of warning rung loud in her ears, propelling her forward.

Savina took the next turn slow but slammed on her brakes so not to hit the man standing in the middle of the road. The car jerked and stalled. His imaged blurred from the pounding rain pushed off the car's windows by inadequate blades. Time stood still with the click, click, click, click of the wipers.

A gun went off in time with the next click . . . into the radiator, killing the car.

She screamed — then threw open the car door. Standing in the mud, the rain soaking her, she found herself looking down the barrel of a shotgun. "What are you doing?"

"That you, Savina?"

"Good God, yes! What are you doing, Cole Farlow? Why d'you shoot my car?"

"I just came from the shootin' at the cook shack, I thought ya was a scab. What, ya gonna arrest me?"

"Who got shot, Cole? Who?"

"Don't know. Don't rightly care."

He staggered a step or two and swayed, staring at Savina like a starved dog after a hunk of meat. The car hissed. Steam shot out of the grill and from under the hood.

Alcohol clouded Cole Farlow's eyes. Savina could smell it through the rain. Staggering toward her, dragging his rifle behind him in the mud, a chew of tobacco swelled his lower lip like a bee sting.

"Well, well, well. If it ain't the purty little whore belongin' to James Curtis Nettles," he slurred. Cole smiled and swung his gun over his shoulder. "I heard ya been spendin' some time up in Nigger Holler. Y'ain't been cheatin' on James with some old nigger man, have ya? Ain't you and James sup'osed to be gettin' hitched soon?"

"What I do in my spare time is none of your business, and you know I'm engaged to James Curtis!" She had to yell above the roar of the rain.

"Too bad. Every man in Widen's got a hard-on for ya. Maybe ya need to spread it around some, 'fore ya give it all away to young Mr. Nettles."

"Stop it. Enough of your foul mouth. Who got shot? Is my daddy okay? Have you seen him?"

"Seen a couple fellers with bullet holes through their damn heads. Must've scared the piss right outa their peckers too." Cole laughed and pulled a whiskey bottle from his pocket. "So what the hell ya doin' out here?" He unscrewed the cap and took two long gulps.

"Better question is, what are you doing here? What'd you do at the cook shack? You runnin' from somethin'? Did you shoot somebody, Cole? Tell me. Why you been drinkin'?"

He slid in the mud another step closer. His clothes were torn and his unshaved face bled from deep scratches, like he had run through a patch of briars surrounded by barbed wire. "My, you're an awful nosy little gal." He took a quick step forward and jabbed the gun barrel into Savina's chest.

Fear spread through her belly like a spray of ice water. His finger twitched on the trigger. "You need to go home, Cole. Go home and sleep this off."

"I think I'd like a little taste of what James Curtis has been chewin' on." He yanked the gun back and jabbed it again, hard this time. Savina stared down the sleek black barrel of an old hunting rifle, used for small game and shooting cans off fence posts. He leaned toward her over the gun that connected them like an iron bridge.

"Why don't you and me get in the back seat of that dead car?"

Savina put the tips of her fingers against his cold hard chest. "Stay away from me, Cole, you hear? My daddy'll skin your hide while you're still alive. I'm gonna turn around and walk back to town. You can crawl in Daddy's car and sleep." She pulled away slowly and turned her back to walk in the direction she had come from. Fear seized her by the throat in the chilling rain cutting her breath in two. Frightened, she slid in the mud and fell hard on her hip, but stood quickly and continued moving, cold mud covering the right side of her body.

The gun went off. Savina's head snapped sideways, her body turned just enough to see Cole lurch, stagger, and then lean against the car, having shot his gun up in the air. "Get back here. Ya always was a tattle tale little bitch." His eyes glowed a bloodshot red through the downpour.

Savina turned her back and continued walking.

"I said get back here!" Another shot blasted into the air.

She kept walking.

Cole Farlow was a better shot drunk than sober. At the moment of impact, the third bullet burrowed through Savina's back and bull's-eyed into her heart. She was dead before she fell into the mud on the Widen road.

Word spread quickly of the shootings at the cook shack. By noon, the mine had closed again. Thirl had left early to meet with the heads of The Elk River Coal and Lumber Company.

When there was no work and he couldn't meet Savina at the cabin, James Curtis found solace in drawing pictures of Powells Mountain or listening to Elvis Presley or Chet Atkins sing their latest hit record. He had shut the door to his room and turned on his radio.

From the moment Highpockets left her front porch, dread ignited like a small burst of flame in the center of DeDe's stomach. She stood on the other side of her son's door and wept. Some time later, she wiped tears from her face and found the courage to knock.

"That you, Mama?"

The door creaked when DeDe opened it. She avoided his eyes and sat down heavily at the foot of her son's bed. "Oh, James," she breathed deep and searched for words. "There's been an accident. Doc Vance sent Highpockets to the house." Her face twisted. Tears slid down fast as though she'd been waiting until this moment to allow herself a full measure of grief.

"What do you mean?"

"It's Savina." Her hands came to her face and covered her opened mouth. She inhaled sharply through her fingers, and then closed her eyes. "She's been shot . . . on the Widen road. Her car broke down and she got out. She was trying to find Odie. Warn him not to go to the cook shack. It was Cole Farlow that shot her. His mama found him drunk in the back seat of Odie's car. He took off. Nobody can find him."

DeDe had dreamed of Savina — her tiny body, bloody, slumped on the ground. She saw her dead, though she didn't want to believe it was anything more than a dream. The vision was a cold pain inside her now.

James let his gaze fall and sat for a moment, silent, his eyes focused on his hands and the tear that had dropped into his lap. Jumping to his feet, he grabbed his rifle. "Where is she?"

"Don't, James! Don't do this . . . you can't take a life for this . . ."

He stopped at the door. "Is she dead?"

DeDe could only go by her damned premonition, but this time it wasn't enough. "I don't know . . . she's at Doc Vance's office. Cole's mama found her, too, and took her to Doc's."

DeDe drew closer to her son, attempted to hold him. He wept quietly and thoroughly, as she couldn't remember him weeping since he had been a small boy — long shuddering inhalations, and then a gentle high keening as his inheld breath came out. He pulled away and shrieked, "I'm going to see her!" He looked back at his mother. "Tell Daddy, I love him."

Her eyes pleading, she sensed a sorrow she'd not felt since the day they pulled her grandfather out of the mine in pieces. "Stop, James . . . come back here this instant! You can't raise her up; only God can do it

. . . only God can do it . . ." DeDe followed behind him, grabbing his coat and clutching his arm. Great tears coursed wild down her pale cheeks.

James escaped the grip of his mother's fists and drove off in his truck. DeDe fell in the road, the coal cinders cutting her knees, the mud sucking her life out . . . the sound of her son's cries still in her head and piercing her heart.

Time passed in slow motion again. DeDe managed to pull herself up by the gate in a drizzling rain. In the mist, she saw Thirl's car speeding up Nicholas Street. He nearly hit the fence post where she stood before he braked fast and rushed to her side.

"I heard." He held her tight in his arms. She allowed herself to be comforted then pushed away from him, wanting to talk but not finding the strength. Thirl's shirt was wet where she had leaned against him.

"How did it happen?" he asked at last, keeping his voice gentle. "When?"

She seemed stricken again at the question. Her eyes swam and grew larger but she held on and whispered, "Savina was trying to find Odie and bring him home. Herald Wingate, the visitor from Pennsylvania that knew her mother . . . he'd told her of the danger before he left town today, but he wanted her to come pray with us, not go after Odie. Oh, God." DeDe held tight to Thirl as if she might faint or be sick. "This afternoon. In the rain. Her car broke down on the Widen road. Highpockets said it was shot in the radiator. Cole Farlow. He was drunk and . . ."

Her body became too heavy for her legs to hold. She slumped by the gate again. Thirl eased her back into the yard and down to the grass where she sat and held fast to her husband. Gulping for air, she managed to squeak out her words. "Oh my God, Thirl, he shot her in the back. She's at Doc's. James went to her. But I know he's gonna go after Cole, Thirl, he's gonna kill him, or be killed . . . we got to stop him . . ."

Before she'd finished, Thirl had jumped up, swung himself back into his Plymouth, and barreled back to the middle of town, to the clinic, and to find his son.

A stench in the back room of Doctor Vance's clinic seeped from the cracks between the wooden floorboards. The smell of death and remorse — sweet and pungent.

Savina's body made a small lump beneath the sheet like a bundle of firewood. James picked up an unresponsive hand. It laid motionless in his palm. He stared at it with sorrowful compassion and talked to her like people talk to their babies in the womb, hoping she could hear him. He bent down and kissed her lifeless cheek. Someone had washed the mud off her body, but her hair was still damp. Dirt and blood had formed a crust along her hairline and the corners of her mouth. The table was moist with the stink of an overused dishrag. Her bloody dress had been cut off and thrown into a corner. She deserved better than this.

Doctor Vance stood obscurely by the bed. "She's in a better place, James Curtis. You must be strong for her."

It stuck like a thorn in his mind. He swung around and stared at the doctor. "You don't know the half of it," he cried.

"You'll recover from this, son. You have to go on."

"To what? Die in the mines like the rest of the crazy men in this town. No thanks, Doc." His cheeks wet with tears, he turned back to brush her hair from her face. "We was leavin'. We had plans. But they're all wasted. All wasted."

The state police arrested 52 that evening, incarcerating all including one woman and two small boys in the county jail at Clay. Bill Blizzard protested, but for the first time was ignored by Governor Marland. The police confiscated a twenty-gun arsenal from the cook shack and from the trucks around it. Warrants were issued for the arrests of Odie Ingram and Cole Farlow — the two who remained at large.

The evening light was strong enough to show the road ahead of him. James Curtis drove along the washboard road with ease. He knew every pothole.

Coasting his truck past Cole's house, a group of men had gathered on the porch and eyed him as he drove by. James figured they were kin. Cole's dad had died during the invasion of Normandy. He lived with his eccentric mother and grandmother; both had refused to leave Widen after the war.

James recalled the day he stopped at Cole's house — the day after Cole turned sixteen, quit school, and started working in the mines. His mother came stumbling in, drunk, screaming and yelling. She hit him when she found money in his shirt pocket, then disappeared for two days. Word in town was she got saved last summer during revival. But that didn't save Cole from finding trouble. "Bad seed," Doc Vance had said once as he stitched up James Curtis' eye from a punch Cole had thrown over a lost game of pool.

As boys, they had played in an abandoned mineshaft on the opposite side of South Mountain dug by the sweat and blood of miner's backs. Men who had worked the earliest mines in Widen at the turn of the century. The old cave was unlike the new coal mine with its main shaft located near the tipple, and the underground maze of tunneled streets that ran sixty miles from Clay to Nicholas County.

At fifteen, Cole had built a moonshine still close to the opening of the old mineshaft, and James Curtis had donated ingredients from his mama's fruit cellar. But when Thirl found out, both boys had been immediately introduced to the wrath of God and the rod was not spared. Neither boy could sit down for a week. In spite of warnings to never go in the dangerous mine again, it remained a place of risk and adventure for the boys and young men of Widen.

The night of their high school graduation James Curtis, Cole, and several boys from their graduating class filled a washtub with ice and beer and carried it into the mineshaft. They spent the night drinking, playing cards, smoking packs of stolen cigarettes, and puking after hours of pretending to be men.

Driving in the dark, his eyes stung as he wiped his tears with his bare hands. James determined he would have ended up like Cole, alone, with no direction in life, had it not been for Savina.

Rumors spread quickly that the authorities had rounded up every striker involved in the cook shack shootings, all but Odie and Cole.

He'd heard it before he left Doc Vance's office. Still, James couldn't imagine Odie not knowing about his daughter. Somebody had to have gotten word to him by now, even if he and Cole were hiding out. Odie, a seasoned hunter, was well acquainted with every mountain and trail in the state. With access to a good horse, James figured he was probably miles away by now.

As for Cole . . . James knew his hiding places. The first on the list was the old mineshaft.

Pulling his truck up as far as it would go, James stepped out into the tall grass and weeds leading up to the cut timber logs that framed the opening. The wind blew colder after the sun had gone down, but the rain had lessened since morning. He shook visibly, but not from the night air or from fear. Ravaged by grief, insanity had begun to seep into his pores like a cold rain. Rage twisted tight around his head as if caught in a vice squeezing out all reason. He switched on his flashlight and pulled his shotgun off the front seat.

"Cole! It's me, Cole. We need to talk!"

James walked to the edge of the mineshaft. The light from a small fire cast flickering shadows on the walls of the mine. He tossed the flashlight into the weeds. Cole crouched like a feral cat against a pile of rusted metal. The remains of their moonshine still sat crusted with several years' worth of dirt, the recipe still hung on ancient wires from the ceiling. An empty whisky bottle lay in the dirt. Coatless, Cole's clothes were covered in dried mud. His lifeless green eyes fixed on James Curtis.

"It was an accident, wasn't it? You didn't mean to kill her, tell me that. You owe me that. Tell me you didn't mean to kill her."

Cole stood and smiled a ragged gap-toothed grin that was both knowing and mean. Another half-empty bottle of whiskey dangled from his right hand. "I don't owe you jack shit."

He was large and chinless, with an enormous adam's apple and sideburns like Elvis. At school, his breath was like coffee and cavities. But all James could smell was the dampness of the old mine and wafts of his 100-proof breath.

Cole dropped his bottle to the ground, shook out a Lucky Strike, tapped it on the side of his lighter, lit it, and then blew a stream of smoke toward James. He had tucked his filthy T-shirt in tight and had another pack of cigarettes rolled into his right shirtsleeve. Levi cuffs were turned up around muddy work boots. Black hair and big round ears made him almost comical to look at.

Sweat rolled down James's cheek. "Did you do it on purpose? Did you touch her?"

Cole flicked his smoke into the dirt and stared, shooting James a don't-mess-with-me smirk, the drink long gone to his head. He snarled like a rabid dog. "I shoulda shoved her in the back seat 'fore I shot her, now I'm gung fuggin kiw you!"

A war scream pierced the darkness and echoed through the mine, then dust rose as James hurled himself at Cole, dropping his rifle in the dirt.

James got him first with a left hook. Cole wheeled and came back at him and drove a vicious blow right into his nose. It sent James reeling. He felt the crack and went to one knee, his eyes welled up and a fountain of blood erupted from ruptured vessels, pouring like a faucet thrown on. He wiped blood from his face. It dripped from his hands, as his nose seemed to disappear into its cavity.

The blood appeared to unnerve Cole. He let James crawl up the side of the wall to steady himself.

Through eyes blurred by tears and blood, James caught movement coming toward him again. Struggling to hold on to his bearings he crouched low, preparing for the strike. He ducked Cole's fist and it landed high above his head into the rock wall. He could see it sent a bullet of pain up Cole's hand and arm.

But Cole's advantage was clear. Swooping in from above he rushed James once more, whirling his pained fist squarely at his head. Fighting back a sudden wave of nausea from a pungent mix of tobacco smoke, alcohol, and Cole's unwashed body, James forced himself to push off with his feet, turning his body slightly, and caught the blow in his right arm instead of his face this time. He somehow managed to snake his arm around Cole's, his hand winding up on Cole's shoulder. Making full use of their combined momentum, James sidestepped Cole, allowing him to trip over his feet and tumble to the ground.

A sickening pop echoed off the rock walls of the mine, followed instantly by a hideous scream of pain and anger. James had maintained his hold on Cole's arm, forcing it farther and farther back, then letting him fall into the dirt. Squinting through swelling eyes, James bent over Cole where he lay, face down, moaning and clutching his wracked shoulder.

Mercilessly hooking the toe of his boot under his armpit, James rolled him over onto his back, meeting with another wretched cry. Staring up with eyes blinded by rage and pain, Cole used his legs and good arm to skitter away. James stalked after him, adding fear to the hatred that glared back at him. Cole's attempt at escape was cut short as he rammed into a wall of railroad ties.

Eyes darting from side to side like a cornered fox, he accepted escape was not to be found. Fumbling at the top of one boot with his good hand, he produced a Bowie knife from its sheath, satisfaction replacing some of the fear. Undeterred, James drove forward with a purposeful stride, dodging a feeble swing of the knife but tripping over Cole's deliberate swipe with his feet, landing flat on his back in the dirt. Cole rolled, stood and placed the heel of his boot squarely on James' stomach, just below his rib cage, the knife at his neck drawing blood. James grimaced and let out another gasp of pain.

But the pain from Cole's arm caused him to stagger backwards a little, lifting his boot from James' chest. James heard the wheezing sound of air being forced back into his own lungs. Cole staggered forward again; his hand flashed out from behind his back, trailing after it a reflection of the metal that swung toward James in a sweeping arc. He flinched instinctively, but his blurred vision hampered his reaction; too slow to save him from the unexpected attack.

James rolled, but not far enough. This time he felt the jolt, then the sting. A sharp smell cut through his swollen nostrils, a damp stain grew across his arm, then the loud whine of his own voice pierced the dead air of the cave. Cole, also fighting against his own pain, rocketed through the air and stabbed ruthlessly at an unsuspecting James again, this time slicing his cheek open with the tip of the knife.

Half crawling and half falling, Cole stabbed at him again but missed entirely and bowled over from drunken exhaustion.

James rotated to his hands and knees, breathing fast and hard. His head wanted to explode from the pain, his arm throbbed with his heartbeat, blood soaked his coat; he felt vomit stirring inside. Picking up a rusted pipe near the fire, he struggled to his feet and swung at Cole's head, hitting him square in the mouth. Cole's lips burst open, shooting blood everywhere. He backed up against the mineshaft wall; his face, sideburns, and shirt were instantly soaked in blood.

"Yer fuggin dead," he muttered, spitting a tooth into the dirt. A wicked smile twisted on his mangled lips, causing James to wince as the expression tugged at the flesh and bone of his busted nose. Through the slits of swollen eyes, he saw the terror and humiliation that now held Cole in their sway. Cole swung the knife loosely in his hand.

James Curtis took a breath as if to say something, but words seemed inadequate and insufficient to account for the years of humiliation Cole lived with on a daily basis from an over-bearing mother and taunting men from the mine. A cry from a distant hollow rung in his ears and pulled at his heart. James raised his hands; sanity replaced his adrenalin.

"Cole . . . enough."

"It'll never be 'nuf." Cole lunged with the knife again, trapping James against the twisted metal of the old still. The strength poured out of James's injured arm; his futile attempt to fight off his adversary made Cole laugh. "Yer just like her. She walked off, refused to fight me, and she paid fer it."

Cole pricked the point of the knife through his enemy's shirt and into his chest, surprised at the ease with which the sharp blade penetrated. James' swollen eyes popped wide as the knife entered his body. Driving the knife deeper, Cole felt some resistance of the blade biting through to the bone. He shoved harder until it plunged deep into James' lung. He coughed and gasped. Blood oozed out of his mouth. Cole tore the knife through his skin, spilling more blood out of James' chest wall and down his shirt.

Without a word, Cole yanked out the knife and backed up. Stumbling toward the dying fire, he bent down with his uninjured arm, picked up his whisky bottle, and then took a long swig. He swayed back and forth, feeling his way back along the rock wall until he tripped over James lying on the floor of the mine.

Sitting in the dirt, he finished the whiskey to numb his pain then leaned over and pulled James' truck keys out of his jacket pocket. Getting to his feet, he staggered back to the mine opening and found James' rifle lying in the dirt. He picked it up.

Cole looked back into the darkness and laughed. In minutes, he was spiraling slowly down the mountain in James' truck . . . looking for a store, or a bar, and another bottle of whiskey.

James heard her voice; it was Savina, he was sure of it.

Blood seeped from every orifice in his body. He tried to whisper her name but his lips only motioned what his tongue would have spoken.

Then he stopped his breath. Not breathing came as a relief from the shortened, labored gasps his breath had become over the last few minutes. Was the voice real, or imagined? *Savina.*

He sunk down through depths of darkness, the darkness of slumber. It was the last thing James Curtis heard as the fire died in the cave.

~ Friday, May 8, 1953 ~

DeDe sat on a log near the old church in the cemetery as the rain fell pitilessly upon her. The trees offered little protection. It was as if someone had poked a hole in the awning of green overhead.

It wasn't a cleansing rain. She knew it wouldn't renew her. Instead she expected it to wear her down, obliterate her features, and allow her to dissolve back into the earth like warm rain on snow.

Leaning forward, she crossed her arms on her lap and hung her head low as the fat drops turned her auburn hair into a twisted brown mop. She wore a thick yellow housecoat, now drenched and clinging to her thin body like a wet rug. Her pale feet were covered with mud, striping her naked flesh like wounds. She cried huge heaving sobs.

DeDe had felt certain Thirl would find him, safe. Drunk, maybe. But not dead. The devastation and grief in her husband's eyes had told the story. Her head pounded from crying jags and a restless night's sleep. But when Thirl returned at dawn with Pastor Jessie, no one uttered a sound. DeDe instinctively knew her son was dead. Still in her robe, she bolted from the house as one who had lost their mind. Careening down the street to no place in particular, her march ended at the cemetery behind the church staring down the hole that had been dug for Savina's funeral.

DeDe rose on shaky legs. It was still morning. She felt Thirl standing behind her. It was only natural that he would follow her. She took a breath to gather her strength, turned around and stepped closer to her husband, narrowing the distance. Pounding her breast with her fist, emphasizing each word, she said in a voice betrayed, "God has allowed my child to be stolen from me. He has deceived me!"

Thirl caressed her face in his hands. His voice was low and hoarse. "You don't mean that. He loves you, Deanna." His arm steadied her, and his kiss to her forehead spoke of a love come down from God, a love she would have to trust more completely in the days ahead. He led her to his car and gently put her in.

The rain poured down once more, and the old Plymouth's defroster sputtered and coughed against the fogged windshield. Just as Thirl and DeDe got back to the house, the storm subsided. Sunlight washed over the leaves of the dogwood in the yard and the tree glowed. It lit up and sparkled like tiny flashlights had been attached to every branch. *Flashlights through the valley of the shadow of death.*

That's when they saw them: the neighbors, half the town scattered across the lawns.

They just got in their cars and drove to Nicholas Street, or opened their front doors forgetting to close them, and walked into her yard and her neighbor's yards, and stood there — silent. On her tiny lawn and porch, they all held some part of themselves: an arm pressed to a chest, a hand up across a forehead. Union sympathizers and men and women loyal to the company, mixed together for the first time since a gunshot maimed Thirl last September.

Edith Holcomb wore only one shoe. Tessa Butcher clutched her newborn to her chest, her other three children strung behind her as she ran across the street. By mid-morning there were twenty more people draped across the porch, front room, and at their kitchen table — sniffling into their handkerchiefs, wiping their tears.

Opal Hamrick's scream broke the silence in the yard. "Goose Digg told me, but I couldn't believe it."

Some people wanted to know where the Farlow boy was hiding out. Some of the men guessed which paths over the mountains he'd take.

"This is in God's hands. The sheriff has all his men out on this." Thirl spoke in spurts, barely audible. "There's been enough killin'. Leave it alone, boys."

Whenever anyone opened the front door, a breeze blew in the windows and the front room became a sea of floating white chiffon — surreal and ominous. The clergy from area churches descended. Pastor Jessie with his wife and two daughters in tow organized food, spoke to Jugg about the double funeral, and started a prayer circle in the Nettles' front room.

DeDe had dried off and changed her clothes, but her face never dried completely. Continually wet with tears, it felt chapped and raw to the touch from so much wiping.

The world was silent in trickles. Then Dewey Wilson ran across the road in his stocking feet, his shadow flung out in front of him, painted long by the early sun. He arrived at the front steps heaving for breath, a newspaper in his hands. "They're callin' for an end to the strike!" He gathered his paper, folding its fragile leaves of print. His socks were soaked with morning dew. "Where's Thirl?"

Lottie Digg, a nervous, pinched woman in a blue housedress, stood on the porch, her hands around her Bible. "Where d'you think he is, Dewey? He's in the house with DeDe."

Dewey bolted inside and laid the paper gently in Thirl's arms. "This won't ease yer pain none, but looks like the strike might be over. It's over because this town's finally come to its senses. This town and them vultures in Charleston. James had to die for it to happen, but it ended it." He turned to DeDe. "I'm sorry, Deanna. I'm sorry your boy had to die for all of us."

"Kinda makes me know how God must've felt." DeDe's voice was as dense as freshly poured cement. "But let's remember all the families that've lost someone they love in the past few days. I hear the Frame family is burying Charles today. So many families are mourning in Widen." She nodded in appreciation of Dewey's words and hung her head.

Later, the house filled with another shift of people. Visitors brought food — dozens of casseroles, pots of beans, a ham, a few pies — gallons of tea. The preacher led many in prayer who wept. He asked Lottie to read the Psalms. Her gentle reading voice wavered only slightly. She kept asking the preacher, "Is this God's will, Pastor?"

Thirl wandered to the back yard, his face calm, almost blank. DeDe roamed the peopled rooms of her house, walking from bedroom, to porch, to kitchen, wishing they would all leave. But she didn't have the heart to tell them to go — they were all grieving. She wanted to be alone when the undertaker brought James' body back to the house. They would be quick about it and bury him beside Savina tomorrow.

She stopped and looked out through the rusted screens at the hazy view of the back yard filled with people. They weren't good at much. All they knew was mining. Nobody had made it to college. But the town had one talent: faith.

They believed in the power of Jesus Christ. The same yesterday, today, and forever. They had been raised up in the shadow of this great faith, in the vast floodplain of belief. To DeDe, Jesus was more real than the people of Widen. As she walked to the school or down the path across the creek to the store, she often heard His voice. He was her comforter, her most intimate friend. As far as DeDe knew, Jesus was a Baptist. To say you didn't believe in the existence of God was like saying you did not believe in corn flakes, or sunsets, or that the earth was round. But in the last few hours, His voice had gone silent.

DeDe went into the bathroom to be alone. She sat on the floor. The sun strained through the window, the light bounced off the chrome handles in the tub and shimmered across the porcelain. It filled the small bathroom with an underwater radiance.

It felt like somebody had taken the needle off the record and for the first time, the music she'd heard her whole life, the music that played all around her, just stopped. She'd never heard such silence. DeDe rubbed her ears for a moment and thought perhaps she'd gotten something stuck in them, some water from the rain that morning. She shook her head back and forth. But there was nothing. Just silence. And sorrow. She'd had no premonition of her son's death. She felt betrayed.

When the last mourner had gone and James Curtis was laid out in the front room, Jugg Pyle, Widen's undertaker, closed the casket's lid for the night. DeDe hoped Jugg thought about the morning he and Dewey had stood in her kitchen and argued with James about shoving the strikers off the hill. She hoped they both thought about it good and hard.

"I'll be by in the morning to get things ready for the funeral procession," Jugg said.

Thirl nodded, shook Jugg's hand, and closed the door behind him. Exhausted, he fell into his worn leather chair. His elbows angled on the arms. Turning pages of his Bible — the spine crackled under his grip, his eyes took in each paragraph, quick and hungry searching for answers.

At midnight the house was finally quiet. DeDe sat with her arms outstretched on the kitchen table, her hands folded, staring at a blank wall. She was childless. The emptiness of it caved in on her.

Thirl heard the knock at the back door and sighed. "No more, not tonight. Not at this late hour." But DeDe had already stood and opened it, finding Odie Ingram standing on the back porch in the dark, his hat in his hand.

~ Saturday, May 9, 1953 ~

She'd survived the night. DeDe sat up slowly, feeling the creak and snap of each vertebra. She'd slept in James' bed, or tried to. She wanted to smell him, feel where he had been only hours before. What little sleep she did get was filled with dreams of him as a baby, crying at her feet, toddling behind her as she hung sheets on the line, or playing with a puppy.

Swinging her feet over the side, she put the sole of her foot down on one of her son's drawings sticking out from under the bed. A picture of Savina. James had not shown this picture to her. There was a curious look in her eye; she looked strange . . . different . . . not his best drawing of Savina. DeDe noticed it was dated July, last year. She carried the drawing to her chifforobe and placed it in the box with the rest of his drawings. Until she could bear to put them into a scrapbook in her old age, they would be buried there.

"Bury," she said aloud. The word stuck in her throat.

DeDe wasn't a stranger to burying a child. But she had not known her stillborn son. This was different.

James Curtis had slept his last night in their home. She slid her hand along the top of the closed casket that rested on two sawhorses in her front room. How could she find the strength to put on her blue funeral dress, eat breakfast, and face the crowds again? How on earth could she lower her son's body into the ground and keep on living?

DeDe stumbled into the church, watching Pastor Jessie greet people with a double-handed shake.

"You and Thirl need anything, anything at all, you call me, hear?"

DeDe smiled weakly, but said nothing.

She walked to the front pew and looked into the sleepless face of Doctor Vance; his glasses had steamed up from humidity and tears. She sat next to him. Hands clasped together, twisting in her lap, she avoided his gaze.

"He was a good son."

DeDe cleared her throat. "Thanks, Doc. I just want this day to be over."

He leaned toward her. "But you can't let grief consume you, Deanna."

She nodded. "People give in to grief the way they fall in love. Grief will be my constant companion for the rest of my days." Doctor Vance squeezed her hand, then moved over so Thirl could sit beside her.

The crowd grew quiet, except for a low volume of grumbling and dissension when Odie walked up to the altar where his daughter's casket lay next to James' at the front of the church. He stood disheveled in a wrinkled suit and placed each hand on a coffin. His shoulders heaved up and down until Thirl stood and guided him back to the front pew for the eulogy. Tears ran down his cheeks, unchecked. The crowd of mourners murmured among themselves over such a blatant display of forgiveness.

Aging years since DeDe had seen him last, Odie was frail, hairless, and embryonic. His old man's shoulders, thin and lifeless, moved beneath the fabric of his jacket grabbing hold of James Curtis' casket and hoisting it to his shoulder. DeDe prayed for Thirl's bad leg when he raised Savina's casket to his shoulders. Sixteen men in all carried Savina and James to their final resting places. Sixteen men who were neither union nor company on that day.

Odie had appeared on their back porch to ask his friends for forgiveness and grieve with them. Thirl had contacted the sheriff and requested Odie be allowed to go to the funeral and then get his house in order before they arrested him. The Nettles took responsibility for him, promising the sheriff that he would be at his farm on Monday morning. Thirl made a promise to his old friend that he would sell his farm and put the money in a fund for miners' children.

Thirl, DeDe, and Odie were miner's children who became miners. It was only fitting they carry one another's burdens and share in each other's sorrow on the day they buried their children — together. Buried them under a Golden Delicious apple tree in the church cemetery, two rows down from a tombstone that was barely readable. HERALD WINGATE, BORN 1884, DIED 1909, FRIEND OF C.G. WIDEN, TOWN FOUNDER.

~ Sunday, May 10, 1953 ~

Odie spent the last night on his farm laying his papers and a few pictures of Savina where Thirl would see them as soon as he walked into the house. In the crude barn he'd built after the fire, Odie cleaned the horse stalls and said goodbye to his small herd. He fed his dogs, chickens, hog, and his horses, and then laid the feedbags in the barn where DeDe could find them easily. Hanging his head and dragging his body through the house, he gathered Savina's belongings and what few clothes he owned and put them in two boxes to be given to the Baptist missionary fund. Finally, he collapsed into a chair and stared into a blazing fire until morning.

~ **Monday, May 11, 1953** ~

Outside, the low light of dawn came quickly. The sun won its battle and the storm clouds departed, leaving behind ragged wisps of black and gray streaking the blue sky like soot on a clean sheet.

Odie had one last mission. His car totaled, his truck already confiscated by the authorities, he relied on his bay colt to help him fulfill his last duty to his friends. Seizing the reins, Odie swung up onto his horse's back, knees tight around the animal's barrel of ribs. The horse uttered a great whinny, tossed his head, and broke into a lope across the hill. Odie wiped tears from his eyes with his coat sleeve and headed for Colored Holler.

The sound of a horse brought men and women out to their porches in the hollow. Nappy-headed children peeked through windows. Smoke floated out of every chimney. When the horse stopped in front of Jabo's house, Mama Ola clopped out on the porch, her eyes stern and her lips stiff.

Odie tipped his hat. "Ma'am." He remained on his horse. "Mister Kelly awake?"

"Nawser, you g'wan now . . . git. We don't need no trouble up heah."

Hephzibah stepped out on the dilapidated porch and wrapped a shawl around her mother-in-law. "Jabo's in the house. He be out directly. We're grievin' too, Mist' Odie."

"I know. You loved my Savina, and I appreciate what you done. You know what I come fer?"

"I knows why," said Hephzibah. "You ready to tell the Nettles the truth?"

"I am."

Jabo walked out with his rifle. "You do this, Mist' Odie, you do this right, or ah swear ah hunt you down mysef."

"I promise, Mister Kelly. I promise to make the Nettles' world a little happier today. I'm goin' to prison, probably for the rest of my days. You'll have no fight from me, Sir. Was my bullet that killed Cole Farlow two nights ago. I'm gonna pay for that."

"Come inside then."

The sheriff arrived early to arrest Odie at his house, but when he walked up on the porch he saw a note had been tacked to the door. *Meet me at Thirl Nettles'.*

Squeezing with his feet, he gave a little *hey-yup* and set the horse into motion, waving goodbye to Jabo and his family. He headed to Widen.

Odie passed houses at a slow trot; it'd been many years since folks had seen a horse in the middle of town. DeDe heard the noise of the crowd getting louder as she hung sheets on the line. It sounded as if the whole town was walking up Nicholas Street again.

Thirl stuck his head out the back doorway. "DeDe! Come quick. It's Odie riding his horse up the street. Ya ain't gonna believe this."

DeDe wiped her hands on her dress and walked inside the house. Thirl was already on the front porch. The air in the house was electric. The top of her head tingled and there was music in her again. Her grief moved aside for a moment as she stepped on the porch with her husband.

Odie sat on top of his horse that pranced in the street by the gate. His right hand was wrapped around the chest of a smiling baby boy that sat in the saddle in front of him. He looked to be about ten months old. DeDe ran to Odie and reached up. The book of life had never closed. In moments it was revealed to her mind. Tears flowed as she laid her hand on Odie's leg.

Gazing at the boy for a second, Odie tentatively touched the child's forehead and cheek. He folded the blanket down around him and allowed the baby to slip off his saddle, out of his large hands, and into DeDe's arms. He had James' eyes and Savina's mouth. And red hair. Lots of dark red hair.

"The most powerful force in the universe is gossip," said Odie. "Savina didn't want anybody to know, didn't want people pointing at her baby, calling him a bastard. It was my fault they didn't marry sooner. But they was gonna leave town next month, get married, come back later, after some time had passed. Jabo and his family been takin' care of the boy all this time, that's why Savina spent so much time there. He was born last July fourth."

Thirl walked up behind DeDe and put his hands on her shoulders, then touched the child's head, smoothing down his fine hair. The baby smiled, its toothless little mouth opened with a gurgle. With his finger, Thirl wiped drooling spit from its chin.

"Thirl, meet our grandson. This here is Emery. Emery Curtis Nettles. Son of James and Savina, grandson of Deanna and Thirl, and Josephine and . . . me." Odie choked on his tears.

Thirl unhooked a sack of clothes and diapers tied on the saddle. Odie laid his hand on Thirl's shoulder and smiled.

"We'll take good care of him," Thirl said and nodded. He shook Odie's hand.

DeDe kissed the baby and held him close as a silent police car nosed through the parting crowd and pulled up behind the horse.

~ Thanksgiving 1953 ~

The music dueled in the barn. Thanksgiving held a special meaning this year to the residents of Widen. Groups of men and women played their fiddles, banjos, and mandolins. A few guitar pickers joined in. They danced and sang old mountain songs from their past, and set rows of food for the town to partake together, giving thanks for an end to the strike.

Thirl raised Emery to his shoulders. "Mamaw, you want us to bring you some cider?"

"No, you boys go on. I'm gonna sit here a spell and listen to the music." She hesitated a moment. "Thirl?"

"Yes?"

"I want . . . I want you to know how much I love you."

He smiled down at her as he patted his grandson's legs hanging around his neck. "You're a fetching woman, Deanna."

She smiled back. He had been her rock. She wanted him to know.

Watching her husband carry his grandson with the same love and affection he once carried James Curtis in the Thanksgiving barn, the pain of loss pulled at her insides. She'd grown weak in her mind.

Mournful. Raising Emery only put a Band-Aid on the infected wound of losing her son. Even Doc Vance worried about her — part of his rounds to sick folk included a visit to the Nettles family every week.

Her foot tapped in time to the music. She shoved stray hairs back into place and closed her eyes, absorbing the low cry of the steel guitar.

"Nobody cares if you can't dance well. Just get up and dance."

She recognized him. Herald Wingate. DeDe turned toward the voice; her mouth opened but remained silent.

He hiked up his same nasty boot on the bench beside her and rested his arm on his leg. "God will not let you suffer what you're not able to bear."

"I cain't bear anymore." Anger filled her throat like she was choking on a piece of meat.

"He knows that. But you've got to find the strength He sent you a while back to raise this young'un."

"What strength? When?"

"The night you heard the angels sing. That was for you, Deanna."

"Just who are you? Why did you come back here?"

"He sent me, to tell you that. Who I am doesn't matter. Your suffering is over. You're to be a witness to those who will still have some suffering to do."

"That's my purpose? To help others get through their suffering?" She turned away from him, indignant, and stared straight ahead to watch people dance.

"Yes, and to raise their child. They're watching you, you know. They're proud of you."

DeDe continued to stare, ready to match him word for word. "Who's watching me?"

No answer.

Jugg Pyle's fiddle began to play *Angel Band,* and the aroma of apple blossoms filled the room. She turned to speak to his face, but his face was gone. Along with the rest of him. Nobody had seen him that night, nobody but DeDe.

❦

Odie's trial lasted for months. He was found guilty of first-degree murder and given life in prison. The Clay County grand jury handed up a series of indictments, from holding up the railroad and stealing dynamite to blowing up the bridges, and the murder of Cole Farlow.

In November 1953 the evidence gathered by the FBI was finally laid before a federal grand jury in Huntington against the UMW strikers. More of the striking miners found themselves doing time in a federal prison. The United States Department of Justice regarded the indictment as the most important attempt to deal with labor violence under civil rights statutes. Widen's reign of terror was over.

~ May 1954 ~

Spring came again.

In the mountains, near the shadows of town, side by side in their graves, the young lovers slept under the apple tree. Close by the humble walls of the little Baptist church, in the heart of Clay County they laid, unnoticed. Daily the tides of life went ebbing and flowing beside them. Every Sunday throbbing hearts filed past where theirs were at rest. Every Sunday Pastor Jessie searched the scriptures, but their minds were no longer busy. Their eyes were closed for eternity. Every Sunday the toiling hands of the Pastor shook those of his congregation while their hands ceased from their labors and a thin gold band laid forever buried under a stone in a cabin now abandoned. Every Sunday weary feet drug into a sanctuary to rest from a weeks' worth of backbreaking labor in the mines, but their feet had completed their journey. Every Sunday the Pastor reached across his pulpit for the souls of his congregation, but their souls had walked to the light.

As Pastor Jessie concluded his sermon, his gaze fell upon Thirl, DeDe, and their grandson asleep in his grandmother's arms. He stretched his arms above his head, and held his black King James Bible in his right hand. His voice bellowed and he wept aloud.

"The United States Government may have ended the strike, but Savina and James Curtis ended the hatred of family against family, brother against brother, man against himself. Their love was not in vain. God's ways are not our ways, His thoughts not our thoughts. Who are we to know the plan of God?"

"The violence and sorrow in Widen will not be put away and forgotten like an old picture book, but passed on for future generations to never forget what has happened here. This tale of woe is not the sole possession of one family, but of all families in this town. For all are punished. Let us pray and let us remember."

He played coal miner with his toy truck on Nicholas Street. On warm sunny mornings he could be found sitting in the dirt, a little redheaded boy with brilliant blue eyes and coal dust on his feet.

What Is A Southern Fried Woman?

One warm Carolina day, I said to a certain young woman of mine that the average Yankee man knows as much about a Southern Fried Woman as a cat knows about God's plan of redemption.

"What's a Southern Fried Woman? Lord, Mom, where d'you come up with that?"

I'm great at embarrassing my kids.

So I explained . . . while she sat and dutifully listened, as always.

A Southern Fried Woman's family and friends laugh at her dreams. But Southern Fried Women have learned not to boil over about it and make a mess. They fry all the criticism out of their heads, admiring and tasting the occasional golden brown results . . . when nobody else does.

Boiling it down, they're women born below the Mason Dixon line and range in age from sixteen to ninety-six. They're not only fried, they're burnt out on empty promises, dead-end jobs, junk cars, making ends meet, and cheating husbands. Southern Fried Women are what Faith Hill, Loretta Lynn, and Patty Loveless sing about. Patsy Cline, Marshall Chapman, and the Judds are fine examples of Southern Fried Women.

Not being perfect, Southern Fried Women live to love again, believing the next set of dreams won't give out.

For years, Southern Fried Women have fled northern cities like Detroit, Cleveland, Pittsburgh, New York City, and Chicago. They escape the bitter cold of bad relationships and weather and return to the peace they once thought was boredom. They travel back to a life they once ran away from to achieve dreams that over time turned into nightmares.

Searching for the comfort of their roots, the Southern Fried Woman packs her car, her kids, and sometimes her husband, and heads home. Home to the "hollers" and coal towns of West Virginia and Kentucky, the Blue Ridge and beaches of Virginia, and the North Carolina Mountains and Outer Banks. The Low Country and battlefields of South Carolina whisper to her daily. Her eyes close and the plantations and bayou of Louisiana flash on her brain screen. The peach groves and rural dirt roads of Georgia call her in her dreams. Cotton fields and shrimp boats in Alabama invade her thoughts. The everglades, horse farms, and keys of Florida beckon. A vast river called the Mississippi winds through her memories. All roads lead to the Great Smoky Mountains and the back roads of Tennessee for some Southern Fried Women. The lakes, rivers, and farms of Arkansas reach out and pull her by the hand. The Southland draws her to a place she once called home, or to a new place that something reincarnated in her must find.

Before she reaches the Ohio River, she hears the call of the whippoorwill, the wind rushing through the tobacco fields, and the whir of the cicada. She feels the hot sun on her back, tastes the sweet tea of the local diner where she had her first date and the salty air of the barrier island beaches where she lost her virginity.

A Southern Fried Woman is fed up with promises of something better. She woke up to find she possessed the ingredients for a happy life a long time ago. She's let go of her pain, to hell with her pride. The dream was never any farther than her mama's back yard.

Southern Fried Women not only have all their eggs in one basket, they've fried them up with grits and gravy, hot buttered biscuits, and a pound of bacon and don't give a damn who knows it. Southern Fried Women can't stand to eat alone. When they cook a mess of beans, they want to eat them with a mess of people. But they've been experts at drinking alone.

A Southern Fried Woman knows life is not about how fast you run, or how high you climb, but how well you bounce. They keep away from skunks, lawyers, and people who've been mean to them and learned a long time ago you can't unsay a cruel thing. A Southern Fried Woman's path has had some puddles. They've washed a lot of mud off their faces.

They're not frail and they don't swoon. Southern Fried Women are about as fragile as a pack mule. After all, their mamas taught them how to wash laundry in a Hotpoint on the back porch, hanging miles of wet, heavy sheets and to pray the rain holds off. They iron their own clothes and can do their own hair and nails. They've been preached to, lied about, screamed at, broken, bruised, and just plain FRIED. They never give up; they just go home.

So you ask me, what is a Southern Fried Woman?

She's any woman brave enough to start over again, darlin', never gives up her dream, wherever she decides home is.

Pamela King Cable
April 2006